THE WOUNDED BREED

THE WOUNDED BREED

JAMES S. KELLY

This is a work of fiction. All of the characters, names, incidents, organizations, and dialogue in this novel are either the products of the author's imagination or are used fictitiously.

Archway Publishing books may be ordered through booksellers or by contacting:

Archway Publishing
1663 Liberty Drive
Bloomington, IN 47403
www.archwaypublishing.com
1 (888) 242-5904

ISBN: 978-1-4808-6592-1 (sc)
ISBN: 978-1-4808-6593-8 (e)

Library of Congress Control Number: 2018909349

Print information available on the last page.

Archway Publishing rev. date: 8/7/2018

OTHER WORKS
by
JAMES S. KELLY

Mysteries
I Didn't Forget
Interned
Not in My Backyard

Westerns
A Man of Breeding
A Breed Apart

Autobiography
Muddling Through

ACKNOWLEDGEMENTS

My wife, Patricia

Children

James S. Kelly Jr.
Mark Raymond Kelly
Nancy Jean Leachman
Michelle Patrice Leachman

Friends

John and Nancy Orchard
Robert and Marilyn Lang
Don and Noreen Pate
Lyndon Beauchene

Relatives

Jim and Ethel Lancaster
Thomas Kelly
Maryann Kelly

PROLOGUE

1900

CHRISTMAS was still ten days away, and retail sales were booming in spite of the early rain storm. Puddles were everywhere on the streets, yet that had little effect on the shoppers. The gravel streets were full of townspeople; carriages were everywhere. Children were out of school for two weeks and they were playing in the rain while their mothers were shopping in stores or having their hair fixed. Merchants had huge smiles on their faces while the two restaurants and thirteen saloons were doing a rush business. To stay in the Yuletide spirit, the town constable was only arresting half of the cowboys who had too much to drink and were shooting at crows flying by.

Santa Claus was sitting on the Central Hotel Porch and a line of children, ranging in ages from three to twelve, were lined up all around the building. Santa was a big attraction, but so were the warm cookies and lemonade provided by Saint Mary's Catholic Church.

Across the street in the Santa Ynez General Store, holiday sales were brisk. The assistant manager, a young man of twenty-six, years was asked to work on his day off to handle the additional workload. He didn't mind; he did exactly the same thing last year at this time; all the other employees were married. There was no one at home waiting for him, no girl friend, and no one that depended upon him. Over the past two years he'd been able to progress from stock boy to assistant manager, though he didn't see much of an increase in his salary. He accepted this as the way it was for a young man trying to get ahead. Being at the manager's beck and call, though, had its perks. He was able to take time off when he needed and the few times he was late weren't even mentioned. Everyone at the store thought he was a polite young man who took his job seriously. Little did they know of the dark secret he held within and what mayhem he was planning.

Disguising his feelings to all who came into contact with him was necessary. The years of being patient would pay off; his plan was complete and he was confident of success. Tonight, he would strike.

"John, I have to leave early today. Do you mind locking up for me? My wife's not feeling well." The owner/manager was standing in the doorway to his office, at the rear of the store. John was making a list of items that needed to be restocked on the shelves of the Santa Ynez General Store. He was concentrating so deeply on his obsession that he nearly jumped when his manager called out to him. He hesitated for a few seconds before responding. "No, sir. I can handle that."

"Good. Have a nice evening."

"Thank you, sir."

At eight o'clock, John closed out the cash drawer and

put the day's receipts in the floor safe in the manager's office. He padlocked the back door, left the lights on in the storage area, and secured the front door on his way out. The owner had an elaborate security system in place, even though they'd never been robbed.

The rain had ended, leaving the streets slightly muddy. Standing on the porch of the general store, he saw several patrons leaving the Lucky Lady Saloon and staggering to their horses. He was able to make his way to his small room, a short distance from his place of employment, without encountering anyone he knew. It was sparsely furnished with a bed, small desk, kitchen sink with pump and a wood burning stove. He ate some dry bread and cheese he kept in a metal container inside an overhead cabinet and then washed it down with a glass of water. As he undressed and changed into a black sweater and pants, he mentally reviewed his plan. He covered his face with black ash from the stove and put on black gloves and a black cap. He was fairly certain that he would be camouflaged on this moonless night; yet he didn't want to take any unnecessary chances. He looked in the mirror attached to the bureau, made sure his clothing was appropriate, and noted that he wasn't nervous.

It was too early to make his move, so he decided to take a nap. He had nearly two hours to wait. His target was a man of predictable patterns. Every Monday evening, he went to the Grange Hall, played cards until ten, and then walked back to a room at the rear of his barber shop. John wanted to exact his revenge on a more meaningful date, but that would come later. Today would be his first act of retribution; he was excited.

Rising about nine-thirty, he made sure that the lights were out in the widow's bedroom in the house next door. She had a direct view of his only exit and she seemed to be looking out her window every time he came home or went out. He approached her one day and asked her not to spy on him. When that didn't work, he plastered mud on her windows. She complained to his landlord, who laughed it off; apparently, the spying wasn't confined to him alone.

It was a few minutes to ten when he turned out all his lights, slipped out his door, crossed over the slightly muddy Sagunto Street and made his way into the alley behind the livery stable. His position, and the absence of any light in the alley, gave him cover and a clear view of both the barber shop and the Grange Hall a few doors away. He watched as a young man and woman stopped in the shadows and kissed each other longingly. He heard the young woman protest her partner's advances; soon they moved on.

A few minutes after ten, four men came out the front door of the Grange and stopped to talk to each other under one of twelve street lights installed by the power company in Santa Ynez. John recognized his prey, but not the other three. He distinctly heard them gossiping about the widow Smith and who was bedding her this week; all four laughed. Finally, each said good night and walked off in different directions. John went down the alley and quickly made his way behind the barber shop and waited. Soon, he heard someone whistling as they approached his position. The street light cast a shadow of a man; his mark was near.

Just as the man turned the key in the lock on the rear door of his barber shop, John moved quickly, and came up behind him. The target must have heard someone approaching because he instinctively turned toward the noise. It was too late. John hit him on top of his head with a small lead pipe and then held him up as he started to fall. Pushing the limp shape through the door and dragging him to the bed at the far corner of the room was a strain.

John checked outside, closed the door, made sure the windows were covered, and lit a match to illuminate the room. He looked around the room; it could easily be his. It was stark and had no feeling. He wondered if the man spent much time in his room. Striking another match, he confirmed that the man was the barber. It wouldn't do any good to attack the wrong man. He placed a gag in his mouth, rolled him onto his stomach, tied his hands behind his back and lashed his legs together before turning him onto his back again.

As the barber began to stir, he realized that he was tied up and strained against the ropes. He was simultaneously scanning the room and trying to free himself. He stopped exerting himself when John approached and stood over him. "Do you recognize me?"

The light was dim inside the room and the barber strained to look at John. Soon, he nodded his head, yes.

"I remember you. You were one of the soldiers that I heard laugh while you were firing indiscriminately at my family. I'll never forget that day. I'm going to kill you and I'm going to do it slowly, so you'll have time to think about what you and the others did."

His voice was shrill and he knew he had to calm down. What he was about to do would take concentration. There was a look of sheer terror on the barber's face and he kicked out trying to loosen the ropes that bound him. His was a medium-sized frame, but John could see the muscles in his face contort as he strained to move his hands. Gradually, the barber seemed to give up the effort. John waited until the barber was exhausted and perhaps, resigned to his fate.

Standing five feet ten inches tall and weighing nearly one hundred seventy-five pounds, he was the same size as the barber. But John's hands were large and strong and this set the two men apart. He put his hands around the barber's throat and slowly squeezed until the man's face turned blue. He released his hold and allowed the color to return. His target couldn't speak because of the gag in his mouth but his eyes seemed to be pleading. John performed the ritual several times just to torment him; the adrenaline was flowing. The utter hatred he felt for this person was overwhelming. Finally, he decided to put an end to the ritual. When it was over, he felt a sense of relief and one of redemption. He sat back on the bed next to the dead man and tried to regain his composure; he was mentally exhausted.

It was past midnight before he removed the ropes and put the garment over the barber's head, slid it over his shoulders and around his body. The hardest part was putting the man's arms into the sleeves. Once the clothing was in place, he propped the body against the headboard of the bed and looked at the costume; it seemed appropriate. He painted the barber's face red and cut a lock of hair from the nearly bald man. When he was ready, John opened the door and looked out to see if anyone was between him and the post office. With no one in sight, he went back inside, pulled the barber's hands toward him and lifted the body onto his shoulder. It was a short distance to the post office, and though the dead weight of the barber was significant, John easily carried the body and put it on the wood flooring in front of the post office. He leaned the dead man against a structural roof post.

The post office sign was mounted on a six-by-six-inch beam jutting out three feet from the building. John fashioned a noose and threw it over the extended beam. He fastened the other end to the hitching post rail directly below the end of the sign. He pulled on the noose to be sure it would hold the barber's weight. When he was satisfied, John placed the noose over the victim's head, lifted the body onto his shoulder and then slowly let the body hang free. The dead man's feet were touching the ground and his knees were bent. John stuck his head between the man's legs and lifted him higher while pulling on the rope he had double looped around the hitching post, just as it started to rain. John was able to get out from under the body while holding onto the rope with both hands. Through sheer strength, he was able to tie the rope to the hitching post and keep the dead man's body off the ground. The many hours he spent during the last five years lifting heavy bales of hay was paying off. Before he left, he placed a tin cup with a lock of the victim's hair at his feet.

As he started to move away, he heard thunder in the distance, and then a bolt of lightning illuminated the area around him. A shiver went down his spine as he looked at the body being lashed by the rain. Lines of the red paint streamed down on the shirt.

CHAPTER 1
1900

SARAH eased herself out of bed early Sunday morning, slipped on her robe and slippers and made her way to the kitchen. She wanted Tommy to have a few more minutes of sleep on this cool December day. There were still some embers in the kitchen fireplace, so she threw on some kindling that was stacked on the side of the hearth. As soon as the fire rose, she placed a few small logs on top and warmed her hands before starting breakfast.

Last night's biscuits were set on the stove top to keep them warm. Ham was fried, and when she heard him moving in the bedroom, she scrambled his eggs. As he entered their kitchen, Sarah put a pot of coffee and his breakfast on the table. He kissed her on the cheek, rubbed his hand on her bottom, and sat down in the nook. "Don't wait for me, Tommy, your eggs will get cold. Mine will be finished in a few minutes and I'll join you."

Their spacious kitchen had a nook nestled in the east corner, while the stove was on the opposite wall. The kitchen was finished off with a fireplace on the south side. Most family meals were shared at a large table in the middle of the room; the nook was used mainly by Sarah after the children left for school. She'd fix a fresh pot of coffee and sit in the nook looking out over her flower garden and enjoying the many sunlit days in the Santa Ynez Valley. Once in a while, Naomi and Naiwa would join her after they finished their early chores.

Tommy was picking at his breakfast and barely touching his coffee. Sarah placed her hand over his. "I know this is sad day for you. I'd like to spend it with you, if you'll let me. Perhaps we could go to the mission and talk with Father Michael. I know you and he share a friendship; perhaps he can help. If not, I can find something to do if you have other plans."

He smiled back at her. He wasn't a handsome man, but his sharp features, light chocolate skin and hazel-brown eyes were an attraction she couldn't explain.

"I appreciate your concern, but I think I'll take care of something that I've put off for too long. We lost a calf this week and one last month in the south pasture. I saw mountain lion tracks around the carcass when I rode out there two days ago. That cat is getting too bold and needs to be stopped. I'll take two hounds with me and hunt it down. They can use the tracking experience, and it'll give me some time to contemplate. I know you want to help, but I won't be good company today. I should be back no later than the day after tomorrow. I hope you don't mind?" He reached out and ran the back of his hand down her cheek. She grabbed his hand and kissed it.

Although they'd been married for less than seven

years, it was as though they've known each other all their lives. They were not only joined at the hip, but they were soul mates. They could sense each other's moods and knew when it was time to give the other space. She moved from her side of the nook over to him and sat on his lap. She put her arms around his neck and kissed him passionately. "It's okay. Get it out of your system and come back to me refreshed."

Sarah prepared food for two days while Tommy was getting the hounds ready. Raul Mendoza, the ranch foreman, saddled a horse and placed Tommy's favorite rifle in the scabbard on the right side of the roan. In addition to the rifle, Tommy took a bow and quiver of arrows in the event he had a chance to bag the animal with that weapon; he liked to maintain his edge. He checked his saddle and made sure that his spiderlike Dreamcatcher was fastened to the right side. Tommy was not a superstitious individual, but it was hard to break from old customs. The intricate small circular web was made by his mother and given to him on his thirteenth birthday.

The legend behind the Dreamcatcher was that good dreams would pass through the center of the web-like symbol to the sleeping person. The bad dreams would be caught in the web. He knew it was silly to believe in such things, but he'd been raised in that culture and it was hard to let go. Tommy kissed Sarah goodbye. "I'll be okay. I just want to get away for a few days. You know."

"Are you sure you don't want me to put you in a really good mood before you leave?"

He smiled and blew her a kiss as he went out the front door.

Sarah wanted to give her husband space and allow him to deal with this sad anniversary. But Sarah had another reason for wanting to be with Tommy on this day. This was the date her mother and father and most of the members of their wagon train had been killed by a Sioux raiding Party. Sarah could remember the events as though it happened yesterday. Only she, her brother and three other children were spared. Her mother was shot by one of the raiders as she was protecting Sarah. She died in her daughter's arms. Sarah was still angry to this day at the callousness of the raiders. She was torn away from her mother who was dying and trying to say goodbye to her daughter. Helga Hansen was the best mother a young girl could ever have. Sarah felt she'd been cheated out of her childhood and was going to make sure that Thomas and Helga didn't go through what she had experienced.

Tommy reached the carcass near the fish pond after a two-hour ride. The distinctive paw prints of the lion were unmistakable. Four paws about three and one-half inches in diameter were leading south toward the Santa Ynez River. He spent some time making sure the hounds were able to pick up the scent of the carnivore, though it was obvious to Tommy that the predator wasn't trying to hide. Several scat leavings were visible just off the trail as it made its way toward the river. In addition, this lion had a distinctive habit of dragging his rear foot and then urinating on a small log nearby, probably to let others of his species know that this was his territory. Mountain lions lead a solitary life and generally maintain a discrete territory.

As the sun was receding, Tommy set up camp near the river and decided to continue the hunt first thing in the morning. Ancient Indian lore suggested that the setting sun signified the end of the day or the end of life. He hoped that the former was in store for him. Sitting by a roaring fire, he ate some of the chicken that Sarah had prepared and opened a bottle of wine from their vineyard. He reached into his saddlebag and took out his favorite pipe; he had made it when he was a young brave. This was but one of the many skills he learned as he was growing up. Relaxing with the two hounds brought back memories of other times when he had camped out.

Growing up as an Indian Brave, he learned to live in intimate contact and friendship with nature. From childhood, he was trained to be a man, then a warrior and subsequently, a hunter. While white children were read nursery rhymes, Tommy heard lullabies of hunting and heroic exploits of battles or feats of endurance. He could not forget his roots and the symbolism of an outdoor culture. Today was December 15, 1900, and the tenth anniversary of his father's passing. For the past ten years on this anniversary, he went off by himself and reminisced about his days with Sitting Bull.

When Tommy was sixteen, his father took him to a favorite campsite in the mountains and shared with him some of his thoughts and dreams. Sitting Bull wasn't a bloodthirsty savage as portrayed by eastern newspapers. To his people, he was a Sioux patriot who tried to protect his people and lead them to a better life. During their last camping experience, his father told him that it was time for him to make his way in the outside world; the life they knew and loved couldn't be sustained. The white man was too numerous and too aggressive. Any treaty the Sioux signed with government representatives wouldn't be respected. Soon all their lands would be taken and they would be confined to a small area that couldn't sustain their lifestyle.

Tommy was hesitant to leave the nest; yet, he didn't have any trouble finding his way. He was lighter in skin than his brother, but he had Sitting Bull's facial features. They were the same height and weight, with thick eyelashes, sharp features and a pointed nose. Both men were thick in the chest. He prayed that he'd be half the man his father was. His early jobs on ranches and livery stables brought him into contact with many Mexican laborers, and as a consequence, he became fluent in the Spanish language. The six Sioux virtues of silence, love, reverence, generosity, courage and chastity taught by his father and the village elders were his standards to live by.

Luckily, his mother, Elizabeth Kelly, taught him English and how to read and write, so language skills were not an impediment. His mother was a small woman, with red hair and a slight limp. Her white influence probably softened his facial features. Most people he came into contact with didn't realize he was Sioux. His mother had been hit by an arrow during her capture and the wound became infected. As a captive, she didn't receive any medical help and consequently, her leg wasn't set straight. She seldom spoke, and although a captive, she was cherished by his father. It was a tragedy that she died so early in life, as did many female captives; their life was hard and often brutal. She died before his fifteenth birthday. He often wondered what he could've done to make her life more pleasant, but there was nothing he could do; it was the way it was.

The reemergence of the Ghost dance had given the Sioux hope that things would change. Sitting Bull was a skeptic, fearing that it would only serve to activate hostile voices on both sides. Instead of being a promise of fulfillment, the dance became the vehicle for destruction. Jack Wilson, née Wovoka, the sponsor of the dance, told everyone that the dance would bring back their hunting grounds, the buffalo would then reappear and the white man would leave the range. History showed that Sitting Bull was correct in his skepticism. The Ghost Dance wasn't even an original innovation by Wilson. A form of this dance had been practiced in prehistoric times, with the participants forming a circle while holding hands and swaying from side to side.

Six months prior to his father's death, Tommy had witnessed a large Ghost Dance ceremony at the Pine Ridge Reservation. There were nearly 300 tents placed in a wide circle around a large pine tree, adorned on all sides with strips of cloth covered with eagle feathers, claws, stuffed birds and odd-shaped horns. A medicine man and others who said they were experiencing visions stood near the pine tree. Chanting dancers formed a circle around the medicine man inside the tents and raised their eyes to the heavens. As greater numbers joined the dance, the group enlarged the circle. Men and women clasped hands and swayed from side to side, keeping rhythm with the dance. Women wore ordinary dresses, while the men wore a typical shirt. However, the dresses and the shirts bore the same type of ornaments that decorated the shirts hung from the teepees. The collars were blue and the sleeves had red painted stripes down their entire length. Eagle claws and animal bones were sewn on the back of the dresses and shirts.

But this wasn't the only dance indigenous to the Sioux and other Plains Indians. The Sun Dance was the most practiced ritual of the Sioux. The rite included fasting, singing, drumming and self-torture. It was held once a year, normally in June and July, lasting about eight days; it was a sort of regeneration of life.

As Wilson stirred up the Sioux Nation, the American government became increasingly alarmed that the Ghost dance would revive old feelings and there'd be an uprising in the Indian Nations, similar to that experienced at the Battle of the Little Big Horn. Settlers were wary and called for their government to take action. The War Department, fearing that hostility with the Sioux was imminent, issued an order for Sitting Bull's arrest. General Miles, head of the Western U.S. Army, was directed to apprehend the great Sioux chief.

But Miles was concerned that an arrest would cause more problems than it would cure. He asked Buffalo Bill Cody, a friend of Sitting Bull, to accompany him when they arrested the great leader. James McLaughlin, the Indian agent at Standing Rock Reservation, wouldn't wait. He sent Native American policemen to arrest Sitting Bull before Miles and Cody could reach the reservation. A confrontation occurred, and when Sitting Bull resisted arrest, he was shot and killed by the native policemen. The Native American policemen fled the scene as Sitting Bull's followers rallied and attacked them. But they escaped from the village and fled to a ravine outside the reservation, where they were holed up for a week. Eventually, a small detachment of cavalry rescued the policemen. The death of his father left a void in Tommy's life. His confidant and friend could no longer provide guidance.

He was happy with his life and especially with his wife, Sarah. She brought warmth and meaning to their existence. He always wondered what would have happened if they hadn't met. From his first experience away from the reservation, he'd been able to survive and gradually build a small business empire, but money wasn't everything. He wanted a home, but most of all he wanted roots. The need to impart his knowledge to his children, the same way Sitting Bull did for him, was paramount in his life. He considered himself a prince of the wilderness.

His camp selection that evening was nearly two hundred yards back from an animal crossing at the river. The brush and vegetation at the creek was dense and often used by predators to stalk their prey. Just to be safe, Tommy kept the fire going all night so the lion wouldn't sneak up on them. He sensed the animal must be close because the two hounds were jittery. He slept some, but kept his rifle in his hand until daybreak. Sioux lore said the rising sun spread out over the entire earth beginning a new day. Early the next morning, he rose and performed a series of calisthenics, including stretching and deep breathing. After breaking camp, he turned the hounds loose and crossed the river behind them. Rainfall was below normal this year, so the river was only about a foot deep at the spot he chose. Within thirty minutes, the hounds got on the scent and Tommy moved quickly to keep up with them.

But something unexpected happened. The hounds suddenly veered to the left and then back toward his location. Instinctively, he knew what had happened and dropped his gear. With his rifle in front of him, he looked high and low trying to find the lion, or at least sense where it was. The animal had backtracked on the hounds and he could hear it snarling as the hounds kept their distance. He knew the lion was close and he was ready. Just then the lion leaped out of a medium-sized thicket to his right and sprang at Tommy. He raised his rifle ever so slightly and shot the animal, but it was only wounded, and that made it dangerous. The lion's momentum carried it into Tommy's chest and he was knocked over. He quickly got to his feet just as the lion attacked again. His coat was torn and his leg was cut. He pulled a knife from his boot and stabbed the lion repeatedly as he and the lion stood eye to eye trying to gain an advantage. Though it seemed like an eternity, the animal finally succumbed and fell dead at his feet. He lay down on the ground trying to recover. After a few minutes, he sat up and examined his body. In addition to his leg, there were scratch marks on his face, his right sleeve was torn away, and his right forearm was bleeding.

He confirmed the lion was dead and then checked its paws. This was the lion he'd been tracking. The hounds were still agitated and kept their distance from the carcass, even though the lion was dead.

It was easier to skin the animal here than to carry it back to the ranch. But first, Tommy crossed over the creek and retrieved his saddle bags. Inside were bandages and liniment, which he applied to the cuts and scratches. When he took off his coat and rolled up his sleeve, he could see the deep gash in his right forearm. Still, he thought he looked worse than the actual injuries. When he felt that he'd recovered and was once again in charge of the situation, he took out his knives and made the first incision in the animal's remains. As a brave, he had learned to skin buffalo before he progressed to mountain lion. The animal he shot was average in size, measuring five feet from the buttocks to the neck. He started peeling the skin away from its body, as his father had taught him. It took him about forty-five minutes to complete the action. He kept the pelt, left the carcass for other animals, and started home. A light rain started just as he began his trip back, so it took a little longer to complete his journey.

It was nearly three in the afternoon when he arrived at his ranch. He knew that Sarah wasn't expecting him for another day, still three dogs came out to greet him and he called them off. That's when he noticed Juan's horse tethered to the rail in front of the main barn. Tommy turned the hounds over to Raul, his foreman, who came out to see what all the barking was about. "Nice skin," Raul said as Tommy handed it to him.

When he looked at Tommy's face, he said, "My God! What happened to you, Patron?"

"The lion didn't surrender peacefully. I had to use a knife at close quarters. I'm fairly certain this is the one that killed our two calves. He was a mean one. He back-tracked on me and the hounds."

As Tommy approached the house, Juan came out to greet him. "Welcome home, Patron. Did you bring home dinner?" Juan stopped in his tracks and said, "What happened?"

"I had a run-in with a lion. I'm okay, but I know that Sarah's going to have a fit. It was of nice of you to come all the way from town to welcome me."

Though Juan was technically his stepson, the two approached their relationship as brothers. Juan was the son of Sarah and her Indian husband, Crazy Horse, the hero of the Battle of the Little Big Horn. Like Tommy, Juan was a half-breed and was experiencing some of the same prejudice that haunted Tommy in his early life.

"Well, I had something else on my mind. There's been a hanging in town."

"Okay. But why should that affect me?"

"The victim was found swinging in the breeze in front of the post office; he was wearing a Ghost Shirt."

CHAPTER 2
1900

WHEN they entered the house, Sarah and the children rushed to greet him. "I thought it would take you at least two days," and then she saw the scratches on his face, the torn sleeve and the bandaged arm. She pulled back initially; her hand went to her mouth, and then she regained her composure.

"Children, please go play while I take care of your father's wounds." The children had shrunk back and she could see the terror on their faces. They'd never seen their father wounded.

He settled in the rocking chair by the kitchen fireplace while she went for bandages and ointment. "Did you have to perform hand-to-hand combat with the damned lion?" she asked as she pulled off his shirt and examined his wounds.

"The lion was a little anxious and tried to get me. I couldn't wait. I look worse than I feel. The wounds are primarily superficial."

"Are you serious? There's a two-inch gash on your right arm. You probably need a couple of stitches. But the face is what bothers me. You could have lost your eye. One claw mark is only a half inch from your eye. I'm going to use alcohol on the cuts and scratches. It's going to sting, but it serves you right for scaring me." She could feel him tense as she dabbed the alcohol on the cuts. His right pant leg was torn, so Sarah cut the pant leg up the side. The gash on the leg was minor, and she swabbed it with alcohol and bandaged the wound.

"I suggest a glass of whiskey and a hot bath. I can have Naomi prepare it now."

"Let me have the whiskey first, and I'll take a bath later. I want to hear what Juan has to say about the hanging."

"Tommy, you have to take your wounds seriously."

"I'm fine. If I wasn't, I'd tell you so. I want to sit here and listen to what Juan has to say."

"Darn it, you're going to give me a heart attack. I'll get your whiskey."

Juan pulled up a chair in front of Tommy. "Jerry Knudsen came upon the body, about six in the morning. Needless to say, he was shocked. It was a little eerie, because there was a breeze and the body was swinging back and forth. He ran down Sagunto as fast as he could and woke up the Town Constable, who in turn got Dr. Cunnane out of bed. By the time the Town Constable reached the scene, there were twenty people milling around. The constable didn't know what to do; someone suggested he send for you. Rather than go out to the ranch, he came to our law office and asked me to get you."

"You haven't told me who was hanged."

"It was Simon Higgins, the barber."

Sarah was standing behind Tommy's chair as Juan related the incident. "I know him. He's an ex-soldier who worked for us. You remember him, don't you, Tommy?"

"I do. I didn't know him well, but he seemed like a pleasant sort. Who'd want to hang a barber, unless he cut some customer's hair too short?" Tommy laughed and then winced and grabbed his arm.

"He was your barber, wasn't he? I've heard you complain about him several times. In fact, you said he cut one side shorter than the other," Sarah laughed.

"Yep, but I was out of the area when this happened."

"A likely story. The only one that can corroborate that is a dead lion."

He couldn't help but smile as he turned to Juan. "Where's the body now?"

"As far as I know, it's still hanging from a beam in front of the Post Office. The constable doesn't want to proceed until you look at everything. You're not going, are you?"

"I don't see why not. We can take the rig and you can drive."

"Tommy, you look a mess. They'll think you had something to do with it," Juan said.

Sarah brought in a fresh pot of coffee, some warm muffins for her husband and son, and placed them on the table in the nook. "I gather they want you to take a look at the body and explain the Ghost Shirt. Juan told me that some people are worried there might be a Sioux uprising."

"You mean eighty-year-old Little Bear and his sixty-year-old son, who can't walk, are seen as threats to our community?"

"Well, there are you and Juan, aren't there?" Sarah laughed.

"Don't make me laugh, I hurt all over."

"The Town Constable is asking for my help. He and I are hunting buddies. What harm could it do if I went into town and looked at everything? It's still early. Juan can take me in the rig and then bring me back."

"You had a traumatic incident, and I'm worried about infection. I don't want you to go."

When he didn't answer, Sarah shrugged. "I know I'm not going to win this argument, so I'll fix something you can take with you. I want you to promise to have the doctor put some stitches on the right arm while you're in town."

Tommy put his arm around her waist, letting his hand slip much lower as he pulled her to him. She leaned down and he kissed her gently on the mouth.

Juan laughed. "That's my mother you're taking liberties with."

"I know. I know." The three laughed.

"Juan, you make sure he gets stitches in his arm."

"Yes, mother." Juan ducked as Sarah playfully swung at him.

"You men are all alike."

The sky was clear, the light drizzle had ended, and the temperature was still in the fifties when Tommy and Juan arrived at the post office. He was greeted by Charles Little, the Town Constable. A crowd of maybe twenty people were gathered in a circle around the body. The victim, Simon Higgins, was still hanging from a beam outside the post office. An odor was obvious, but a slight breeze was keeping it down somewhat. The body had been hanging for at least fifteen hours; rigor mortis had set in. Tommy walked around the body, carefully taking into account the rope around Higgins' neck and the boot marks on the ground below the body. The rope holding the body was secured to the hitching post in front of the building. Tommy noticed a couple of men he knew. "Can you help the constable take down the body? It's stiff, so be careful."

They laid the body on the wooden flooring outside the post office entrance and Little removed the rope from around the victim's neck. Tommy estimated that the barber was five feet eight inches tall and weighed about one hundred sixty pounds. "I don't see any foot prints other than these distinctive boot marks."

He pointed to the many diamond-shaped marks on the ground under the sign. Tommy tried to see if he could determine where the boots led. After twenty feet, the marks disappeared into the gravel-lined Sagunto Street.

"It would take someone pretty strong to lift the body up and tie the rope to the hitching post. There may be more than one person involved," Little said.

Tommy asked the constable to take off the Ghost Shirt so they could look at it. While he was doing that, Tommy looked at the rope burns around the victim's neck. "Charles, look at these marks on Higgins' neck. In addition to the rope burns, there're bruises as well, probably thumb and finger marks. Someone may have tried to strangle him. Maybe he was strangled first and then hanged here."

"Who'd want to do that?" Little asked.

Tommy shrugged and turned to Dr. Cunnane. "Maybe you can do some sort of autopsy and confirm how he died. He may have been strangled." The doctor nodded.

"Who do you think did this?" Little asked.

"I don't have a theory, but putting that Ghost Shirt on the victim seems like a message to me."

"Do you recognize the Ghost Shirt?"

Tommy picked up the Ghost Shirt. It was made of white cloth and painted blue around the collar. There were figures of birds painted on the front, while the back held crude images of a bow-and-arrow and drawings of the moon and sun. Down the sleeves were rows of feathers tied by a quill and left to fly in the breeze. "I've seen Ghost dances and I've even performed in one, but I was gone from the reservation before the craze swept the Sioux Nation. From what I remember, this shirt is similar to those used in Ghost Dances at the Standing Rock Reservation."

"There are a couple of other things that point to Lakota rituals. Painting the face red is something that my people did with the dead. The lock of hair with the tin cup at the victim's feet is part of that same ritual."

"You think the Sioux did this?" Little asked.

"Could be, and then again, someone may be suggesting we look that way. Charles, I suggest you take pictures of the rope, the body, the marks around his neck, the boot marks on the ground, the tin cup, the paint on the victim's face, and especially the Ghost Shirt. It may turn out to be nothing, but at least you'll have something to refer to if there's another instance."

"You think there may be other hangings?" Little asked.

"I meant to say that you'll have a record of the crime, if you take photos. There's a photographer in town. Tell him what you want. I need a couple of stitches in my arm. Juan will take me to Cunnane's brother. I was mauled by a lion this morning, but I'll be back in an hour. After you take pictures, you should let Dr. Cunnane take the body."

The crowd, including a very interested young man, gathering around the body, seemed to be in shock. After Tommy left, the young man asked one of the bystanders who the Mexican gentleman with the bandage on his arm was.

"That's Tommy Sanchez, and I don't believe he's Mexican. The word is that he's a Sioux half-breed and the son of Sitting Bull. The word is also that he's not someone to antagonize."

"Do you think he could be involved in the hanging? He's pretty banged up."

"No. The constable told me that he was attacked by a mountain lion this morning. He's pretty savvy and someone who helps out the sheriff once in a while; he's probably the best tracker in the area."

Tommy and Juan returned in an hour and were told by the constable that photos had been taken as suggested and that Dr. Cunnane took the body to his office. "What did you do with the Ghost Shirt?" Tommy asked.

"The doctor has it. Do you want to keep it?"

"No. I just want to know where it is. The rope used in the hanging is very coarse. You might want to see who sells that brand in this area. It could give you a lead. The boot marks are also distinctive. Check the general stores and see if they carry boots with that kind of tread." Little acknowledged the suggestions.

"Have you looked at Higgins' room in the barber shop?" Tommy asked.

"No. I was waiting for you."

"Let's go."

Higgins lived in a solitary room in the back of the barber shop, across the street from the post office. They lit a kerosene lamp on one of the tables and looked around the room, searching for anything that might give them some information as to why the barber was killed. They found his birth certificate and 1896 discharge papers from the U.S. Army in the top dresser drawer. "I know he was discharged from the Army in 1896 and worked for me soon after that, both at our ranch and later on the old Singleton spread, after we bought it," Tommy said.

"I've seen Higgins around town, but as far as I know,

he kept to himself and was never married. He was thirty years old," Little said.

The bed was in disarray and there were muddy footprints on the floor. "Charles, these boot marks look similar to those found under the corpse. He may have been strangled here and then carried to where he was found."

Little looked at the boot marks on the floor and made a note of their existence. "I would suggest that you try to recreate the last few hours of Higgins' life. He may have met someone tonight. I also think you need to seal off this room until the sheriff gets a look at it. It's up to the sheriff to follow up," Tommy said.

"The Pinkertons have an office in Santa Barbara. I suggest you call and tell them what you know and ask their advice. They may have some information that could help you, and then again, they may not. I've done all I can for you. Let me know what you find out."

As Tommy and Juan got in the carriage and left the area, their every movement was watched by a young man looking through the front window of the general store.

CHAPTER 3
1900

SIMON HIGGINS was a convert to the Catholic religion. His funeral service took place at the Santa Inez Mission, which was founded in 1804. The Spanish-style buildings were located midway between Mission Santa Barbara and Mission La Purísima Concepción. The complex was built primarily to solve the overcrowding of the other two missions. Soon, the Padres and Mexican settlers turned to farming and candle making, and became quite proficient in making leather goods, especially hand-made boots. In the early days, there was a continuous rebuilding due to the earthquake destruction in 1812. Subsequently, a fire and then a Chumash revolt wrecked the main buildings. During the revolt, many of the itinerant workers from the three missions attacked Mission Santa Inez because a soldier had beaten a young Chumash Indian boy severely. The Chumash burned the soldier's quarters and soon the church was engulfed in flames. But it was the Chumash who put out the fire and protected the priest's vestments.

Recently, the assistant pastor, Father Alexander Buckler, and his sister, Mamie Goulet, with the help of some of the homeless, started restoring the mission. Tommy and several of the ranchers had furnished workers to help the priest complete the restoration.

A funeral mass was performed by Father Michael, the pastor, who was also a friend of both Tommy and Sarah Sanchez. Interment was outside the church in the cemetery on the north side of the complex. Though sparse in attendance, it had significance for three men who stood at the periphery of the small crowd. Their names were Hiram Whitman, Jarod Butler and Samuel Spenser. "I hadn't seen Simon in six months. What about you two?" Whitman asked.

"I saw him last week; he didn't indicate he had any problems. Someone must have really hated him to hang him like that and leave him swinging in the breeze. He was always a pleasant sort, so I don't know how he could have an enemy that hated him that much. He and I kept in touch often after we left Altura Prado. He would've told me if he had any problem with someone here," Butler said.

"He was like a younger brother to me. Though we enlisted at different places, we spent our entire Army career together. We were in the same barracks and assigned to the same detail while we were at Fort Robinson. You get to know someone pretty well after six years shoveling horse manure and fighting the Sioux. He was a good man," Spenser said.

"I didn't know him as well as you two, but we went hunting in the mountains to the south a couple of times.

He was a good shot, and although not overly outspoken, he was nice to be with around a camp fire," Whitman said

When the mass was over, Tommy and Sarah thanked Father Michael for a splendid service. "I don't see you as much as I see Sarah. You know you're always welcome. If you're uncomfortable coming to church, we can always go fishing some afternoon. I hear that you have some nice fish in that pond you made on your lower forty."

"It sounds to me that you're a fisherman and are angling for an invitation. Well, I'm not going to give you a specific invitation. You can fish on our pond anytime you want."

After bringing the priest up-to-date on their children and new grandchildren, Tommy and Sarah moved on to acknowledge some of their acquaintances in attendance. While Sarah was promising one of the widows her recipe for apple pie, Tommy scanned the crowd in attendance. The young man who'd been in the group milling around Higgins' body when Tommy examined the murder scene was there as well. Tommy wondered what his relationship was with Higgins; he seemed out of place. He led Sarah over to the three men, who were now standing by the uncovered grave and expressed their condolences. The men worked for them in the past. "Do you know anyone that could have done this?" Tommy asked the three.

"No, sir. It's as much a surprise to us as it is to you. Higgins was the type of individual that'd go through life and you never knew he was there. He was a good man. What about the Ghost Shirt? I've seen them before when

I was at Fort Robinson, but never in this area. You're Sioux, aren't you, Mr. Sanchez? What do you think?" Butler asked.

"I'm half Sioux. I've seen the shirts when I was young, but like you, it isn't something I would expect to see here."

"What about you, Mrs. Sanchez? I heard you were a captive of the Sioux for many years," Whitman asked.

The history between Whitman and the Sanchezes wasn't good, and therefore Sarah and Tommy didn't appreciate his question. Whitman had made subtle and not so subtle advances toward Sarah when he was employed at the ranch. Sarah didn't want to bother her husband with the issue, but she spoke to Raul, who said he'd take care of it.

Tommy happened to walk into the barn one afternoon at the exact moment that Whitman, who'd been working under Sarah's supervision, let his hand slip to her bottom. The next thing Whitman remembered was getting off the floor and then rushing at Tommy, only to be met with a sharp right hand. This time he got off the dirt floor slowly and didn't return to the fray. Tommy fired him on the spot.

"I've seen them before, but I'm as surprised as my husband at their appearance here in our valley." Sarah tightened her hold on Tommy's arm, signaling him she wanted to leave.

They excused themselves and went to talk to the postmaster, mainly because Higgins was hanged in front of his building. Tommy asked him if Higgins had a confrontation with anyone who was working at the post office. "I don't know of any problem. Higgins seemed to get along with everyone. He was always on time, did his work and never complained. Although he was quiet at work, we're all going to miss him."

The three men watched Tommy and Sarah walk off, and then got on their horses and rode into town to have a beer. When they had first come to the valley, they'd get together at least once a week, but as they grew older, they seemed to drift apart.

"I think you'd better be careful, Hiram. Sanchez and his wife don't appreciate you ogling her like you do," Spenser said.

"Oh, I'm just having fun."

"That kind of fun can get you killed. He kicked your butt before, and I could see in his eyes that he wanted to do it again. Had it been any other place, you'd probably be missing some teeth right now. Sanchez isn't someone to joke with about his wife. There a story going around that a man named Jason Brown took a fancy to her and he turned up dead. Now, I don't say that Sanchez killed him, but if I were you, I'd look elsewhere for your fun, if you know what I mean," Spenser said.

"Oh, I can take care of myself," Whitman responded.

"I'm thinking of getting married," Butler said, trying to lighten up the conversation.

"Who's the unlucky woman?" Spenser asked.

"Mary Westcott. She's a widow with two boys. We've been seeing each other for a year and it's gotten serious.

I couldn't make a move before, because I was trying to build up enough stock so I could make a decent living. I can support them now. My place is small, but the quarter horses I own are first class. Sanchez has been very good to me. He's helped out a lot, so I agree with Spenser, forget about Mrs. Sanchez. By the way, I expect to see all of you when I get hitched; in fact, I need a best man."

"Who's going to marry you?" Spenser asked.

"You are, and Whitman's going to be my best man, but he better keep his eyes off my Mary." They all laughed, toasted their deceased friend, promised to stay in touch with each other more often, and then rode off separately.

CHAPTER 4

1890

IT'D BEEN RAINING the past two days and it was an effort to keep dry. His job was to make sure that water didn't flow into their living quarters. He trenched around their teepee the first day and again the second day. Keeping dry and warm was always a problem in the winter. He felt that this was woman's work. Why must he, a brave, have to do such menial work? It was humiliating. And then there were the young maidens who taunted him, saying he wasn't much of a brave if he was doing woman's work. He'd scowl at them and then chase after them but they wouldn't let him get too close; they'd laugh and run away. But they always seemed to be near; perhaps the fact that White Bird was a handsome youth had something to do with it. Whatever he thought of his chores, he kept that to himself rather than chance the ire of his father. His older brothers were out gathering firewood for the night; that was more like work for a brave.

Today, the sun was out; it was warm for this time of the year. Days like this were few in the winter time. His father was at a tribal council meeting, so he and his brothers decided to play the Corn Cob Game in a field within sight of their village. Most of the young men and women played the game. Contestants would place a corn cob on a rock four to six feet away. The object was to knock the corn cob to the ground by throwing a stone at the cob. To score a point, though, the corn cob had to fall in front of the rock it was resting on. Daniel White Lance had scored two points, Dewey Beard had one, while he and Joseph Horn Cloud hadn't scored yet. He concentrated and finally made his throw just as he heard multiple shots. All four turned to look in the direction of the village. Then a succession of shots followed, and all four ran to see what happened.

They were out of breath by the time they reached a group of villagers. Their apprehension eased when they saw their mother and father standing with others in a circle around men lying on the ground. In the middle of the group was Sitting Bull, lying on his back with his head cradled in the arms of one of his supporters. Blood was saturating the front of his shirt and he looked lifeless. Eight other tribesmen lay dead or wounded near him, while the uniformed Indian Police, who'd come to arrest Sitting Bull, left seven lifeless colleagues lying on the ground. Afterward, the remaining police fled the scene and hid out in a treed ravine outside the village. They were afraid of retaliation by Sitting Bull's admirers.

With a great deal of anxiety, he looked around but couldn't see Maiden Dream or any of her family. His mother was crying, while others were chanting songs of the dead; others of his tribe stood in mute silence. It was as though a veil had been dropped over the mourners, and their faces reflected a feeling of hopelessness; their leader lay dying. "How did this happen?" White Bird asked his father.

"Be still. You and your brothers take your mother back to our lodge. I must help with the dead."

"What can we do?" White Bird asked.

"Do as I say and you'll be helpful."

Their father, Running Bear, was one of the tribe elders who met immediately after the slaughter to determine what action should be taken. There were twelve men on the council. Most were elderly and represented various divisions within the village. Two of the council members were young. But the only action over the next few days was more meetings and no action. The presence of a cavalry unit that came to rescue the Indian policemen who shot Sitting Bull caused more indecision. That wasn't to say that the meetings weren't contentious. The two younger members of the tribe's council were highly volatile and wanted revenge. "If we don't strike now, we'll never strike, and the soldiers will consider us weak. They've broken the treaty and taken most of our land. They expect us to cultivate this semi-arid area of the Dakotas without water and without equipment. They cut back our rations by one-half and they say we are lazy because we can't grow anything. With the buffalo gone, we'll all starve within a few years. What do we have to lose? Living like this is not worth living." This theme was echoed by both younger braves throughout their meetings.

The older members of the council pleaded for caution; the village was without a leader. "Our weapons are few in number and there's no one to rally around. Sitting Bull died last night, Spotted Elk is in Cheyenne and Jack Wilson, who brought back the Ghost Dance, has fled," Running Bear said.

"Let's elect a new leader," the younger two shouted.

"But that would be disrespectful to Sitting Bull, who hasn't even been buried."

But the members of the council were being drowned out by the more vocal faction. So the elders ended the meeting abruptly, leaving the two younger braves without any resolution. Running Bear stayed behind. He tried to placate the younger members by saying that their choices were few. "The soldiers have the weapons and they control the food supply. We must not antagonize them, or we'll all starve."

"Isn't that what we're doing now?" one of the more active young braves said as Running Bear left.

The next morning White Bird and his brothers went back to the scene of the bloodbath, but it was as though it had never happened. The area had been cleaned and the bodies removed. The four brothers were told by one of the women that plans were being made to bury Sitting Bull and the other members of the tribe who were killed. The dead Indian soldiers had been taken back to Pine Ridge Reservation. Still, no one spoke of reprisals. "How can we just accept this?" White Bird asked his brothers. They hung their heads and didn't respond.

Rather than have a continual confrontation, the elders met without their younger members for two days, but nothing happened. As the days passed, talks of reprisals were few and then none at all. At the end of ten days, his father told the family to prepare to move. They were going to join Chief Spotted Elk, who was leaving the Cheyenne River Reservation with over two hundred of his followers and traveling to Pine Ridge Reservation to seek shelter and protection from Chief Red Cloud

"But why must we leave our home?" White Bird asked.

His mother, Little Paw, who seldom spoke out, wrapped her arms around her son. "It's not safe here, and there's not enough food to feed us. The Indian agent asked us to grow crops, but the land with little or no rain won't support any crops; then they cut our rations in half. We know how to raise crops. Before our ancestors had horses and followed the buffalo, we raised corn and grew berries. We must find a place where we can live without fear of being shot or of starving. Chief Red Cloud has promised to protect and feed us."

It wasn't as though his family was rich, but they did have some possessions that meant something to them. Running Bear told them to trade their possessions for food. They needed all the food they could carry for the three- to four-day trip to the Pine Ridge Reservation. White Bird had a small headdress that had been given to him by his paternal grandfather. He loved the colors of the feathers and was reluctant to part with the treasure, but his father said he couldn't take it with him. Rather than trade the prized possession, he gave it to his best friend, Morning Eagle, who was staying behind.

CHAPTER 5
1900

TWO WEEKS had passed since the barber's body was found hanged from the post office sign. Charles Little had contacted the Pinkerton Agency in Santa Barbara and the Santa Barbara County Sheriff. No clues had turned up, nor had the other law organizations been able to provide any guidance. Boot marks on the ground and the rope used for hanging Higgins, which seemed to be significant leads, turned into a dead end. Most people believed the killing was the work of somebody passing through town. Most felt that it couldn't have been committed by any of the peace-loving people in the valley.

This was the sixth year Tommy, Sarah and the family celebrated the holidays on their ranch. It was also the sixth consecutive year they invited friends, neighbors and business people to their home for a barbecue and a glass of Christmas cheer. They sent out invitations for guests and their families to come on December 29, 1900, at two p.m.

A local combo was hired to play for the group, while a couple of Tommy's vaqueros set up a dance floor in their backyard. Raul was the resident master chef; he and three of his vaqueros cooked two half cows over an open fire. Invitees began to arrive around two in the afternoon and mingled around the vaqueros cooking the beef until dinner was served at four. Guests from Santa Barbara were housed overnight in the bunkhouse; some had been invited every year of the cookout. Picnic tables were fashioned from lumber used on the ranch and kerosene lamps lighted the rear landscape. The tables were covered with red, white and blue cloths.

Holiday decorations were everywhere and would remain in place until a week after New Year's Day. Red and white rosebushes, which had been pruned, dotted one side of the one-thousand-foot entryway into their ranch. A ground covering of ivy covered the other side of the lane. Pasture fencing, lining the road, was decorated with all kinds of Christmas ornaments. Sarah was in charge of the decorations and Tommy was in charge of the beer and wine. Needless to say, the wine came from their boutique winery, while kegs of cold beer were delivered from the Lucky Lady Saloon in Santa Ynez.

Close to four o'clock, the dinner of beef, baked potatoes, carrots, salad and dessert was served on the patio. Nearly seventy people lined up at the serving table and carried their plates back to the tables spread over the back lawn. Guitar music kept the diners entertained during their meal. Later, Tommy served after-dinner drinks, and one of his friends, running for councilman, gave a quick speech. It was Sarah who ended the evening by wishing them a Merry Christmas and Happy New Year after Father Michael offered a short prayer.

Sarah had lived on the ranch for nearly ten years. When she married Thomas Sanchez, they bought the adjoining parcel owned by Don Ortega and built a vineyard and expanded the cattle operation that Sarah had started. Once the ranch was making a sustained profit, Tommy turned his attention to raising quarter horses. His herd had risen to almost thirty; he was ready to start selling to the public.

Jarod Butler, who, like Higgins, Spenser and Whitman, had worked at the ranch, started a small spread in the valley and wanted a couple of mares to breed to his stallion. He'd been looking in the valley for a few months, without too much success. The problem was that most sellers wanted cash. As luck would have it, he was able to talk to Tommy Sanchez over a glass of Christmas cheer at the party. He took advantage of that meeting to ask Tommy's advice.

"You have some great stock, Mr. Sanchez. I admired them when I worked here. I know you're selling a few at a time, and I'd be grateful if you'd sell me two mares, if the price isn't too high."

The price Tommy quoted was too high for Butler. "I know your stock is first-class, but I may have to look elsewhere. I just can't afford that much."

"What if I were to keep my price, but let you have them for half down and the balance payable, quarterly, for two years?"

"That's more than fair. I believe I can handle that. I won't let you down."

"One thing I've learned in the short time we've known each other is that you're a hard-working man and one I can trust. I'm happy to be able to help you. If you'd like, I can have Raul bring them over tomorrow morning, say about eleven. Why don't the three of us talk before you leave? Eleven o'clock will give you enough time to get funds from the bank before he arrives. He'll have the bill of sale and a contract reflecting the balance to be paid in two years."

"There's one more thing, Mr. Sanchez. I'm getting married next Saturday at noon to Mary Westcott. My friend, Spenser, is performing the ceremony at his small church. I wonder if you and Mrs. Sanchez would come. We're going to have a small reception at my place after the ceremony. I know you're a busy man, and I'll understand if it's inconvenient for you."

Tommy looked around and saw Sarah talking to a friend from Santa Barbara. He signaled to her and she came over to the two men. "Jarod is getting married next Saturday and has invited us. Do we have anything going on that day?"

"Not that I'm aware of, and even if we did, I'd move it so we could attend."

The look on Butler's face didn't need to be explained. His mentor was taking the time to be with him on his most important date.

Around seven, many of the local guests started to

leave. The last one to leave was Jarod Butler. He made arrangements with Tommy and Raul to deliver the two horses Tommy had sold him. Raul said he'd deliver them the next morning at eleven o'clock.

John had never met Tommy Sanchez, but he had been one of the onlookers when Sanchez took down Higgins' body. Later, he saw him and his wife at the funeral of Simon Higgins. John was impressed with how Sanchez looked over the murder scene, pointing to the distinctive boot marks and the quality of the rope. He hadn't realized that Sanchez was Sioux until one of the other men watching the scene told him. He wondered if Sanchez knew where the Ghost Shirt ornaments had originated. Everything he heard about Tommy Sanchez pointed to an individual who would be a formidable adversary.

The annual party at the Sanchez ranch was the big social event of the holidays in the Santa Ynez Valley. Friends and business associates were invited; his employer was there, but John wasn't. It was dark around six that evening as he lay hidden behind some shrubs at the entranceway to the Sanchez Ranch. The gate to the ranch had been left open, so no was looking in the direction of his hiding place as they rode through. He dressed in black, as before, with a black cloth hat and gloves; the Ghost Shirt and rope were carried in a paper bag tied to his belt. He hoped that Butler would be the last to leave. It was known around town that he was very friendly with the Sanchez couple. John had learned a good bit more about Tommy Sanchez. Shooting the hats off Ed Meade and his two friends on Sagunto Street in Santa Ynez was a legend in these parts. Equally impressive was the story of the beating he subsequently gave Meade when he ordered him to leave town. Tommy Sanchez, by everyone's account, was the most lethal man alive.

John couldn't help but wonder how he'd fare against Sanchez. Though slightly bigger and much younger, he knew he wouldn't stand a chance with a gun. However, with a knife, John backed up for no man; it would be interesting. Christmas music was flowing from the ranch house and he caught himself singing along, but he stopped when he saw a carriage coming down the entryway. The face wasn't distinguishable, but the individual driving was the same size as Butler.

Crouching near the open gate, he waited for the rig to go through and then stop. The driver jumped out just as he passed the gate and walked back to close it. John rushed the man from behind and hit him over the head with a zap and the man staggered, falling to his knees, but he quickly recovered and began to rise. John struck him again and the man fell again but rolled onto his side. John dived on top of him and flailed away, but the quarry was holding his own until he was hit in the head again several times with the zap. John looked around to be sure he was alone before he turned the fallen man over, struck a match and looked at the face of Jarod Butler.

The limp weight of the man posed a problem, but John exerted himself and dragged him back to the carriage and gradually lifted him onto the front seat. He tied Butler's arms behind him, bound his legs with a rope and placed a gag in his mouth. John closed the gate and drove to the Butler Farm. He didn't encounter anyone on the trip there.

There were livestock in the corral, and two dogs on a leash were barking as he passed by the small house. It was light enough to make out that the barn door was open enough for John to drive the carriage in. Butler hadn't moved during the two-mile trip. Once inside, John closed the barn door and checked to see that no one was inside, though he knew that Butler lived alone on his small spread. Butler started to stir and made a moaning sound. John hit him over the head again with the zap and Butler slumped forward and didn't move. John had to work fast. He cut the restraints on Butler's hands and placed the Ghost Shirt over his head and around his body. He refastened the rope around Butler's hands before he placed the noose around his neck and pulled it tight.

He had been nervous when he hanged Higgins, and didn't complete the rituals he felt were necessary. He had plenty of time now, because no one else was living on this remote ranch. He opened the small can of red paint and painted Butler's face red. Then he cut a lock of the man's hair close to the scalp and put it in a tin cup. The adrenaline was moving through his veins and he was excited. He raised his hands and communicated with the spirits, attempting to gain wisdom and strength. "This is for you, my parents and my loved one."

The carriage was under the main beam traversing the

barn, and John threw the rope over the rafter and tied one end to a vertical beam on the side. He pulled it tight so that Butler's body was forced upright in the seat. John got in the cab from the other side and pushed the unconscious man off the seat. Butler swung to an upright position with the tip of his toes barely touching the floor of the barn.

The jolt awakened the rancher, but he was groggy. He tried to determine what was happening to him while his body was twisting. His face was turning blue and he tried in vain to keep enough weight on his toes to allow him to breathe. It took him some time to realize that someone else was in the barn and smiling at him; in fact, the man had a glass of liquid in his hands and seemed to be toasting him. Butler was a rugged man, and he spent the last thirty minutes of his life trying to stay alive. He struggled with the ropes binding his hands and then those holding his legs before he gave up and his head slumped to his chest. John waited another hour before he removed the bindings around Butler's legs and arms. He smoothed out the Ghost Shirt, placed the tin cup with the lock of hair near Butler's feet, and left the barn.

CHAPTER 6
1900

AFTER giving the vaqueros their tasks for the day, Raul met with Tommy and was told which horses had been promised to Butler. "Those are two of your best young mares, Patron. Are you sure you want to part with the white one? It would make a great quarter horse."

"I know, but I like Butler, and this is kind of a wedding present from my wife and me. It's always good to treat your neighbors like you'd like to be treated."

The two young horses were still green and a little spirited, but Raul was an experienced equestrian, and the mares soon learned who was in charge. It took him nearly two hours to lead the young stock to Butler's small spread in the Happy Canyon section of the valley. He didn't see the owner anywhere, so he put both animals in a holding pen. The dogs were tied up and barking, but that didn't bother him. He understood that Butler might be at the bank this morning getting funds for one half the agreed-to price of the two mares. Tommy told Raul to wait for the money and have Butler sign a promissory note for the balance. Since no one came to greet him, Raul walked up to the one-bedroom adobe and knocked on the door. No one answered, so he went around the back of the house, but he didn't see anyone.

He decided to see if the owner was in the barn and just hadn't heard him arrive. He opened the barn door and immediately stopped where he was. Butler was hanging from the center beam. As far as Raul could tell, he was dead—and was wearing a Ghost Shirt. Raul was torn between going back to the ranch and telling Tommy Sanchez or letting the town constable know what happened.

The constable was in his office when Raul arrived. "My God, not another one," was his response when Raul told him, in fractured English, about finding Butler.

Raul wasn't sure what to do, so he went back to Butler's farm with Little. "Raul, I want you to go to the ranch and tell Mr. Sanchez what happened. Tell him I need him again. I'll wait here until you and he get back here."

"I'm going to take the two horses back and let Mr. Sanchez decide what to do."

Finding Butler's body hanging in the barn had unnerved Raul. Just last night the two had talked about delivering the two mares the next day and about his wedding next week. Butler was in such a good mood, perhaps due to the wine he drank, but certainly because of his good fortune. He invited Raul and Naiwa to come. The foreman was reluctant to tell Tommy what happened, but he knew he had to. He found Sanchez coming out of the main barn as he rode up to the ranch house. When he saw the two young horses tied up the rail, Tommy asked what happened. Raul told him in Spanish how he found Butler, his subsequent trip to the town constable, and the law enforcement officer's request to see Tommy. Sarah joined the two men as Raul rode up and overheard the dialog between the two men. Tommy looked at Sarah. "You might as well go with him. You know you want to," Sarah said.

Tommy decided to stop at the constable's office first before going to Butler's place. Little had just returned and the body had been taken to Dr. Cunnane's office. After the two discussed the hanging, they rode back to Butler's farm. "Cunnane doesn't plan to do an autopsy; he accepts the fact that Butler was hanged. I kept the rope the killer used and the Ghost Shirt for you to look at. As you'll see, I cordoned off the area around where the body was, so you could see the boot marks."

Tommy spent the next hour analyzing the crime scene and the surrounding area. When he was finished, he sat on a hay bale and examined the Ghost Shirt. He noticed the similarities with the one found on Higgins.

"The two killings used the same brand of rope, had the same boot marks below the body, and then there's the Ghost Shirt. I think whoever is making these shirts is Sioux and probably from the Standing Rock Reservation where my father lived before he was killed. I remember several teepees that were decorated with many of these same ornaments. There are two other elements of this murder that may or may not have any significance, I can't tell."

"What are they?" Little asked.

"First, it appears that Butler and the killer came here in Butler's carriage. So my question is, where did he intercept Butler and how did he leave here? Our ranch is a good two miles from town. The killer probably intercepted Butler somewhere between our gate and Butler's farm. That's quite a range to search. It's also possible that he had an accomplice who had a horse waiting here. I took a look at that option and followed the boot marks outside and through the entrance gate. The killer started down the road into town and I lost his tracks when he cut across Anderson's field. My guess is that he walked to the place where he neutralized Butler, and after he hanged him, he walked home."

"What's the second?"

"Simon Higgins was hanged on the anniversary of my father's death, and Butler was murdered on December 29th, the anniversary of the Massacre of Wounded Knee in 1890."

"You're suggesting that these murders are symbolic," Little said.

"It's possible; the question is how to tie those two events to the two men who were killed. I know that Butler and Higgins were friends and in the Army at the same time and were discharged on the same date along with Whitman and Spenser. All four came to the valley together and worked for me. That raises several questions.

Was there something that happened while they were in Army that has come back to haunt them? Another question that seems obvious is, did Spenser or Whitman or both kill their two friends? If they did, what was the reason? I think Higgins and Butler were close friends. I also know that Spenser was going to marry Butler and Mary Westcott and Whitman was to be his best man. Did they know something about either or both of the other two? If I were you, I'd ask the sheriff to question Spenser and Whitman to see what they know. They may not be involved, but they may know what lies behind these killings."

"Is the rope similar to that used to kill Higgins?"

"My best guess is that it is similar. You were going to check on these two items. What did you find out?" Tommy asked.

"Nothing. The general store doesn't carry that brand of rope, or boots with that distinctive sole. The young man I talked to at the store said he never saw those brands and doesn't know where to find them. I forgot to tell you that Butler's face was painted red and some of his hair lay in a cup at his feet."

"That's definitely a Sioux ritual," Tommy said.

CHAPTER 7

1890

ONCE the decision was made to move to Pine Ridge Reservation, they had but one day to prepare. Though raised to be stoic, White Bird couldn't control the tears that ran down his cheeks. This was the only home he knew. Where they were going was unknown, and he was apprehensive. Leaving his friends, and especially Maiden Dream, was disheartening. Last week she let him kiss her and fondle her breasts, and now he was going to leave, and some other brave would have that privilege. How could this be happening to them? He wasn't actually courting her in the Lakota tradition, but the understanding between the two of them was meaningful.

During their initial stages of courting, he'd wait behind a tree until she came down the path to the small stream outside the village and pretend that he just happened to be there. Soon that progressed to the point where each was anticipating meeting the other. She even suggested other spots where they might come upon each other. He was two years older than she, but she'd reached the age of puberty and soon would be of the marrying age.

That evening he went to her teepee; her father was out, so the two young lovers clasped hands and walked to a grove of sycamore trees outside their village. "I don't want you to leave. Why can't you stay here with another family?" Maiden Dream was crying.

"I asked Eagle Feather, my best friend, but he said they didn't have enough food for themselves, let alone another. My brothers and I have hunted most everything in this area for food, but lately it's as though the animals are trying to wait us out."

"I can ask my father to let you stay with us; I'll share my portion with you."

"I don't think he likes the way I look at you." Although there were tears on her cheeks, she couldn't help but smile.

"I want to be your woman. Take me now. My father will have to agree that we are meant for each other if I am with child. I don't think he's promised me to another."

He'd never gone beyond kissing and feeling the girl's breasts, but he heard from his brothers what it was like and how to bed a woman. He kissed Maiden Dream passionately and then began to undress her; she moaned and helped him. Just as they lay down side by side, her father, Drift with the Wind, came upon them. "Get your clothes on, Maiden Dream, and go back to our lodge. I will talk to you later."

The girl scurried away, dressing as she ran. "I know your father; he wouldn't be pleased at what you were doing with my daughter."

"I love Maiden Dream. I wouldn't do anything to

hurt her. We would've waited but, I'm leaving tomorrow and I probably would never see her again."

"Even more reason to be a man about this. You would leave my daughter with child and no husband. You are a little boy, not a man."

"Let me have her. I will take care of her. I am a man. You will see."

"You may have your chance. My family is joining the trek tomorrow. I want your word that you and Maiden Dream will wait until I give my permission. She is only fifteen. I want you to prove to me that you can take care of her. If you can do that in the next year, she is yours."

"You'll never be sorry. I will cherish her and take care of her; you will see."

"All the young men in heat say the same thing. I don't want words; prove to me that you're the man she needs."

"Can I tell my parents of your promise?"

A smile crossed her father's lips. "I have already spoken to your father."

When he told his parents of his good fortune, his mother smiled and kissed him on the forehead. His father said, "You have a year to prove yourself. Don't let your mother and me down."

Twenty families began their trek on December 26th to Pine Ridge Reservation. Most families walked in a light snow storm. Those who had ponies constructed a travois to carry their belongings. Two long teepee poles were crossed and strapped to the animal's back, and a carrying platform was fastened behind and between the two poles. Many of the small horses had been swapped for food with those staying behind. Relatives and friends gave those leaving as much food as they could spare, but it was only enough for one meal a day. White Bird and his family were one of the lucky ones. Even though their horse was old, it was able to carry everything they'd been able to bring. Maiden Dream and her family walked beside White Bird's. When they thought no one was looking, they'd hold hands as they walked; once when they thought no one was looking, they kissed. His mother saw them and smiled.

Heavier snow fell the first night of their trek, and exacerbating the situation was the absence of wood along the trail to keep the fires going all night. White Bird's family huddled together to keep as warm as best they could. They woke up the next morning to six inches of snow. Two older members of the trek died in their sleep and were quickly buried. Another family lost their horse; their belongings were divided up and carried by others with animals, and on they moved.

The second day of travel was tiring because of the amount of snow that had fallen the previous night. Trails had to be cut by some of the younger men to help the families. White Bird and his brothers took turns breaking trail and carrying personal items for the older tribesmen and women making the tedious trek; they fell asleep early that night. There were few trees and no water along their route. The group camped in a small ravine and used blankets as shelter from the cold and the howling wind. White Bird saw very little of Maiden Dream that day.

On the afternoon of the 28th, their small group caught up with Spotted Elk and fell in behind his people. The trail was broken by Spotted Elk's followers, and the walking was much easier. Soon thereafter, the entire group was met by the U.S. 7th Cavalry, commanded by Major Whiteside, who escorted them the next five miles to Wounded Knee Creek, where they made camp.

After he'd completed his chores and ate a meager dinner, White Bird asked his parents if he could spend some time with Maiden Dream. His father was reluctant, but his mother convinced the father that it was okay. Her family didn't have a fire and they cuddled close to each other to keep as warm as possible. Maiden Dream suggested to her father that another body would provide some more warmth and the young couple couldn't do anything with her parents so close. The father was tired and gave his consent; the two young lovers made the most of it and held each other until morning when White Bird went back to where his family had bedded down.

That evening Whiteside was relieved of his command by Colonel Forsyth, who brought with him additional troops. The Sioux and other members on the trek were now outnumbered five hundred to three hundred fifty. In addition, Forsyth showed up with four Hotchkiss mountain guns, which was like bringing a gun to a knife fight. The Indians were cold, tired and hungry. The significance of the maneuvers that Forsyth was performing and the reason for the additional firepower was lost on them; they were exhausted and perhaps didn't care.

In the morning, just after White Bird returned to his family, Forsyth lined up the Hotchkiss mountain guns on a ridge overlooking the Indian camp site, which was covered with snow. Soldiers surrounded the Indian encampment, while Forsythe used a bullhorn to order the Indians to relinquish their weapons. The soldiers aggressively went through the crowd, but less than fifty weapons were confiscated. Those were stacked in a pile between the Indians and the soldiers.

Antagonism started slowly at first, with insults being traded back and forth. But soon both sides increased the rhetoric, and the more volatile ones on either side were egged on by their compatriots. One Indian donned a Ghost Shirt and started to perform the Ghost Dance; another refused to give up his weapon. Soon a scuffle broke out between that individual and a soldier; a weapon was discharged. Then more guns were fired, and many around White Bird's parents were shot and fell to the ground. Initially, the soldiers were firing their rifles at close range into the mass of Indians gathered together in one place. With no cover, and no weapons, the slaughter lasted but a few minutes. To those under fire, it seemed like an eternity. Some tried to flee, and soldiers ran them down and shot them; some were bayoneted. Forsythe ordered his gunners to fire the Hotchkiss guns into the entire camp of men, women and children; the onslaught was devastating. Some women tried to flee to a ravine to escape the rain of bullets from the soldiers but were run down and killed. Many soldiers finished off the wounded with bayonets and rifle fire, while some mounted their horses and ran down those trying to escape the deluge.

Maiden Dream had come to his side when the shooting started and grabbed his hand. White Bird had seen his father and mother clutch their chests and fall among the others. They'd been shot point blank by four soldiers standing in front of White Bird. He stood immobile at first, but when they trained their guns on him and Maiden Dream, he pulled her into the mass of humanity and they burrowed themselves under the bodies. The shooting continued to intensify and bodies seemed to fall in rapid succession, many on top of each other. White Bird lost track of his brothers, but not Maiden Dream. When he decided to rise, the number of bodies falling around them blocked any exit and they fell back. Three more bodies fell on him, which may have saved his life. Though they were dazed and pinned down by the bodies on top, they could see women and children being run down by soldiers: some were shot, others were bayoneted. Those who could escape ran for the ravine with weapons they took from the pile of confiscated weapons. Soon they fired on the soldiers.

All around him and even above him were the sounds of women moaning and children crying. This must have incensed the soldiers, because they came back and shot those who were still alive. Several bullets barely missed him; he didn't make a sound or make any movement that would give away his position. Maiden Dream was not as lucky. A stray bullet pierced the left side of her head and before he could say "I love you," she was gone. He could barely see through the bodies above him, but what he did see indicated that the soldiers were making sure the dead were really dead by firing multiple shots into the bodies around him. The shooting was over in less than an hour, and that's when he heard the soldiers coming back. They were calling out to anyone who might be alive, but White Bird didn't trust them. He remained where he was, holding onto the cold hand of his love.

CHAPTER 8

1900

WITH the twins and Sarah's two Indian grandchildren back in school, she and Tommy had some time to themselves and decided to play house. It started in the back yard when Sarah sprinkled water on Tommy's head and he chased her inside. He grabbed her dress from behind and both ended up on the floor. He pulled her to him and they quickly started to undress each other. "As much as I'd like to do it here, I'm afraid that Naomi or Naiwa would be embarrassed if they saw you fucking me on the kitchen floor."

"I got the message." He lifted her in his arms and with his pants around his feet, he stumbled into their bedroom and onto the massive four-poster. There wasn't much talking after that, just a lot of panting and moaning over the next few minutes. When they were finished, they lay side by side and looked at each other and smiled. "Not bad for an old married couple, if I might say," Sarah said.

"Madam, at this point you can say anything you want."

Their bedroom, with a large picture window lined

with laced curtains, was on the north side of the house. It looked out over the front yard and the entryway to their ranch. Lying in bed, they had a direct view of the entrance road. A lone rider was slowly coming up their road. He didn't seem to be in a hurry; it was as though he'd been here before. As he came closer, they could see who it was and hurriedly dressed before going outside to greet James Jefferson, their friend, and a Pinkerton detective.

After shaking hands with Tommy and embracing Sarah, he mentioned that Sarah seemed flushed. "Are you okay?"

She was quick to respond. "I was doing some baking, and it's a little warm around the stove." With that comment she walked into the house.

Jefferson turned to Tommy, who raised his eyebrows and smiled. The detective had been a frequent visitor to the valley over the last few months. As part of his investigation into Jarod Butler's murder, he'd come into contact with Mary Westcott, who'd been Butler's intended. Though she was at least twenty years his junior, he and the widow had been keeping company. She was a delightful woman, and Tommy and Sarah had encouraged the relationship by having them to dinner at the ranch on two occasions.

Jefferson followed him into the kitchen and sat down at the nook. Sarah offered coffee, and Jefferson accepted some biscuits she placed on the table. "This isn't strictly a social call, though it's always a pleasure to see such good friends." He had their attention as Sarah slid in next to Tommy.

"The Ghost Shirt murders have the entire county nervous, and no one knows what to do. Women and children don't want to go outside at night. I think everyone sees an Indian uprising on the horizon."

"I gather that there's a reason why you're telling us this," Tommy responded.

"I don't know whether either of you have seen yesterday's *Santa Barbara Register.* There's an editorial that you need to read; it's on page five. It was written by Samuel Jacobs, the new owner and editor." Jefferson handed the paper to Tommy.

He opened the paper to page five and laid it on the table in front of Sarah so she could read it as well. They read without speaking.

"The recent murders in the Santa Ynez Valley have been investigated by the Santa Barbara Sheriff's Office and their consultant, the Pinkerton Agency. They have a reputation as a first-class detective agency with forensic science capability. This reporter doesn't understand why a major portion of the investigation was headed up by Mr. Thomas Sanchez of Santa Ynez, who is the legitimate son of Sitting Bull. The father is the same killer who slaughtered the 7th cavalry and their famed commander General George Armstrong Custer at the Battle of the Little Big Horn."

"What's this all about?" Sarah asked.

"Read on, there's more."

"The corpses of the two men hanged in Santa Ynez were desecrated with a Ghost Shirt, which was the symbol for the Sioux to rise up and force the white man from their land. It's also interesting that Sitting Bull was arrested because he was involved in the Ghost Dance, which the U.S. Government felt would lead to an Indian uprising. So here is the son of Sitting Bull, a former Sioux brave, leading the investigation of the two Ghost Shirt murders. This reporter feels that a more qualified and independent person should be hired as a consultant, if the Sheriff doesn't believe in the capability of the Pinkerton Agency. Having Mr. Sanchez as your consultant is like having a fox guard the hen house. I haven't met Mr. Sanchez, but his reputation as a gunfighter shouldn't be the credential for leading this investigation."

"It seems to me that the editorial is suggesting that you either had something to do with the two murders, or you're impeding the investigation," Sarah said.

"Why is he suggesting that?" Tommy asked Jefferson.

"He wants to increase circulation and make a name for himself at the same time. Since you are the son of the great Sioux Chief, he feels that you're good copy and will certainly enhance his readership and circulation."

"Where's he from?"

"Back east. I believe someone told me that he grew up in Boston. He came out here last year and bought the paper after the previous owner died."

"Well, it wasn't something that I volunteered for. I was asked by the Town Constable to help out. I'll stay out of it, if that's what you want. I have enough on my plate without some distraction, such as this."

"You're the most qualified man I know, and I want you to help. The hell with Jacobs—just ignore him."

"I hope it's as easy as that. Once someone stirs up old memories, it's hard to put them back where they belong. An accusation has a life of its own, and it doesn't have any idea who it will attack. I think I'll watch from the sidelines for a while," Tommy responded.

"Do you think there will be more hangings?" Jefferson asked.

"I liked both men who were hanged. There may have been something in their past that they wish hadn't happened, but while they were here they were solid citizens. I think someone holds a grudge and may not be appeased by just two hangings. You need to look to the past, because that's what the Ghost Shirt is; it's the past. I have another suggestion. There were four men who were mustered out of the Army at Fort Robinson at the same time. The same four worked for us for about six months. I'd interview the two survivors to see what they have to say. Perhaps, they're on somebody's list as well."

"Even if you won't get involved, I hope that I can call on you for advice?" Jefferson left the couple and rode into town.

On Wednesday of the next week, the four children came home from school and immediately went to their rooms. Sarah thought that was odd, and knocked on Thomas' room and asked to speak to him. Reluctantly, he opened the door and came out into the hall. Sarah was shocked. His face was swollen; there were scratch marks on his cheeks and his nose was red, with some remnants of blood in his nostrils. His shirt was torn and his pants dirty.

"Thomas, what happened?"

"Nothing, I just fell, that's all."

"This looks more like fighting than falling."

Thomas didn't respond, so Sarah took him by the hand and walked him into her room and applied some lotion to his scratches and washed his nose. She then took him into the kitchen, got some ice, and put it in a handkerchief. "I want you to hold this against your cheek to bring the swelling down. You can go to your room now, and we'll talk about this at dinner."

At dinner time, she rang her bell. Everyone came but Chatan. She called him but he didn't respond. "I'll get him," Tommy said.

Tommy walked down the hall and knocked on the boy's bedroom door. "Chatan, it's time for dinner. Come on."

"I'm not hungry. I'm not feeling well."

Tommy sensed something was wrong. "Chatan, open the door. We have to talk."

Within a moment, the door opened slowly and Chatan emerged, with swollen eyes and scratches on his face. "What happened, son?"

"It's nothing. I had a fight at school."

"Who with?"

"Some guys."

Tommy led the young man into the kitchen and his mother, Naiwa, became hysterical. Sarah was calm; she took Chatan into her room, washed his face and put lotion on the scratches, and brought him back to the table.

It took some time before the story unfolded. Three bigger boys had started picking on Chatan at the beginning of the school year, and it got progressively worse. Initially, it was because Chatan was new, and later because he was a little slow and didn't catch on as fast as others his age. It wasn't simple bullying; there was a new element to the abuse. The three older boys said that Tommy hanged the two men in Santa Ynez and that Chatan was probably a killer just like Tommy. Young Thomas came to his rescue, and he got the same treatment as Chatan. The two girls, Wachiwi and Helga, confirmed what happened. "They've been picking on Chatan because he's different, but they always call Thomas an Indian lover," Helga said.

"Give me the boys' names," Tommy demanded.

The boys were apprehensive at first, but after further entreaty on Sarah's part, Thomas told them it was Fred Grimes and the Heller brothers, Nick and Roger.

"Why, they're ten to twelve years old! Thomas and Chatan didn't have a chance. Doesn't Heller's father run the Sagunto Saloon in Santa Ynez?" Sarah asked.

"I think I'll pay him a visit."

"Be careful, Tommy, that newspaper article may have stirred up a lot of people."

"Probably, but I think it's time we take a stand and

make sure that our children are not singled out because of me. The Heller boys didn't dream up this harassment by themselves."

Sarah tended to the children's homework while Tommy went to his office and reviewed some invoices. Around eleven that evening, he kissed Sarah and made his way into town.

The Sagunto Saloon was a local watering hole on Sagunto Street in Santa Ynez, where Tommy and Sarah purchased kegs of beer whenever they had a party. It closed at midnight on week days, so Tommy arrived about eleven-thirty and waited in the shadows outside the back door. At twelve-thirty, Phil Heller locked the back door and started walking toward his home.

"A word with you, Phil?"

Heller stopped and looked around, but he didn't see Tommy. "Who … who is it? I'm not carrying any money."

Tommy stepped out of the shadows and walked up to Heller, effectively blocking his path. "Oh, it's you, Mr. Sanchez. Why didn't you come in and have a drink? Why wait out here?"

"What I have to say is between you and me—and how long we talk is up to you."

Heller was starting to understand that this wasn't a friendly visit. "I've never done anything to you. I don't want any trouble."

"My son and grandson, who are five and six years old, came home today with black eyes and scratches all over their faces. They were told by your two sons that I hanged the two victims. Now why would they say something like that? My guess was they heard you say that." Heller took a step backward and Tommy took a step forward. The move wasn't lost on Heller.

"Now wait a minute, Mr. Sanchez, my boys wouldn't do anything like that, because I never said anything against you or your wife."

"Your boys are ten and twelve. Isn't that right?"

"Yes, yes, sir, but they didn't do anything. I swear they didn't. This is just a misunderstanding."

"If either or both of your boys ever lays a hand on my son or my grandson again, for whatever reason, I'll visit you at night at your home and give you what they got. Do you understand?"

"You can't threaten me."

Tommy hit Heller in the stomach with his left hand and brought his right hand up and hit Heller under the chin. Heller fell on his back. Tommy straddled Heller with both knees on his arms and took his knife out of his boot. Heller cleared his head and that's when he saw the knife in Tommy's hand and started to scream. Tommy put his hand over his mouth and muffled the sound. "I'm going to cut off your right ear lobe, so you know I'm serious."

"Please don't. I'll make sure my boys won't hit yours again. Please, I'm sorry, please, don't."

"My children are going back to school tomorrow. I don't want any problems. Do we understand each other?' Tommy flicked the blade on Heller's right ear, drew some blood and the man cried.

"I don't care what the newspaper said. I liked both men; they worked for me at the ranch. Do we understand each other?"

Heller shook his head and mumbled something like, "I'm sorry."

Tommy stood up over Heller and then disappeared into the shadows, got on his horse and rode home. He knew where Grimes' father was. He'd take care of him tomorrow. The word would be out by that time.

CHAPTER 9
1900

TO SAY that theirs was a love affair was truly an understatement. From their first encounter, Sarah was mesmerized by Tommy Sanchez, even though she didn't remember how they met until years later. The Hansen family from Pennsylvania had travelled by stage to the jumping-off point, Independence, Missouri, for their trip west. Sarah was thirteen, blonde, and wore her hair in pigtails. Her brother James was fifteen and beginning the transition to manhood. One night they wandered away from the family wagon just to see what it was like in this midwest town. They milled around until Sarah saw some horses in a livery and James followed her inside.

Sarah was skipping around until she stopped in front of a light brown pony and began to stroke its mane. Just then, three young men, who appeared to be wranglers, came out of shadows and grabbed Sarah and started to fondle her. James came to her defense and was knocked to the ground by the largest one of the three. The other two, medium in height, already had Sarah on the barn floor and were pulling off her undergarments. James tried to fight back, but he was overmatched and was lying on the floor bleeding from a cut on his face. When his assailant decided to join the other two in abusing the girl, a slender young man with sharp features and long black hair, tied in a pony tail, hit the larger man on the head with his revolver. The other two were so busy looking at Sarah's nakedness that they didn't see the young man until it was too late. He hit both with the handle of his gun, and they slumped to the floor.

He helped the young woman up and did the same for her brother. "Why don't you dress and then leave. I'll take care of these three. They won't bother you again."

Sarah struggled with her clothes and was too scared to be embarrassed by her nakedness. She and James ran back to their wagon train as fast as they could. They were so scared that they didn't even bother to thank the young man. Sarah came back later with her father and a couple of men from the wagon train, but no one was there. Her father wanted to thank the young man who had come to her aid. They also wanted to punish the ones who took advantage of the two children. Sarah always wondered who that young man was. She never saw his face.

Years later, long after Crazy Horse was killed, she and her brother were vacationing in Santa Fe, New Mexico. They'd entered the Silver Lode Hotel to exchange some money at the First National Bank, which was housed in an annex off the hotel lobby. Just as her brother produced a draft, two men walked into the bank and demanded the cash in the teller's tray. As the two robbers exited into the hotel lobby, a distinguished-looking Mexican gentleman was standing on the stairs, facing the two outlaws. He was dressed in a black tailored suit, a white Stetson hat, and a light brown vest. He told the two gunmen to drop the money on the floor and leave town.

"Shoot him," one of the robbers said, but the man on the stairs didn't make a move; he just stared at the two desperados.

The older robber paused and looked at the man on the stairs. "Wait a minute, Billy—I've heard that voice before. If it's who I think it is, we're looking at death in the flesh."

"Are you the man from the Saddle Back Saloon in Wyoming?" the robber asked the man, whose arms were relaxed at his side.

"Yes."

The older of the two robbers said, "Lay the bags on the floor, Billy. We can always rob another bank, but we may not get out of here to spend it today."

"There're two of us. We can take him," Billy said.

"I've seen him shoot. It isn't worth the risk," the older brother said.

The two robbers laid the money bag on the floor, exited the hotel, got on their horses and rode out of town. All this time, the man on the stairs just watched them. When the robbers were gone, he walked down the stairs and exited the hotel as the teller was retrieving the bank's cash. Sarah and James were stunned. They couldn't believe what had happened. They walked over to the hotel clerk. "Who was the man on the stairs?"

"That's Mr. Thomas Sanchez. I never saw anything

like that before. I don't think he had a gun, but the bandits were afraid of him. He always seemed like a polite man. I wonder who he really is?"

That evening, she and her brother were having dinner in the hotel when Mr. Sanchez came into the dining room and sat down at a wall table by himself. "James, go ask him to join us, please."

James went cautiously to the man's table and passed on his sister's request. Sanchez looked at the beautiful blonde young woman and accepted the invitation. When he arrived at the table, he kissed Sarah's hand and introduced himself as Thomas Sanchez. He thought he recognized her, but he couldn't place where they had met. Sarah couldn't stop staring at him, and blushed when he kissed her hand. He ate very little that night and talked mostly about how wonderful Santa Fe was. After coffee, he excused himself, citing a pressing business problem. Sarah learned from the hotel clerk the next morning that Sanchez sold his livery stable last night and left town.

"Where did he go?" she asked the hotel clerk.

"I have no idea, but wherever it was, he was in a hurry."

• • • • •

Her wagon train departed Independence, Missouri, two days after she and her brother were attacked in the livery stable. They never learned the identity of the young man who helped them that day. The wagon train was out eleven days when it was attacked by a Sioux raiding party. The members of the train fought valiantly but were overwhelmed by sheer numbers. Sarah and Thomas fought side by side with their parents under their wagon. Her father was the first to succumb, and then her mother, who was shot in the forehead and died while her children were being captured. The children didn't even have time to say goodbye to their parents before they were struck to the ground and subsequently fastened to a long rope held by one of the raiders. As a Sioux captive, at the age of thirteen, Sarah had to compete with the dogs for food; at night, she slept on the ground around the fire. She was constantly watched and beaten regularly by the women of the village. For five years, her only thought was of survival. It was only after she became a mature young woman, and the young braves were taking notice, that she was adopted by a family in the Sioux village. From that time forward, she was able to have some degree of dignity after five years of captivity.

Although her wedding to Crazy Horse, the war chief of the Sioux, was a forced marriage, she made the best of it and grew to love the moody brave. In spite of her status as wife of the war chief, she was still an outsider and scorned by the women of the tribe. It was only later that their band found out what a valuable asset she'd become. Her work as an interpreter during treaty negotiations was the first time she felt equal. But it was her affinity for languages in addition to her communication skills during the many interfaces with neighboring towns on behalf of her village that brought her some degree of trust from the tribe elders.

There was no question that her first five years of

captivity were years of depravity and survival, and the later years with Crazy Horse were filled with humiliation. The treaties were broken and the tribe was continually being pushed to its limits with no recourse. She and her family were forced onto reservations, provided with land that could not sustain life, given limited rations by the Indian Agents and became, in a sense, beggars. Crazy Horse could not cope with the shame of being impotent in the face of the white man's push to rid themselves of the Indian problem; it fell to Sarah to keep the family together and fed. She started doing charcoal sketches of the Indian village and sold some to the general stores in the area. In most instances, she traded her drawings for food. But Crazy Horse was restless; he longed for the life of hunting and fishing that seemed forever lost to his people. When Sitting Bull decided to attack the 7th Cavalry, Crazy Horse became his war chief. Rather than leave his family behind, he took them with him and had them wait in the hills during the battle.

From a vantage place overlooking the Little Big Horn, Sarah watched the battle unfold and saw the massacre of the Seventh Cavalry and was embarrassed. Here she was the wife of the war chief and the mother of two of his children, watching her own people slaughtered, similar to what had happened to her father and mother on their way west. The massacre would haunt her for some time. Many nights, she would wake up in a sweat and relive the battle and cry out; she was torn between two cultures.

The only respite during these times was when she and

Crazy Horse travelled to Washington to meet with the Department of Interior. Red Cloud led the delegation of Indian leaders. He wanted to see if they could negotiate a fair settlement for their people. Here was a beautiful blonde woman, the wife of the Indian hero of the Battle of Little Big Horn, rubbing elbows with Washington society. The town couldn't get enough of the couple, who were showered with invitations for dinner and parties during their week-long visit. The last evening they were in the capitol, they were guests at a dinner and dance at the White House. Crazy Horse was stoic and sat at the table while Sarah danced with many of the congressmen. One senator seemed overly amorous and let his hand slide down her back and squeeze her bottom. He tried to put his hotel key in her hand. "Senator, my husband has killed twenty-six people that I know of; six he skinned alive. If I told him about the liberties you're taking with me, I dare to think what he would do." The senator flushed and excused himself. He departed immediately, leaving Sarah on the dance floor alone.

When she went back to the table, Crazy Horse asked why the senator left so early. Sarah laughed. "I told him if he didn't stop squeezing my rear, you were going to scalp him." Crazy Horse smiled.

This trip was the highlight of her life with Crazy Horse. From that point forward, he was arrested, released and arrested again. And then one day he was shot and killed while she was with him. Being a widow and a white woman with two half breed children was difficult. She had no money and very few prospects; she couldn't live on the reservation without a husband to support her. James, who was rescued from the Sioux, had returned to their home in Pennsylvania and discovered that his parents' farm had huge deposits of oil. He became wealthy overnight. But he couldn't reconcile his hatred for the Sioux for the murder of his parents with his sister's marriage to Crazy Horse. He visited his sister during her trip to Washington, but didn't divulge his fortune, nor did he offer any financial help; she was on her own.

Sarah was a good person who was liked by all who came into contact with her. General Miles had led many of the treaty negotiations between the Army and the Sioux, and Sarah was the prime interpreter for the Sioux. She became very friendly with the older gentleman, and when she was forced to leave the reservation, Gen. Miles made arrangements for her to stay at Fort Robinson and teach the garrison's children.

To the women of the fort, Sarah was too beautiful, too available and too Indian to suit them. It took an order from Miles to the garrison's commander to have the children attend school. Well, they'd let her teach the children, but they wouldn't socialize with her, nor would they talk to her as they passed her on the dirt roads inside the fort. The young officers fancied the beautiful young woman, and that by itself made her more of a piranha than before. During this time, her son, Lars, became a malcontent and eventually ran away, organized a gang of like-minded young braves and committed small misdemeanors throughout the territory. Her daughter had grown to be a young woman, and at seventeen, Naiwa became the bride of a young brave and moved to the Standing Rock Reservation with her husband. Sarah was all alone with not much of a future ahead of her.

Subsequently, her brother James had a change of heart and came for her and brought her home to Pennsylvania. Sarah took up art and became a proficient artist, specializing in portraits. But this show of brotherly love lasted but a short time. James became enamored with a girl from Philadelphia who didn't approve of Sarah's background as the wife of a blood-thirsty savage. Sarah was ostracized by her only living relative, and, out of desperation, she moved to San Francisco with her constant companion, Naomi; it was there that life finally started to show some promise.

Her first glimpse of the Santa Ynez Valley was when she travelled with her brother James to the west coast, after he rescued her from Fort Robinson. Later, she would travel by sailing ship with her lover down the coast of California. Unfortunately, they ran into a severe storm at Conception Point. The boat crashed against the rocks and her lover drowned. Sarah and Naomi survived and came to the valley, where she set up an art gallery at Mattei's Tavern and met Tommy Sanchez again.

When Sarah was in San Francisco, she hired James Jefferson, a Pinkerton detective, to find her son, Lars. The reunion between mother and son wasn't friendly. Lars resented his mother being white and wouldn't return home with her. Later, when she married Tommy Sanchez, she asked his help in reuniting with her son. Along with Jefferson, he found Lars. The initial meeting was not cordial, but Lars got the message that Tommy Sanchez was a fair-minded man, but was not someone to trifle with. Reluctantly, Lars came to live with Sarah and Tommy, changed his name to Juan Sanchez, and studied the law. From their first encounter, Juan and Tommy became like brothers, with Tommy filling the role of confidant and teacher to Juan.

Sarah invested her royalties from the oil field located on her family's farm, and with her art work was now financially comfortable. Tommy was rich, having worked hard his entire life amassing a fortune from his investments in cattle and land.

The couple was generous to those who were less fortunate and sponsored an Indian orphanage in Montana. Still, they felt resentment toward them. Tommy was respected and feared, but not loved. He was considered a half-breed, and therefore shouldn't be smart enough to have the financial standing he had. Some felt cheated by their success. Sarah was looked upon by many as a fallen woman, having first married that killer, Crazy Horse, and now to a half-breed.

CHAPTER 10
1890

THE HOURS passed so slowly; yet, he was afraid to move, or even breathe too loud for fear of being heard. People were calling out to loved ones, but no one near him answered. He thought one of his brothers was calling out for his father and mother, but he was so distrustful of the soldiers that he thought it was a trick; he wouldn't respond. While still holding Maiden Dream's cold hand, he pushed one of the bodies to the side so he could see outside. *Thank God for the snow and the cold,* he thought. It held the smell of decaying flesh to a minimum.

It was afternoon as he walked through all the bodies and distanced himself from the soldiers who were back and loading about fifty disoriented Sioux into wagons. Those must be the survivors, he thought. Still he wouldn't call out, because he wasn't sure where the soldiers were taking those who survived. Fear was directing his thoughts, and White Bird thought the soldiers were rounding up his people so they could shoot them. He believed that the soldiers didn't want any survivors. He was torn as he watched the wagons with his people disappear;

still he would not show himself. There had been snow flurries during the massacre, but last night, the snow started in earnest: it would last for three days.

After the soldiers left with the survivors, White Bird returned to the mass of dead bodies and tried to assess what he had to do to survive. He saw Maiden Dream lying among the bodies and began to cry; the tears ran down his cheeks. His mother and father lay near her. He found some fry bread in his mother's clothing. He didn't want to desecrate his dead mother, but he wanted to live; he was sixteen years old. He found clothing that had been discarded by those who were running away and were subsequently shot and killed. As he looked around, he saw Spotted Elk lying on his side; blood was pooled around him. As the snow began to pile up, White Bird had to create some form of shelter.

He walked some distance from the dead and began moving the snow with his hands. Soon, he built a small enclosure with snow walls about four feet high and six feet square. He laid enough sticks and branches on top of the walls, hoping it would support a cloth roof. He fashioned a bed inside the hut with discarded clothing and rags. The better ones he used as a blanket. During the night, the weight of the snow accumulating on his makeshift roof forced him to get up several times to toss snow off the roof. But that wasn't the only reason for the interruption in his sleep. He heard wolves in the distance, and he sensed what a pack of wolves would do with the bodies. As he lay back down, he sensed he heard human sounds, but believed it was his imagination playing tricks on him. Nobody could be alive, he thought. The next morning he fashioned a roof with thicker branches he found in a creek nearby and laid more clothing on top. After two days alone, he believed that he would survive. He went through the dead bodies again looking for food; he found enough for a couple of days. The prize, though, was the two rifles with eight cartridges lying between two bodies. He took a nice pair of moccasins off a dead brave. At first he felt guilty, but soon he didn't care. He tried to make a fire with some kindling, without success.

Near noontime, with rags for gloves, he went in search of food. Frozen bodies littered the landscape. Women with young children were lying dead in the snow nearly two miles from where they were camped. Down by the creek, he found some rabbit footprints and remembered what his father taught him. He set some snares and hoped for the best. He didn't sleep much that night during another snow storm which reached blizzard condition. The howls of the wolves were getting closer; it was only a matter of time before they'd come in packs; it could even be tonight. He loaded both rifles and waited for their attack, but that didn't come. In the morning he returned to the creek and found the snares intact, but no game.

The next day brought some success; he caught a rabbit. With an old knife, he skinned the animal and ate some of the raw flesh. He packed the remainder in snow outside his makeshift hut and spent the remainder of the day scavenging for food and useful items, such as weapons. Being able to hunt for his food gave him a feeling of confidence; he knew he could survive on his own. Burying his father and mother and Maiden Dream was his priority. He dragged their bodies down to the ravine, which was fifty yards away. He fashioned a sharp point on a stick to scratch the ground until he had enough dirt to cover their remains.

He tied together some sticks with rags and made crosses. He placed them in the dirt on the graves and said a small prayer. He wanted to come back some day and have a fitting burial for his young love and the two people who raised him.

That night three wolves started invading the bodies. White Bird tried not to have any feeling for the dead, but it tore at his soul. He took aim and shot one of the wolves and the other two ran off, but he knew this was only temporary; they would return. That night, they waited outside the perimeter of the massacre and howled. With only seven cartridges left, he tried to use restraint and only fire when necessary. He assumed the reason they hadn't immediately returned was that they were concentrating on those who ran off and were shot. He checked his traps the next morning and found another rabbit caught in a snare. He reset the traps and skinned the one he caught. He would save this one for later. That afternoon he slept for a few hours. He was sure the wolves would return that night.

CHAPTER 11

1900

RAUL AND NAIWA, Sarah's daughter, had been keeping company for about six months and decided to marry. They divulged their intentions to Sarah to see what her reaction would be. She was concerned that they didn't know each other long enough, and Chatan and Wachiwi still hadn't become acclimated to their new surroundings. However, the main problem, from Sarah's perspective, was that Naiwa was a very immature adult. She tried, but she just couldn't assimilate into a predominately white society or accept her responsibility as a single parent. She basically withdrew into herself and was only comfortable around the family. It was as though she sensed a threat from everyone who wasn't a family member. The children were slowly adjusting to their new world, but Naiwa couldn't comprehend what they wanted and what they were experiencing. When there was a problem at school, it was Sarah who acted as the parent. This wasn't lost on Chatan and Wachiwi.

But after watching the two together, and recognizing that Raul was a mature adult, Sarah finally gave her approval and told Tommy. He shared her concerns, but knew that the couple liked each other and it would be a good match. They planned to marry in April. Tommy suggested they build a small frame home on the ranch for the couple, but another option appeared feasible. Sarah and Tommy had purchased the five-hundred-acre Singleton Ranch five years earlier, after Singleton and his friends were convicted of bank robbery. They didn't tell Naiwa and Raul what they had in mind. This would be a surprise on their wedding day.

The *Santa Barbara Register* moved the Ghost Shirt murders to the back page and was concentrating on a land speculation scam in the south part of the County. The four children went back to school, and although there were comments made about Tommy and the Ghost Shirt murders, no one made any attempt to harm them. Like all kids, they took most of what was going on in stride and went about being kids. Tommy talked to Fred Grimes' father and was promised that there wouldn't be any more incidents.

It was the first week in February when Jefferson came up to the ranch; he planned to stay for a few days. He'd been contacted by the sheriff to do some follow-up on Tommy's suggestion and interview Spenser and Whitman. They wanted to see if either or both knew anything about the two murders or if they knew anything that would help in the murder investigation. The assumption was that if there was anything in the past of the two now deceased, the remaining two would know.

Jefferson spent an afternoon interviewing Hiram

Whitman after Tommy told him about the significance of the dates of the two hangings. "I took an immediate dislike to the man. It wasn't just how he said the only thing that the four had in common was the Army, it was his attitude. He seemed to sneer at everything. I wanted to punch him in the mouth. I'm supposed to be a skilled investigator but I lost my cool."

"The most relevant thing he had to say was about the skirmishes they had with the Sioux, one of which was at the Battle of Wounded Knee. Whitman said they just did what they were told, nothing spectacular. I asked him if they were part of the twenty soldiers who received the Congressional Medals of Honor for their exploits at Wounded Knee. Whitman shook his head and said the four of them had only minor parts in the action. I asked if he killed anyone, he reluctantly said he might have. He said they were young and everything happened so fast. Their officers were screaming at the soldiers to fire and the men around him were afraid they'd be shot by the Indians, even though they didn't have any weapons. The only thing he knew for sure was that a lot of Indians were killed that day, and reluctantly, he might have killed one or two. To my question about being at any of the reservations, he stated that he'd been at Pine Ridge. He was part of the detail that acted as an honor guard for the Medal of Honor recipients. He never visited the Standing Rock Reservation."

"All four men were friendly with each other. When they first arrived, they spent all their time together at your ranch. Later, after they left your employ, they spent most of the time trying to earn a living, and socialized infrequently. He and Spenser were looking forward to Butler's wedding; he was happy for Butler, who asked him to be his best man. It was his suggestion that the four come to the valley after their enlistment was up. He'd been in contact with Earl Singleton, his cousin, and the four had been offered jobs on the Star Ranch. They were shocked when they arrived and found out that Singleton was in jail. Reluctantly, he admitted you did a fine thing by giving them jobs."

"I know you and Singleton had a major run-in and he went to jail. But I didn't know that you and Sarah bought the Singleton Ranch."

"It seems as though Singleton had a lot of cousins. Jason Brown, an old friend of yours, was a cousin of his. Maybe they're all from a bad seed."

Jefferson knew too well what Sanchez was talking about. He'd been hired to track down Brown, who had robbed a bank in New Mexico and fled to the Santa Ynez Valley. Along the way he murdered a law man and eight bandits before hiding out at Singleton's place. Brown took a fancy to Sarah Sanchez and abducted her. Tommy followed them into the hills, and he and Sarah came out alive. Brown was found a week later by a couple of Chumash hunters; he was dead from a gunshot wound to the head. No one admitted to the killing and the sheriff decided to let it be. Neither Tommy nor Sarah ever mentioned the incident, and Jefferson didn't ask.

"When do you meet with Spenser?"

"Later today. What do you think of him?"

"He seemed like the leader of the four, at least while he was here. Perhaps it was because he was a few years older, or it could be for another reason. He got religion a few years back and has a small congregation. I was only friendly with Butler, though I liked Spenser and Higgins. I fired Whitman."

"Tommy, I'm not sure about Whitman. He could be our man, but there's nothing in my interview that would lead me to him. Why don't we talk after I meet with Spenser?"

• • • • •

Raul had a few errands to run in Santa Ynez. He rode his favorite horse, Sammy, into town and stopped at the post office to mail a package to his mother in Guadalajara, Mexico. His father had passed away ten years ago, and Raul sent money every month to his mother and sister, who lived together. He wanted to bring them here, but he hadn't been able to put aside enough money. Hopefully, he'd be able to accomplish that goal in the future. Perhaps the Patron would raise his salary. As he walked inside the mail room, he glanced up at the beam where the barber had been hanged.

Sammy was pawing at the ground when Raul came back out. On closer inspection, Raul noticed that the horse's right front shoe was loose. So he decided to lead the horse to Whitman's Livery Stable and have him replace the shoe.

The barn door to the livery stable was locked, so Raul

walked around to the rear of the building and tried a small door, but it was padlocked on the outside. Something didn't seem right, because Whitman kept the livery open day and night. In fact, Whitman lived in a converted stall. He walked around to the far side and looked in one of the lower windows. It was covered with dust, so he took a rag out of his saddlebag and wiped one of the panes. He looked inside once, stepped back, and then looked inside again. Whitman was hanging from the main beam in the center of the barn. Raul ran up the street and found Charles Little sitting in his office.

In broken English, Raul explained what had happened. They walked back to the livery, and the two of them broke the lock on the rear door and went inside. Little untied the rope holding Whitman, and he and Raul eased the dead body to the floor. The first thing each noticed was the Ghost Shirt. "I want you to get Tommy Sanchez and have him look at this. We'll keep the barn locked until he gets here," Little said.

"My horse has thrown a shoe. It'll take about ten minutes to fix it and then I'll go."

Raul borrowed some of Whitman's tools and reshod Sammy's front hoof. He felt uncomfortable working next to a dead body, so he hurried, and then rode to Altura Prado. Sarah greeted Raul after he knocked on the front door. She could tell he was agitated, and immediately took him to Tommy, who was working in his office at the rear of their home. Raul's English was still poor, in spite of the lessons from Naomi and Sarah, so he conversed with

Tommy in Spanish. Tommy didn't seem surprised by the news. He went into the kitchen and told Sarah what had happened. "I'm going to find Jefferson. He went to interview Spenser and is probably still at the church. Raul's concerned that it was he who found the last two bodies."

"Are you taking Raul with you?"

"No, I'll leave him here. I've never seen him this worried."

He found Jefferson inside Spenser's church. The interview appeared to be over; the two men were talking about fishing when Tommy entered the church. Tommy took Jefferson aside and told him what Raul had reported; the two rode to Whitman's barn and banged on the rear door of the livery. Little opened the door and the two rode inside the barn. Tommy looked around the barn and asked the constable to open the front door so they could have more light; their investigation took thirty minutes. The three sat down on some bales of hay piled on the side of the barn.

"Charles, this doesn't look good. Whitman was hanged nearly the same way as Higgins and Butler. The Ghost Shirt is nearly identical to the ones found on the other dead men, the boot marks on the floor around the body are the same, and the type of rope is similar. Then there's his face that's painted red like the other two, and the lock of his hair in a cup at his feet. It's either a Sioux ritual, or someone who knows about our history is leading us in that direction," Tommy said.

"Whitman was one of four soldiers who came to

the valley at the same time. Each worked for me for six months before they went their own way. Three of them are dead; Spenser is the only one left living. Jefferson talked to Spenser within the past hour and Whitman a few days ago. I'll let him tell you what he found out."

"The first Ghost Shirt that Spenser saw wasn't on Higgins. It was at Wounded Knee when one of the Indians who camped there put on the shirt and performed what they thought was the Ghost Dance. Whitman felt that the shirt on Higgins was similar to the one he saw at the massacre. Not that Spenser would recognize any survivor of the massacre, but he did look around Santa Ynez Valley to see if there was an Indian here that could be a survivor of that action. So, yes, he was aware, more than the others, what might be the root cause of the hangings. He was more forthcoming than Whitman. He said they were standing on one side of a pile of weapons confiscated from the Indians, who were on the other side of the cache. Agitation started between both sides as they stood out there in the cold. The only difference between the two groups was, one side had weapons; the other didn't. When a gun was discharged, all hell broke loose. The problem was that no one knew who fired that shot, and after that, none of the soldiers cared. The soldiers went berserk for a few minutes and fired indiscriminately into the Indian masses; they killed anything that moved. They even shot some who they knew were dead. It didn't matter. Women and children were slaughtered as they ran. All Spenser could say was that it was horrible. Neither Higgins nor

Butler felt they were targeted, or at least they didn't raise the issue to Spenser. When the first two were hanged, Whitman asked Spenser if he hanged the two."

"Do you think these are revenge killings?" Little asked.

"Yes. But I don't know what the revenge is about. My best guess is that one of the survivors of Wounded Knee or some other battle is committing these acts. Whitman even wondered if Tommy was behind the hangings," Jefferson said. Tommy smiled.

"We know that the three who were hanged, plus Spenser, were in the valley for the past four years. There are a few young men who have come here during that time, but none appear to be of Indian ethnicity. The other thing that puzzles me is, how did this person or person find the three men who were hanged? It seems unlikely that someone came here and saw the four in the valley and recognized them from the massacre. I believe that he knew they were here and he knew what they looked like. If the cause is Wounded Knee, then our killer was there and either remembered the four or he tracked them down before they left the Army. We need to ask Spenser if any civilian made friends with them while they were in the Army, probably close to their discharge date," Jefferson said.

"Where do we go from here?" Little asked.

"I think Spenser has to be cautious. Perhaps a body-guard or a sheriff's deputy as his companion would be appropriate until this is settled. Why don't you contact the sheriff and share our concerns?" Tommy said.

"I don't think there's any more we can do here today, Charles. I assume that Dr. Cunnane will find the same results after he performs an autopsy on the body. Let me know what he finds. I've been retained by the sheriff as a consultant for these murders. You can always contact me at Mr. Sanchez' ranch. If you're ready, Tommy, let's head back to the ranch," Jefferson said.

"No. I'd like to talk to Spenser before we head back."

They found Spenser in his church, sweeping the floor. He seemed surprised, because Jefferson and Sanchez had left him about an hour ago. "Did you forget something?"

Jefferson spoke first. "Whitman was found hanged in his livery. We just came from there."

Spenser staggered and the broom fell from his grasp; he then sat down on one of the pews in the hall. Tommy and Jefferson pulled up chairs and sat across from him. "You don't think I did these killings, do you?"

"I think we're way past that now. The body was warm, so my guess is that you didn't do it. I'd like you to think about Wounded Knee and whether anyone made contact with you and the other four while you were at Fort Robinson or on your trip to California," Tommy asked.

"The only Indians that I saw were at Pine Ridge Reservation when I was part of the honor guard for the Medal of Honor recipients. I don't remember seeing any at the fort or on our trip here."

"What about a young man who was white or a light-skinned Mexican?"

"None that I can recall … Wait a minute. There was a young white man with long hair who took a picture with us after the medal ceremony at Pine Ridge. We took several pictures and sent one to him in Sidney. He said he worked for the railroad. Come to think of it, I saw him at Fort Robinson once, and then in Sidney before we boarded the train west. He said he was on railroad business. Do you think a former soldier is hanging my friends?"

"I don't think he's an ex-soldier. I think he's an ex-Sioux brave, who is white and hanged the other three. Do you have a copy of the photo?"

"I don't, but Butler was the one who took the photos. I don't know if he saved a copy. That's a long time ago."

"Would you be able to recognize that young man if you saw him in the valley?"

"Perhaps."

"I want you to think hard. Is it possible that there's someone in the valley you've seen that could be that young man?"

"Come to think of it, I remember someone that seemed familiar to me at the time, but I couldn't remember where I'd seen him before."

"Where did you see him?"

"I don't remember. Let me think about it and see if I can recall."

"We're going to ask the sheriff to assign a deputy to you. We think you're in danger."

"I'd appreciate it."

They rode down Sagunto and Roblar Streets before they turned onto the road toward Los Olivos; Altura Prado was two miles west of them. "Other than Juan and myself, there are only two Sioux in this valley."

"If Spenser didn't hang the other three, could it be one of the Chumash, or even an ex-soldier who had a vendetta against the four soldiers?" Jefferson asked.

"Everything points to an Indian. I don't think any soldier knows all the rituals that the Sioux use, and that goes for the Chumash too. The paint on the face and the lock of hair in a cup were things we did for our dead. There are, however, certain factions of our tribe that are fair-skinned. Maybe our culprit is such a person," Tommy responded.

"You feel pretty certain about that a Sioux did this, don't you?"

"Yes."

They were about a mile from the ranch when a shot rang out, and Tommy fell to the ground on the side of the road. Jefferson jumped off his horse and unholstered his gun, but he didn't see anyone. His first thought was of Tommy who lay on his side. Jefferson rolled him over and saw blood coming from his left shoulder. Tommy was conscious and started to rise. "Hold on a second, let me look around before you get up. That shot had to come from the field north of us, but I don't see any movement."

Tommy rose and grabbed hold of the reins of his horse. "Let's assume that the shot came from the north. We'll walk and keep our horses to our right until we get to that grove of trees about two hundred yards up the road," Tommy said as he started walking.

When they reached the grove of trees, Tommy sat down and leaned against one of the sycamores, and Jefferson tore open his shirt, exposing the wound. It looked like the bullet entered about three inches below the top of his shoulder and probably exited through his chest muscle, just missing the heart. "Someone tried to kill you just now; you were lucky. I assume they used a rifle and were behind some boulders, because I couldn't see anyone."

"I think I can ride. I don't think it's wise to go back to the doctor in Santa Ynez. Naomi has treated gunshot wounds before, and so has Sarah. I'll feel better at home."

• • • • •

John Smart followed the two from Spenser's church. He knew that Sanchez was no fool and would gradually put it all together. He thought of leaving town, but that would definitely point to his guilt. He'd have to take care of Sanchez. It was easy to slip out of town, parallel the main road and hide behind the boulders that covered the landscape. When he saw Sanchez and the Pinkerton man, he took his time, aimed and fired. He knew he hit him, and saw him fall off his horse, but he wasn't sure it was lethal. He waited a few minutes, and when he saw the riders rise and walk toward the grove of trees, he tried to get another shot at the former Sioux brave. When he realized that he couldn't get a clear shot, he decided to head back to town. He was lucky no one came to investigate the shot, nor did anyone see him come back and go to his room.

When they rode up to the ranch house, Sarah came out to greet them. She had a wide smile on her face as she moved to greet Tommy. That's when she saw the blood, and she stopped and put her hand to her mouth. "Oh my God, Tommy, who did this to you?"

"We don't know. Call Naomi, have her probe to make sure the bullet isn't still in there." Jefferson and Sarah helped Tommy off his horse just as Raul ran up to the two riders.

"Who did this, Patron?"

Jefferson spoke to Raul. "We were ambushed about a mile from here. Why don't you take a couple of men and see what you can find? He was hit about 200 yards east of the grove of trees on the main road. I suspect that whoever did this was behind some rocks, maybe a hundred yards north of the road; actually it was between the town and the road." Raul's English was poor, so Sarah translated in Spanish. Soon, Raul and two of his vaqueros rode off toward town,

They gave Tommy a large glass of whiskey, and when he finished, Naomi went to work, with Sarah assisting. They confirmed that the bullet had passed through his body. After they cleaned and bandaged the wound,

Naomi said, “It’s going to be sore for a few weeks, but it doesn’t look like there’s a lot of damage to the muscles.”

“Tommy must be making someone nervous. This was an actual attempt on his life. I’m going to notify the sheriff,” Jefferson told them.

“No. Let’s keep this between ourselves. I don’t want to give whoever shot me the satisfaction of thinking that he was successful. I also don’t want to give that damned editor more ammunition to go after us.”

“Maybe the one who hanged Whitman and the others is getting nervous and wants you out of the way,” Sarah said.

“You may be right. I’ll have to be more careful.”

CHAPTER 12
1900

FOR the past month, the Santa Barbara paper had turned its attention to a potential land grab scheme in the southern part of the county. There was some evidence that one of the supervisors and a land use employee were scheming to defraud the state out of ten thousand acres of land along the Pacific Ocean. The investigating reporter assigned to the case felt that the two individuals named were but a small part of the scheme. The loop included many unnamed executives and county personnel. As titillating as this story was, the hanging of Hiram Whitman brought about a reversal in strategy. The editor/owner threw all his resources into putting new life into solving the Ghost Shirt murders, or at least to increase circulation. Editorials were unleashed from the newspaper on a daily basis with Tommy, Sarah and Raul Mendoza as the main targets. There wasn't any aspect of their life that was off limits. Readership was up, and a smile spread across the lips of the owner every day. His favorite expression to his employees was, "We've got them on the run."

The most vicious editorials suggested that Raul

Mendoza, who had found two of the bodies, was the vassal of Thomas Sanchez, a Sioux warrior living in the Santa Ynez Valley with his blonde wife, the squaw and widow of Crazy Horse. Another posed the question of how Tommy Sanchez could amass such a fortune. It answered its own question by suggesting that it was probably over the bodies of white businessmen. Although they didn't directly accuse them of the crimes, it was obvious from the slant of the editorials that there was no doubt about the paper's intent. Letters to the Editor were nearly ninety percent in favor of having an official investigation into Sanchez' role in the killings and his finances. The other ten percent were seeking vigilante justice. The heat was being turned up daily.

The backlash against Sarah and Tommy was felt closer to home. Friends in the community seemed to shun the couple, and when Sarah went into town to do her shopping, she was met with cold stares from people who normally would engage her in a conversation. The new manager of the Central Hotel removed her paintings from the hotel lobby. He had them quickly replaced when he was informed that Sarah and her husband were minority owners in the hotel. No apology was forthcoming.

Their children were the most vulnerable to the attacks by the newspaper. They went to school daily and had to listen to the taunts and vicious insults from their peers. Sarah refused to buckle under pressure from the school board and rejected their request to withdraw the children from school. Her meeting with the school principal was more productive. Mr. Bogoart was sympathetic to Sarah's concern and assured her that he would personally watch out for the children. He couldn't stop the taunts, but he wouldn't tolerate any physical confrontations. Sarah felt relieved.

Some deliveries to the ranch were either shorted or not delivered at all. On one occasion, Tommy sent a vaquero into Santa Ynez to pick up beer, because the proprietor of the saloon said he was short of help and couldn't make deliveries.

The ranch was self-supporting, not only for the Sanchez family, but for those who worked for them. Other than the beer and some feed supplies, they didn't feel any of the supposed boycotts by some proprietors. Tommy decided to fight back. Rather than sell their beef and wine locally, they shipped it to Santa Barbara. Each day, three wagons transported goods south and picked up supplies on the way home. When they started to feel resistance in Santa Barbara, they started transacting business in Ventura. Tommy was prepared to shop by train, if necessary, as far south as San Diego.

The local businessmen could see that one of the valley's biggest employers and suppliers in the area was actually boycotting them. Faced with the backlash by the Sanchez operations, a committee of merchants drove to the ranch with an olive branch, and an understanding was developed. Sarah didn't serve them coffee or any of her famous biscuits. In fact, they weren't invited into the house; all the negotiations were conducted on the front porch. Some had to stand for nearly an hour. "I will honor our agreement, conditioned that my family is treated with respect." Tommy was determined to have the last word.

Two days prior to the aforementioned meeting at the ranch, Tommy was in the Santa Ynez General Store when he heard two men talking about running him and his family out of town. One of the men had been the recipient of a half steer from Tommy and Sarah when his family's home burned down. Tommy walked up to the two men and suggested that they retract their statements; he wasn't polite about it. The message was clear and the two men apologized. Tommy and Sarah's best defense was to keep a low profile, but soon Tommy tired of being forced to turn the other cheek, and he started carrying a gun. That maneuver wasn't lost on those who came in contact with him and Sarah. No overt move was made toward the family, though there were still Letters to the Editor.

Raul refused to ride into town. He knew that people looked down on minorities; yet, he couldn't believe the degree of animosity he faced; he was scared. Naiwa was always crying, and at one point told Sarah she wanted to go back to the reservation. "This will blow over. They'll find the person who's hanging these men. Besides, you and the children were starving to death at Pine Ridge. You can't go back, and I won't let you," Sarah said

"I don't care. We're going back and you can't stop us."

"Watch me." Naiwa retreated to her room.

That evening after dinner, Sarah and Tommy went for a walk. Even though it was spring, the daytime temperatures were in the high sixties, while the evenings were mild. Sarah had on her shawl; Tommy had on a long-sleeved shirt. They held hands as they walked away from the main buildings. "We can't put up with much more of this harassment. It's impacting the entire family. Naiwa is becoming irrational. Today, she told me she was going back to the reservation and that I couldn't stop her."

"Well, she doesn't know her mother very well. I keep thinking this will blow over, but it seems to be gaining momentum. People who I thought were friends, or at least acquaintances, are becoming vicious. I tried to hire two men this week; no one wanted to work here. Raul is scared, and it's affecting his work. I've started to direct Cesar to manage some of the things that Raul always performed. I've thought of suggesting that Raul bring his mother up here, but I don't know."

"I know the group of merchants that came to the ranch mean well, but sooner or later there's going to be an incident, and we're going to be caught in the middle."

"I know. The killer must be found, and it can't be anyone associated with us. I'll talk to Jefferson and we'll come up with a plan." Tommy kissed her and they walked back into the house.

CHAPTER 13

1900

THE MOST important thing in Sarah's life at this time was the wedding of her daughter, Naiwa. She was going to make it as wonderful as she could, in spite of all the difficulties and stress she experienced in her life. She had been thirteen years old when her parents were slaughtered, along with most of the wagon train, on their way to Oregon. A band of Indians had stalked the wagon train for three days before three of the Indians approached the wagon master and demanded food. Those on the train felt that this was appeasement, and they resisted. It was after two more demands for food that they were attacked. Initially, the wagon train had resisted the attacks, but after two days of repelling the hostiles, their ammunition ran low and they succumbed.

She didn't see her father fall, but her mother died in her arms. Sarah assumed that the victors would slaughter the remaining members of the train, but they spared five children, including her brother James and herself. For the next five years she was a slave to her Indian captors. During the early stages of her captivity, she didn't have time to hate those who killed her parents and friends. She spent every moment trying to survive. Although her status was upgraded when she married Crazy Horse, they were only one step ahead of starvation for most of their married life. After her husband was killed, she was forced to take her two children to Fort Robinson to live. The inhabitants of the Army fort considered her a fallen woman because she had wed an Indian and borne his children.

She wasn't the only member of her family who was disillusioned. Her son was a half-breed and couldn't cope with the taunts and derogatory comments from peers and soldiers at the fort. As soon as he was able, he fled. Soon after, Naiwa wanted to marry, and, reluctantly, Sarah gave her blessing. Now, she was alone, despised by her neighbors and with no hope of a future. It seemed like a miracle when her brother finally came forward and shared the wealth their parents had left them.

Trying to recover from those many years of captivity and the years following Crazy Horse's death drained her. It took years before she was able to cope with the fact that she was a mother and her children needed her. She'd been so happy with Tommy Sanchez that she forgot about her daughter and son. It was Tommy who was able to bring mother and son together. With that reconciliation, she made the effort to reach out to her daughter. She vowed to spend the remainder of her life making up for her presumed failure as a mother.

Sarah did have one reservation about the upcoming wedding of her daughter. Up to this time, Naiwa hadn't been exposed to the white man's world, and she was reluctant to participate. In Sarah's mind, Naiwa was very immature. In the past, her husband and the tribe elders had made all her decisions. Sarah wasn't sure Naiwa could cope with the responsibilities that came with marriage and a partnership in a working ranch. Her new husband might become frustrated with her and cause a split in the marriage. "Oh, well, Naiwa has come this far. I'll just have to work harder to bring her into my world," Sarah told Tommy one evening.

The two women had taken several shopping trips to Santa Barbara in the spring to purchase a wedding dress and set up the flower arrangements. With that determined, the only remaining decision was where the ceremony would take place and who would perform the ceremony. Naiwa was reticent when she asked Sarah if the wedding could take place at the ranch. Sarah readily agreed, and that left the issue of who would perform the ceremony. Raul was baptized Catholic, but Naiwa had never been converted, primarily due to Crazy Horse's refusal to be baptized. Though Naiwa received training from Catholic missionaries who serviced the Sioux reservations, she'd never been baptized, though many of her peers at the reservation had.

On a recent trip, Sarah accepted an invitation for her and Naiwa to stay at a friend's house overnight. Their friends owned an elegant old Victorian on Bath Street in Santa Barbara with a view of the ocean from the guest bedroom. At dinner, Sarah shared her daughter's wedding plans and asked the couple to come to the April wedding.

After dinner, her host and husband served sherry and small cakes in their parlor. Sarah rose early the next morning, went downstairs and out onto the front porch. She sat in one of the rockers and thought how beautiful the residence and grounds were. A maid saw her come down and brought her coffee, which she graciously accepted. The maid also handed her the morning newspaper and asked if she would like to read it.

Sarah opened the paper to the advertisement section. They had decided on a dress in one of the stores in Santa Barbara, but she wanted to see if there were other options. She looked at the ads, but when she couldn't find anything better, she skipped to other sections and finally to the editorial section. She sat up straight when she read the heading of the piece, "Indian Squaw Lets Lover Drown."

She read about her trip down the coast of California on the *Emerald Grey,* with her intended, Jonathan Bird, and how she and Naomi swam to safety and left him to drown. "My God, they're making things up as they go along. Where could they get such a story?" She thought out loud. Then she realized it could only have come from that lout Frederick Heller, whom she dumped, after Naomi took a knife to his behind while he was trying to rape her.

She went back upstairs with the paper and tore it to shreds. "Wake up, Naiwa—we're heading home now." Her hosts were surprised at their early departure. Sarah suggested they come up a couple of weeks before the wedding to have dinner with Tommy and her.

• • • • •

History shows that Father Pierre Jean De Smet was sent by the St. Louis Diocese to convert the Sioux to Catholicism. Many missions were set up throughout the northwest, and thousands were converted. De Smet's success was so broad that the U.S. Government asked him to accompany some Washington bureaucrats to arrange a peace accord with Sitting Bull. De Smet went ahead, leaving the bureaucrats behind, met with Sitting Bull and arranged the treaty. From that point, he was respected by many Indian tribes and moved freely throughout the Sioux nation. Consequently, he was privy to many of the Sioux secrets. On one occasion, a Sioux warrior told De Smet of the vast gold deposits in the Black Hills. De Smet knew what would happen if the Army or the white settlers found out about the potential treasure of gold. He advised the great chief to keep the location of the gold a secret. Sitting Bull swore all the Sioux to secrecy, and the location wasn't disclosed until four decades later.

Sarah, Raul and Naiwa were having coffee in the kitchen when Tommy came in from the barn. His wound had nearly healed and he was only wearing a small bandage. He'd been exercising the shoulder and now was able to raise his left arm vertically. No one off the ranch knew that he'd been shot; that is, except the one who shot him. Raul went back to the site where Tommy was ambushed and looked around the area north of that location. He recovered a spent .56 caliber cartridge behind a large tree stump. When Raul returned to the ranch, he handed the cartridge to Jefferson, who said it probably fit a Springfield rifle. This was a Civil War weapon, and Jefferson made a note to check on anyone who'd been a veteran of the Civil War living in the valley.

"We're trying to decide on who should perform the ceremony. Do you have any suggestions?" Sarah asked Tommy as he sat down.

"What about Father Michael at the mission?"

"I'd like that, and so would Naiwa and Raul, but I don't think it'll happen. Raul is Catholic, but Naiwa has never been baptized. The Catholic missionaries who came after Father De Smet routinely tried to baptize Naiwa, but she refused on each occasion."

"That was in the past. Perhaps she could convert now?"

"I'm sure she'd be receptive, but the church is fairly rigid and wants Naiwa to undergo instructions in the religion, and that'll take a few months. Neither she nor Raul want to wait that long." The couple nodded.

"What about the Rev. Samuel Spenser? He has a small following in Santa Ynez and probably needs the money. He worked here for about six months before he moved on, and was friendly with Raul. I believe he holds services in a small church in Santa Ynez," Tommy told the couple.

"I think that's a good idea. Raul knows Spenser. Why don't you two go out to his place and see if you're comfortable with him," Sarah said.

Raul didn't say anything. "But the people have been mean to Raul and he doesn't want to go to town," Naiwa said.

"There hasn't been any threat toward either you or

Raul. You can drive in, meet with Spenser, and come right back home if you're uncomfortable."

Naiwa looked at Raul, who nodded. That afternoon the young couple borrowed the rig and drove to Santa Ynez. Rev. Spenser was talking to a few parishioners and asked them to come back in thirty minutes. Raul and his bride-to-be walked around the town looking in the dress shop and shoe store. When they were stared at by a passing couple, they hurried back to Spenser's church. Raul introduced Naiwa and explained that they wanted to be married on May 13, 1901, at Altura Prado, High Meadow Ranch, owned by Tommy and Sarah Sanchez.

"It's a beautiful location. In fact, I worked there under you, nearly four years ago. I like Tommy and Sarah; they were good to me and you treated me fairly. Who's going to be your best man and maid of honor?" Spenser asked.

"My mother and her husband, Tommy Sanchez," Naiwa shyly responded.

"They're a solid choice. Have you both been baptized?" Spenser asked.

Raul said he had, but Naiwa said she wasn't. "For me to perform the service, both of you must be baptized. I can baptize you today if you like."

The only exposure Naiwa had to baptism was when a traveling priest baptized members of her village in the river near where they camped. During one such ceremony, a member of her tribe had a heart attack when he was exposed to the cold river. From that point forward, Naiwa saw the ceremony as an omen. Raul knew the story and related it to Spenser.

"I don't want to be baptized," Naiwa firmly responded.

"But all I do is sprinkle a small amount of water over your forehead. There's no danger, nothing like what happened at your reservation."

"I don't want to be baptized." She repeated it again.

"Our congregation has strict guidelines. To be married by me, you must be a member of this congregation; all our members must be baptized. I'm sorry, there's nothing I can do about it. Baptism is not difficult and can be performed in a few minutes." Apparently, Spenser's voice carried, and it sounded to a passing parishioner as though he was angry. A woman looked in to see what the commotion was about. In fact, she came into the church and asked Spenser, "Is anything wrong, Rev. Spenser?"

"No. I must have been talking too loud." The woman seemed to be placated and walked out of the church.

Raul was frustrated. "Can't you make an exception, since we're being married on the Sanchez Ranch?"

"It would appear that would be an option, but I'm trying to build this congregation, and therefore I have to stick to the guidelines that myself and the church board set down. Baptism is simple. We don't have to go to a river. As I said, all I do is sprinkle some water on your forehead while I recite a few religious verses. It's nothing to fear. Do you believe in God?"

"No," Naiwa said.

"Then there is nothing I can do for you. I wish you a

lot of luck. Try one of the other churches. Their guidelines may not be as strict."

Naiwa was in tears, and nothing Raul said could soothe her feelings. She ran out of the church, got in the buggy, and wouldn't look at Raul or respond to him. Several citizens stopped and looked at the couple. This further exacerbated the situation, and Raul drove to the ranch. Naiwa was still crying as Raul tied the rig to the hitching post in front of the main house. Tommy saw them come into the house and he called out to them. Raul joined him in the kitchen while Naiwa went to her room. "What's wrong?" Tommy asked.

Raul told him what happened and the effect it had on Naiwa. "I can't reach her right now. It's best that she get a good night's sleep, and perhaps we can visit it again tomorrow. It's bad enough that she's overly sensitive about her Indian heritage, but when the minister says she has to be baptized before he can marry us, it just adds fuel to the fire. Can you recommend some minister who's not that sensitive about baptism?"

"What about a magistrate? A civil ceremony could be just as effective, and you can still be married here."

CHAPTER 14
1890

ON DAY FOUR, a burial party of civilians and soldiers arrived and began piling bodies into wagons. The Detachment Commander, General Leonard Colby, decided it would be easier to bury the victims at the site of the massacre rather than transport them to the Pine Ridge Reservation. He commandeered both civilians and soldiers alike to excavate a common burial site. The task was arduous, in that the ground was frozen and snow flurries continued throughout the day and into the evening. Many of the deceased were frozen and were difficult to carry, which made the undertaking even more tedious. Soon they filled one wagon and drove a short distance and dumped the bodies into a large pit dug at the bottom of the small rise, below where the mountain guns had stood. The work continued until ten that evening. It appeared that it would take many days to complete the task.

A shout went out about three in the afternoon; someone was found alive. Initially, the onsite commander thought it was a joke. He couldn't believe that someone could survive the massacre. The rescuers were even more surprised to find four babies alive. Initially they didn't hear them. It was only after they lifted a few bodies that they could hear one of the infants crying, and then another, before they found the last two. The four had miraculously survived by being wrapped in their mothers' shawls. One baby had a leather cap on its head decorated with beads showing the American flag. General Colby subsequently adopted the baby.

The babies became the center of attention, and one of the soldiers raised the issue of how to feed the crying children. One individual had some milk; he fashioned nipples out of the fingers in his gloves and fed the infants. This was a significant contrast between the nurturing of the rescued infants by soldiers, some of whom may have fired indiscriminately into the helpless Indians.

One of the officers questioned White Bird extensively on what happened and compared his version with that given by soldiers returning to Pine Ridge Reservation. Another round of questioning ensued, and White Bird was accused of fabricating a story to make the soldiers look bad. "It's just your word against many who reported that the Indians were hostile and fired the first round at the soldiers," the interrogator said.

"Believe what you want. I was here; you weren't," he responded.

"You can get in a lot of trouble by lying about what happened," the officer said as White Bird walked away

When his story was leaked to the soldiers on the burial detail, it didn't sit well, and many of the soldiers were angry. They shouted at him, calling him a liar. Soon five of the more vocal soldiers confronted White Bird and told him to take back his lie. Luckily, an officer overheard the commotion and ordered his soldiers to release the young Indian and go back to the burial site. One of those reluctantly going back told the officer, "This Indian kid is saying our guys are liars—you're not going to let him get away with it, are you?"

"I'll take care of it," the officer responded, and ordered the soldiers back to their task.

He then turned to White Bird. "We're here to bury hundreds. One more won't make any difference. If you don't want to end up in that big hole with the rest, I suggest you shut the hell up." White Bird got the message and walked away.

The relief group had planned to stay two to three days to bury the dead, but with the discovery of the babies, four of the civilians took a wagon back to Pine Ridge Reservation and handed them off to a representative of Chief Red Cloud. This left the relief group shorthanded, and their supervisor wanted White Bird to help with the loading and burial of the bodies, but he refused. "I want to dig a fitting grave for my parents. As soon as I finish, I'll help with the burial of my people."

"I'm not going to have some smart-assed Indian tell me what he is or isn't going to do. You're either going to help dig the graves, or I'll kick your ass until you do. Take your pick."

White Bird realized that the supervisor would

probably shoot him if he didn't do what he was told, but he held his ground, but his speech was less abrasive. "I'll gladly help with the graves, but if you don't mind, I'd like to bury my parents and my woman first."

The supervisor threw him a shovel. "You'd better be back in two hours. After that, I'm going to come looking for you."

He picked up the shovel and made his way to the three shallow graves. With the tool, he was able to widen the existing graves and lower the bodies so that they were covered by at least two feet of dirt and would keep away the wandering wolves. He cried when he laid Maiden Dream into her grave. He said a prayer over his parents' resting place and thanked them for raising him and his brothers. He especially remembered the love they showed him and how grateful he was to have such a family. Just as he was finishing, the officer appeared. "You've had enough time—now report to the sergeant. I'd better not hear that you're not pulling your load."

The number of dead bodies was more than the burial party could inter during one day. White Bird assumed that they wouldn't be completed for a least another two days, so after helping with the loading and widening the burial site, he checked his traps and recovered two more rabbits. That night, he was able to roast the rabbits over an open fire the civilians had made, and he shared some of his food with one of them who'd been kind to him. He did his best to avoid the soldiers he had had the confrontation with, though they shouted many remarks at him while he warmed himself over the fire. White Bird was sure they were going to kill him before they left.

With sentries out to guard against the roving wolves, White Bird went back to his makeshift hut. He didn't divulge the fact that he had two rifles and some ammunition under the rags he was using for a bed. That night he slept with a loaded gun in his hand. He wasn't sure if the five would try to sneak up on him. Twice during the night he awakened, sensing someone was near. He rose and stepped outside his enclosure while shielding the gun, but he didn't see or hear anyone. He knew that he was in a precarious position.

Soon, it became decision time for him. He took great pride that he had been able to survive for four days in the open prairie during a blizzard and keep the wolves at bay. He thought about life on the reservation and what his future would be like. To him, it was going to be an endless chore just to survive, let alone have a meaningful life. He didn't know if he wanted to go with the rescuers when they left; yet, he felt that some of his brothers had probably survived and he had a responsibility to be with his family.

The next morning he found two more rabbits in his traps. He skinned the animals, took the meat back to his hut and took stock of his provisions. He had six skins and food enough for six days. He fashioned two gloves from the skins he scavenged around the area. One of the members of the burial party had given him some matches, so he gathered some kindling, lit a fire and cooked the raw meat. He wrapped the cooked meat in a newspaper, picked up his rifles and ammunition and made his way south from the scene of the massacre. There had to be more to life than a reservation.

As he was walking out of range, one of the soldiers called out to him, but he paid no mind and soon he was out of their sight. Intuitively, he felt that the longer he remained at the site, the greater the probability the soldiers would kill him. He had no idea where he was going, but he knew that it was warmer the further south he went.

CHAPTER 15

1900

WITH the authorities stymied in their investigation into the three hangings, John had plenty of time to plan for his next victim. Because of his hard work, he'd earned the trust of his employer, and if he wanted time for some personal tasks, he was free to pursue them. Still, he didn't want to raise any flags, so he used his lunch hour to stake out the next victim. He'd been walking near Spenser's church when Raul and his Indian girlfriend came running out of the church, hopped into their rig and rode away. He hadn't heard what was said, but Mary Connelly had. She related to John that she heard Spenser shouting at the Indian woman before she ran out of the church crying. The Mexican man went running after her, trying to calm her down.

While the woman was telling her story, John's mind was working. The fact that Raul had a disagreement with Spenser and was the one who found victims two and three might come in handy. John filed that away for the future. He's been able to stay on script so far. No one had been able to find either the source of the rope used in the hangings or the make of the boot with the telltale marks. He had found them in an obscure catalog and ordered them delivered to the post office. He had picked them up late in the afternoon one day and stored them in his room. Neither of the orders was processed through the general store. The Ghost Shirt was unknown to nearly everyone in the area except the Sanchez family. This didn't pose any significant problem for John at this time, but Tommy Sanchez was shrewd. John watched him take over the crime scenes at two of the hangings and was impressed with his thoroughness. He probably overreacted when he shot at Sanchez and saw him fall to the ground. The Springfield was old, but John was an excellent shot. He couldn't believe he missed, but there was Sanchez getting off the ground and walking his horse to the grove of trees. The advantage was lost as soon as Sanchez got up, so John walked off and covered his tracks.

Three weeks after he shot at Sanchez, the man came into the general store and talked to the owner. John couldn't hear their conversation and didn't want to seem conspicuous by standing near the office. When Sanchez left his employer's office, he didn't leave immediately. He walked around the store and eventually came up on John. He looked directly at him while he was stocking some shelves with new merchandise. "I've seen you before, but I can't place where," Tommy said.

"I've seen you in the store, sir, but that's all."

"Where are you from, John Smart?"

"I'm from San Diego."

"That's interesting. I owned a company in San Diego. Where did you live?"

"I don't remember. I was only there for about a year. Sir, please excuse me, I have to finish my work and make two deliveries." As John Smart walked toward the rear of the store, Tommy was impressed at how athletically the young man walked.

Two months had passed since the last hanging. The three murders had changed John. He had been angry with the first victim, and taunted the man before he died. That hatred was replaced with a firm conviction that what he was doing was right. Spenser was the main target all along; he was the one who shot his father and mother. He wasn't sure which of the other three shot Maiden Dream, but he killed all three anyway. He'd become more cautious since Sanchez had talked to him at the general store. The man had a way of looking right through you; it was disconcerting. He wondered if Sanchez suspected him. He obviously had a reason for stopping to talk to him.

The Reverend Spenser was always busy on the weekends for services, funerals, weddings and counseling. Tuesday seemed to be his least busy day of the week; therefore, Tuesday, April 1st, would be the day. Spenser had a habit of locking up his meeting hall at ten p.m. and then retiring to a room in the back. John planned to sneak into the church after dark and hide in the choir loft overlooking the main hall. Since it was light until seven in the evening this time of the year, he waited until nine that evening before making a move. He was dressed completely in black as he entered the front of the church and quickly made his way up the stairs on the east side to the upper level. He tied the rope to the top rail looking down on the empty hall and then tested it to be sure it would hold his weight. He lay down in front of the organ and waited for the reverend to lock up.

Waiting for the bell to toll ten o'clock at the Baptist Church over a block away made him uneasy, but it was necessary. When the bell finally rang, Spenser came into the main hall and walked to the front door, bolting it from the inside. As he was returning, he didn't see John climb over the rail and let himself down to the floor with the rope. When John's feet touched the floor, a board squeaked. Spenser turned and yelled out, "What do you want?"

John leaped at him and struck Spenser on the top of the head with a small zap; the clergyman fell backward on the floor. But Spenser was a big man, and he rolled away just as John jumped at him. The two men wrestled, each trying to gain an advantage. John tried to hit him again, but Spenser grabbed his arm and tossed him sideways into the pews. John got up quickly and rushed Spenser and slammed him up against the rear wall; both men went down again, with John on top. He was in for the fight of his life, but he was younger and more agile. With his left hand he hit Spenser several times in the face, and as his victim turned onto his side to ward off the blows, John put on a choke hold, and although Spenser's strength was formidable, he passed out but was still alive.

Acting quickly before anyone hearing the noise would

come to the rescue, John bound Spenser's hands behind him and secured his legs together. Just to be sure, he put a gag in the man's mouth and hit him one more time with his zap. He carefully dressed the minister in the Ghost Shirt, dragged the body across the floor, sat him against the interior wall and painted his face red. John estimated Spenser's height and fashioned a noose that he hoped would have Spenser's feet just off the floor. The man was bigger than the other three, but not as tall. He found a one-foot stool and placed it under the noose. With the adrenaline rushing through John's veins, he grabbed the victim's shirt in one hand and his belt in the other and slung him over his shoulder. He balanced the man there, stepped on the stool, and placed the noose over the reverend's head. He gradually allowed the body to slip off his shoulders and then kicked the stool aside; Spenser was hanging two inches off the floor. He succumbed before he regained consciousness. John clipped a lock of his hair and placed it in a tin cup at his feet. John waited until he heard the bells chime eleven o'clock, and then made his way through Spenser's living quarters and out into a light but steady rain. He let the rain soak his clothing; he lifted his head to the sky, and a sense of relief permeated his entire being as the rain ran down his face. He stayed like that for a few minutes; it was as though a load had been lifted from his shoulders. He'd accomplished what he set out to do, even though it had taken him nearly ten years to finish the job.

Mental exhaustion set in as he sat on the steps at the

rear of the building. Finally, he removed his gloves and hat, then his boots, pants and sweater. Before he left the hall, he retrieved a bag from the loft that contained a change of attire and shoes. He wiped off the blackening on his face with cream he carried in the bag and stuffed the pants, shirt and boots he was wearing back into it. He discarded the bag in some boxes at the rear of a retail store sharing the same alley as the church, and went back to his room. It took him a couple of hours to calm down, but finally a smile crossed his face; it was all over. "This was for you, my mother and father," he cried.

CHAPTER 16

1900

WHAT A SHOCK the elderly cleaning lady was in for when she unlocked the front doors of the church hall the next morning and nearly walked into the Rev. Samuel Spenser's body, hanging from the choir loft. She fell over on her bottom, letting out a scream that surely pierced the morning fog. From that point, everything moved slowly for the next minute as she looked up at the body hanging there. She scooted back, trying to get as far away as she could from the hanging corpse. At first, she didn't comprehend that Spenser was dead. When reality set in, fear took over and she ran the race of the late Olympians, staggering out of the building and stumbling all the way to the constable's office.

Charles Little was enjoying his morning coffee when a screaming woman burst into his office. She paced around his office and then began walking in and out of the small space. Her speech was nearly incoherent. It took him almost five minutes to determine what she was saying. Mostly, all she did was point and continue to sob. He offered the woman some coffee, hoping that would calm her down, but that didn't work. Finally, he was able to understand that something had happened at the church. She was reluctant to walk back with him, so he grabbed her arm and tried to lead her back, but she pulled away and ran off. The door to the church was open as he walked up the stairs and through the opening. There was the Reverend Samuel Spenser hanging from a rope attached to the rail on the second floor. The thing that caught Little's immediate attention was that the body was clad in a Ghost Shirt with a blue collar and red paint stripes on the sleeves. The constable knew he was in over his head and that Tommy Sanchez needed to see this before he did anything else.

On his way over to the church hall, the constable saw one of Sanchez' vaqueros going into the general store. He hastily shut the front door of the church, ran a half block, entered the store and saw the rider standing at the checkout counter. He approached him, asked if he spoke English, and soon realized that the Mexican didn't understand what he wanted. Rather than take a chance, he wrote a short message and told the vaquero to deliver it to Tommy Sanchez immediately. The constable then went back to the crime scene, shut the doors, and sat on the front steps waiting for Sanchez. They had a serial killer loose in their town, and he didn't have the experience to solve the crimes.

Tommy was surprised when he read the message the vaquero delivered, and yet he wasn't that astonished. His instincts told him that whoever was hanging these men had a deep-seated hatred that wouldn't end with just three of the four men who'd worked at his ranch. When he told Sarah, she became tense. "Do you think this is a vendetta against everyone at this ranch? Could it be that one of us or Raul is next?"

"Those four men came from Fort Robinson and only worked six months for us. It's possible, but I don't think any of us are a target. But I'll double the guard at night if that will make you more comfortable. Right now, I'll put Raul on alert while I'm in town."

"Do you think it's wise to investigate this hanging, especially after the newspaper editorials? The last time you investigated a hanging, you were shot. That killer may not be so incompetent this time."

"I'm not going to hide out on our ranch. If it will make you happy, I'll wear my gun. My left shoulder is almost back to normal. I'll be okay. I'll certainly be more alert this time. But my guess is that the one we're looking for has hanged his last man."

The scene at the church was similar to the other three murder sites. The Ghost Shirt was similar, the rope was the same, and the noose was fashioned exactly like the others. While they were waiting for Doctor Cunnane to arrive and take the body, Tommy walked up the stairs to the choir loft. It was from this loft that the killer tied the rope to the rail. He looked around and saw some black marks on the floor in front of the organ. He scraped the floor with his knife, and the particles on his knife resembled soot from burned wood or coal. "Charles, there's black soot on the floor up here."

"There's no reason for it," Charles responded.

"I wonder if our killer is using soot to blacken his face and thereby disguise himself, if he's seen."

"Could be. Have you taken a look at the shirt and red paint on his face?"

"In my opinion, the shirt is the same as the ones found on the other three and the face is painted similar to the other three. The four who were hanged worked for me at the ranch for six months. Raul was their supervisor. They were discharged from Fort Robinson on the same day and came to the valley to work for Earl Singleton. Fortunately for my wife and me, Singleton went to jail for the Santa Barbara Bank heist. But it impacted the four. They needed work, and didn't know anyone here who'd hire them. I sympathized with their plight and employed them for six months. I felt that would be enough time for them to get acclimated and find permanent employment. Whatever happened to get them hanged didn't happen here. It had to happen at Fort Robinson, or some other place where they were stationed, or perhaps at some encounter where there was a lot of shooting. Someone hates them fiercely."

Tommy noticed that boot marks found at the other crime scenes were apparent on the dusty floor in the loft. He followed the boot prints down the steps to where the body was hanged. From there, they led to the rear of the building and into a small bedroom, which may have been where Spenser slept. He walked through the room and out a door at the rear of the church. It had rained for a short time last night, and although there probably was some activity behind the church this morning, he was able to follow the distinctive prints for a short distance. They led behind a hardware store, but soon he lost them. Tommy walked in several directions, but came up empty-handed. As he started back to the church, he saw several wooden crates against the rear wall of a hardware store. He was curious and looked in all three wooden boxes. That's when he found a cotton bag containing a black hat, black shirt, black pants and a pair of boots with the exact tread pattern found at the murder scenes.

He picked up the bag and returned it to the church. He showed the articles to Little, who asked, "Do you think that's the killer's clothing?"

"It's a strong possibility. The shirt and pants have remnants of soot I found on the loft floor. It's possible that our killer dressed completely in black and covered his face and hands with soot to camouflage his features. The pants and shirt are a little large for me, so I'd say our suspect was probably a little taller than me and perhaps twenty pounds bigger. Since he's discarded the clothing, he may have ended his killing spree, making Spenser his last victim."

By this time, Dr. Cunnane had arrived with his wagon and a helper. Tommy and the constable helped the two lower Spenser's body to the floor and moved it closer to the front door where there was more light. Cunnane started to examine Spenser and remarked that the victim had several lacerations and bruises on his face and his hands were cut. Dried blood covered the knuckles. Tommy picked up the tin cup with a lock of hair in it and handed it to Cunnane. "Perhaps you can check this sample against Spenser's hair, doctor."

Tommy and Little looked at the lacerations and blood. "It looks like this hanging wasn't passive. He took a beating, but apparently the murderer is marked somewhat, because Spenser's knuckles are bruised and cut," Cunnane said.

"We need to be looking for someone who may have lacerations on his face and bruised knuckles," Little replied.

"I've got a couple of errands to run before I head back to the ranch. There's nothing more I can do right now; let me know if I can help," Tommy said.

But it wasn't errands that Tommy had on his mind. He wanted to see John Smart and see if his hands and face had any marks. But he was to be disappointed. The owner said that Smart was delivering some supplies to Ventura and wouldn't be back till the beginning of next week. "John wanted a couple of days off for some personal stuff. He's a good worker, so I saw no reason not to approve the time off."

"Did the young man have any lacerations on his hands or face?"

"Come to think of it, he had a small bandage on his cheek. When I asked about it, he said he cut himself shaving."

Two days later the sheriff and James Jefferson came out to the ranch and showed Tommy and Sarah the Sunday morning *Santa Barbara Register.* The editorial page was not quite accusing Raul of the murders, but it didn't pull any punches when it suggested that the sheriff had a suspect. The article asked the public what the sheriff intended to do. It was a half-page article pointing out that Raul was the one who found two of the bodies and was overheard having a serious argument with the most recent victim.

"The boots and clothing you found are our first clue. If they belonged to the killer, then Raul can't be a suspect. Those clothes and boots are too big for him. I think we need to look at all kinds of catalogs to see who makes these particular boots and see if they were sold to stores in our area or perhaps to an individual purchaser. Hold on to the boots. The killer has made his first mistake," Jefferson told Tommy and the sheriff.

"There's one other thing we need to look for," Tommy said.

"What's that?" the sheriff asked.

"Someone with bruising on his face and hands."

CHAPTER 17
1900

THE RANCH wasn't completely isolated from the surrounding community, but it was far enough away that interaction with the surrounding towns was minimal. Yet those living on the ranch felt the animosity of the townspeople whenever they went into Santa Ynez. Guests were infrequent, and those delivering supplies or buying produce from Altura Prado didn't linger. They transacted their business quickly and left. Though the Sanchez family had many acquaintances, their friends were few in number. One of the exceptions was James Jefferson, now working out of the Pinkerton office in Santa Barbara. Their friendship was strong, and Jefferson could always be counted on to bring them the latest news from Santa Barbara and vicinity. Today, he arrived at about four in the afternoon and was greeted by the two Labrador Retrievers on the ranch. Their barking alerted Sarah to a visitor, and she came out the front door to greet Jefferson. "You're staying for dinner, aren't you?"

"I thought you'd never ask."

"It'll be ready in about thirty minutes. Tommy is out in the barn. Why don't you go out there and tell him dinner is early tonight. I had a premonition that you would be here, so I made your favorite dessert." Sarah laughed and went back into the house.

Tommy was cleaning tack when Jefferson walked in. "Sarah says dinner will be early, and if you don't mind, I'll be your guest."

"Still seeing the widow?"

"As a matter of fact, I am. I think I'm going to marry the lady this summer. You're going to be my best man."

"The last guy who agreed to marry her was hanged. Are you nervous?"

"Naw. I don't believe in omens. I'm like you. I think the hangings are over. What's it been, two months since Spenser's hanging, and nothing more has happened?"

They finished dinner early and were enjoying an after-dinner drink on the front porch when Sarah asked Jefferson to give them the latest news from Santa Barbara.

"It's all about the four hangings and the Ghost Shirts. I know you're not reading the newspapers, but there isn't a day that goes by that Tommy and Raul aren't hanged in effigy. That editor has his spurs in this story and he isn't going to let up on you until someone walks in and confesses."

"But we didn't have anything to do with any of this. We're as much in the dark about the murders as anyone else." Sarah was defiant.

"I don't think it matters. He's got a hot story and he's selling a lot of newspapers, and consequently he's getting a lot of money from advertisers. This is a gold mine for him."

"I think it's rotten what people will do for money."

"How's Raul and Naiwa taking this?" Jefferson asked.

"Naiwa is a basket case, and Raul is in a state of shock. He does his duties around here, but you can see there's no life in him. He doesn't know what to do. We tell him that this will eventually go away and become a bad memory, but it's as though he doesn't hear us. Naiwa is talking about going back to the reservation, and Raul told Tommy the other day that he would be better off in Mexico. They're only simple people trying to make it in life; their breaking point is slowly approaching."

The three had changed the subject and were talking about the impending wedding when they saw three riders coming up the main road. Tommy went inside and returned immediately with his and Sarah's rifle, which they rested against their chairs.

The three greeted the sheriff and two of his deputies. Their tone was cordial, if not apprehensive. They allowed the riders to dismount and attach the reins to the hitching post on the side of the house. None of the three visitors seemed threatening, but Tommy's hand rested on the stock of his rifle as they approached. They waited for the sheriff to speak.

"I've got a search warrant for Raul's room. I have a lot of confidence in Raul, but this is what I'm paid to do. I want you to show us where he's staying." The sheriff looked directly at Tommy as he spoke.

"Hold on here a moment. I want to see that search warrant and who issued it."

The sheriff produced a signed warrant by Judge Remier. "Tommy, I don't like this any more than you do, but I have the legal right to search his room."

"All this because some newspaper editor says he's a suspect."

"Well, it started that way, but the town council and the supervisor for this district agree with the editor. That's who I work for."

Tommy didn't move. He stared at the sheriff and his deputies and made them very uncomfortable. He made them wait a few more minutes before he rose and told them to follow him. He carried his rifle as they went into the main barn. Tommy opened a door near the rear of the large two-story structure and allowed the three lawmen to enter.

Raul's room was spartan, with a cot, a chest of drawers and a closet. The sheriff went through the drawers and turned over some underwear, socks and shirts. After going through the chest of drawers, they moved to the closet. Under the spare saddle on the floor was a pair of worn boots, but the marks on the bottom weren't similar to those found near three of the victims. The sheriff showed them to Jefferson and Tommy. Chaps were hanging from a nail on the interior wall. The sheriff reached down one of the chap's legs and pulled out a Ghost Shirt. It was folded so that it would fit down one of the legs and not draw any attention.

Everyone was speechless as the sheriff unfolded the Ghost Shirt and looked at Tommy and Jefferson. "There's enough here to justify arresting Raul. Where is he?"

At that moment, Raul walked into his room. "What is everyone doing in my room? You never came in here before, Patron." Raul was looking at Tommy, waiting for an answer.

"Where did you get this Ghost Shirt?" The sheriff asked Raul.

Raul looked at the shirt and shook his head, and in broken English said, "I don't know, it's not mine."

"Then what is it doing in your closet?" The sheriff asked.

Raul spoke in Spanish. Tommy translated for him. "He says he doesn't know why it's here. Someone must have put it where you found it."

"Who would do that?" the sheriff asked.

"I don't know, but there are many people on the ranch, and those who visit the ranch have access to the barn and, consequently, Raul's room," Tommy responded.

"Raul Mendoza, you're under arrest for the murder of Samuel Spenser," the sheriff said.

"Patron?" Raul was looking at Tommy.

"Now wait a minute, sheriff. Raul's boots are not the ones the killer used. You have the pair we found in the crate behind Spenser's church along with the killer's pants, hat and sweater, which are too large for Raul. He couldn't be the killer. You're being forced by public opinion, not by evidence. I'm asking you to leave Raul alone and leave my property."

The two deputies drew their guns and pointed them at Tommy. "The Ghost Shirt by itself is enough for me to make an arrest," the sheriff said.

Tommy stared at the sheriff. "I would have never believed that you would draw down on me. I've a good mind to test you." He had his hand on the rifle.

The sheriff realized this was a dangerous situation and turned to his two deputies. "Put your guns away. I'll decide what's going to happen here, not you two."

When the two deputies holstered their guns, Tommy laid his rifle against one of the bales of hay. "I'll get Juan to represent you and we'll post a bond to get you out of jail," Tommy said to Raul.

Tommy turned to the two deputies. "Don't ever set foot on my property again. If you ever aim your guns at me again, I'll kill you. Now get out of here."

CHAPTER 18
1900

HER NAME was Claire Wilson. She was the daughter of Frederick Wilson, a Santa Barbara County Commissioner living in Santa Ynez. In the past, she'd come into the store with her mother. But since graduating from high school, and due to the infirmity of her mother, she started coming to the general store by herself to do the family shopping. Normally, one of the workers in the feed lot would assist her. Today, no one was available, so John asked her to drive her wagon to the back of the store; he personally loaded her supplies and groceries.

This wasn't the first time they had met, but it was the first time John had taken notice of her. After he checked her list and filled the wagon, he boldly asked her if she was seeing someone. "Why do you ask?" she replied with a slight smile.

"I've been in the valley for nearly two years and I've not seen anyone as attractive as you during that entire time."

Claire Wilson appeared to blossom. "If you're that interested, why don't you come to dinner on Sunday afternoon at four? You can meet my family and see what they say about your intentions."

John was flirting with Claire, but was taken back by such a bold response. "Well, my intentions are honorable."

He didn't get to finish. "Oh, I think you say that to all the girls in town."

John visibly flushed, and for a moment, he couldn't formulate an answer. "Well, John, can I tell my mother to expect you for dinner or not?"

He stammered and thought he said yes, but he wasn't sure. He must have said yes, because as he helped her into the wagon, she said, "I'll see you Sunday."

She'd driven away before he realized he didn't know where she lived. He hoped his boss knew. He felt like a complete ninny. He hadn't had this problem with Rosita Riley in Sidney.

The next morning he knocked on the owner's door and asked for a few minutes of his time. "What is it, John?"

"Claire Wilson invited me to dinner at her home on Sunday. I don't know where she lives, and I don't know if it's appropriate for me to bring something."

The owner smiled. "I'll write out the directions for you. I'd suggest flowers for Claire and a box of chocolates for the mother. That is, if you want to make an impression."

He was nervous as he got ready to visit the Wilsons on Sunday afternoon. He took a bath, put on a clean shirt, picked some flowers, and bought a box of chocolates. The marks on his face had disappeared and the scars on his hands had healed. Frederick Wilson met him at the door, and from John's perspective, interrogated him for at least ten minutes before he was allowed into the parlor. He stammered hello as he presented the chocolates to the mother and flowers to Claire. She grabbed his arm and led him into the parlor and asked him to be seated. "Let me put the flowers in a vase, and then I'll come back for you. Dinner is nearly ready."

To say that he was nervous was an understatement. He looked around the spacious living room and his gaze fell on the pictures of Claire's family lined up on the mantel over the fireplace. He was startled when he felt her arm on him. "Are you ready?" she asked.

The interchange between the Wilsons at the dinner table gave John pause. They all seemed to be equal, each giving their opinion on various topics while not surrendering to the other. They discussed county issues, state affairs, and certain books that John had never heard of. He was sensitive to his lack of education and felt that he was at a disadvantage, so he didn't join in. But the family made an effort to have him participate; he was forced to think. When he didn't know the issues or the answer to questions her father posed, Claire would intercede and coach him. Gradually, he began to feel comfortable. He expected dinner to last thirty minutes, but two and one-half hours later, they were still sitting at the table having coffee, yet it seemed like only thirty minutes. John never experienced such an interchange between family members. After he got over his fear of using a fork when he should be using a spoon, he thoroughly enjoyed himself. When it was time to leave, he took every opportunity to stretch out his stay.

Apparently, the father was impressed, for he allowed Claire to see John to the door. He stammered his thanks for the invitation and suggested that they go on a picnic next weekend. Claire put her hand on his shoulder and kissed him on the cheek.

"Well, that would be nice, but father and mother wouldn't be able to come. Mother's health, you know. So I guess if you want to see me again, it has to be next Sunday dinner. Are you up for it?"

"You can't keep me away."

CHAPTER 19
1890

THE FIRST significant town White Bird came across on his way south was Alliance, Nebraska. The unincorporated area had nearly one thousand people within its limits. His clothing was ragged, his hair was long and he was dirty. Consequently, he didn't make much of an impression on the two businesses where he attempted to find work. One proprietor suggested that if he didn't move off his premises immediately, he'd call the sheriff. The local church agreed to feed him two meals conditioned on him working for the food. For lunch and dinner, he worked six hours chopping wood. Afterward the minister suggested he might be happier in some other town. He got the message. It was cold, but there wasn't any snow on the ground as he continued his trek south.

The young Indian brave was intelligent, but he didn't know how to read or write. In the wild, he knew how to endure; now he'd have to learn to adjust to town living, if he wanted to survive. The minister in Alliance suggested he might find work in Sidney, which was at least five days away. He camped at night along the stream bed, paralleling the main trail; it provided him fresh water and some game as well. His skills at trapping small animals, though most were rabbits, was increasing. With a few matches he'd obtained from the church, he was able to light a fire to cook the rabbits, but he was reluctant to keep the fire going all night. He didn't want any uninvited quests stopping by. His knife was sharp, so he cut his hair to shoulder length, but he couldn't do anything about his ragged clothing. He took a bath in the stream and rubbed the dirt off his clothing.

Sidney in those days was a railhead. It was also the terminus for the Black Hills Stage, servicing passengers and supplies to Fort Robinson, the Red Cloud Agency and Deadwood, South Dakota. He camped outside town and first thing in the morning went to the town's only general store and both livery stables looking for work. The store wasn't interested, but one of the livery stable owners needed someone to muck the stalls and feed the eight horses stabled there. After just one day, the owner, who was nearly sixty years old, could see that White Bird was a solid worker. He advanced the boy some money for a new shirt, pants and food. The young brave worked from sunup to sundown and slept in the one of stalls at night. After six months of moving the eighty-pound hay bales around, he put twenty pounds on his lean frame, and most of that was muscle. The owner and his wife took an interest in the polite young man, and it was she who taught him to write his name and gain a rudimentary reading ability. She loaned him her children's elementary reading books, which he read in his spare time. White

Bird was a willing student, and within a year he was able to read a few novels. He especially liked Cooper's *The Last of the Mohicans.*

He told the owner that his name was Jacob Light and that he was from Alliance. His parents were dead and he was on his own. He adopted the name from the minister's sermon he heard while he was working at the church in Alliance. The phrase was, When Jacob saw the Light. During his first few months in Sidney, he kept to himself. There were contacts with boys and girls his age, but he was too shy to tell them where he came from and who his parents were. White Bird was grateful for his job and the respect the owner showed him. When he heard the railroad was hiring, and that the wages were almost twice what he was making at the livery, he made his move and started driving nails for the railroad yard boss. He thanked Mr. and Mrs. Andros for their help, but he was moving on. The gang repairing rails was a rough and a hard-drinking lot, but White Bird avoided the more rowdy groups and tried to stay out of any confrontations. But that was easier said than done.

One day, a shaggy-looking worker took Jacob's lunch that was lying on a log next to Jacob. The other members of the twenty-man gang waited to see what the young man would do. He was seventeen now and had put muscle on to his five-foot, ten-inch frame; he weighed one hundred sixty pounds. He was nearly a man. He walked up to the man and asked for his sandwich back. The other man took a big bite out of sandwich, threw the remainder at Jacob, and moved in a threatening manner closer to the young man. When the two were about four feet apart, Jacob jumped up, lashed out with both legs, and struck the man in the chest with his feet. The impact was so great that the antagonizer stumbled backward and landed on his back with his head hitting an iron rail. That was the last time anyone tried to take advantage of him.

Still, he wasn't sure where his future lay nor where he was going next. He was taking life day by day; yet he hadn't forgotten Wounded Knee. There wasn't a day that went by that he wasn't angry at what had happened to his parents, brothers and Maiden Dream. He'd wake in the middle of the night in a cold sweat and visualize the four men firing point blank into his family. Who were these men, and how could he find them? He started speaking to some of the older workers about the soldiers at Ft. Robinson, but he didn't want to divulge his intentions, so he was careful when he asked questions. One of the middle-aged nail pounders had served in the army at Fort Robinson, which was south of the Pine Ridge Reservation. The older man hadn't been at Wounded Knee, but he knew some soldiers who had been there. From everything he heard, it was a slaughter.

Fortune smiled on Jacob one day when he saw one of the four men who'd fired on his family standing on the train platform. He'd gotten off the train at Sidney and was buying a ticket to Fort Robinson. He got up close to the man, but the soldier didn't recognize him. Well, how could he know him, when White Bird was diving under falling bodies as the shooting began? If this man couldn't recognize him, why should the other three?

He'd been working for the railroad for over a year, so he was known to management personnel. It wasn't difficult for him to find out from the ticket agent that the man taking the stage to Fort Robinson was Hiram Whitman. Perhaps he didn't need to go to Fort Robinson. Maybe he could wait here and see if the other three came through Sidney. Still, he wasn't sure what his next step should be. He'd have to think long and hard. It wasn't as though he planned to live in this town the rest of his life. Each week, he'd saved part of his wages in case he had to move on quickly. Now that he had a few dollars set aside, it was time to move to the next step, whatever that was.

CHAPTER 20

1900

AFTER RAUL was arrested and taken to Santa Barbara, one of the vaqueros was sent into town to get Juan, who responded that he could be at the ranch later that evening. Juan had recently brought a new client into his law firm, and he was working long hours to research his case. The man's name was Jerome Whittington, who was disputing the boundary of a Spanish Land Grant, namely Rancho San Martin. It seems the original grantee became land-rich and cash-poor mainly due to the number of claims he had to defend against his grant. Through mortgage default and excessive attorney fees, he had to sell off portions of his grant. Compounding the problem during this time frame was a decline in cattle prices and a lengthy drought that forced the grantee to finally sell all his holdings.

Whittington bought a large portion of the grant from the land owner. The point of contention was that the former owner had sold a small portion of that which he sold to Whittington to another buyer, who set up fences and cut off Whittington's access to water and the main road servicing his property.

In 1891, the U.S. Congress created the COURT of PRIVATE LAND GRANTS, giving it jurisdiction over conflicts involving Spanish Land Grants. Most of their cases over a ten- to fourteen-year term were based on incomplete documentation of the original grant. Such was the case for Juan's client. The previous owner was confused, because the Spanish described the western boundary of the grant as the skirt of the mountain, which could be the foothills of the mountain or the timberline. Whittington interpreted that his property extended to the timberline of the mountain, while the grantee interpreted the boundary as the foothill of the mountain. He sold the space between the two descriptions to another. Other discrepancies Juan found that were compounding the issue were that the Spanish used metes and bounds and Americans used acres. Additionally, the Spanish length of a yard varied from time to time.

Juan had completed his research and felt very comfortable that he could defend Whittington's position. However, in his law firm, junior partners did the research and prepared the briefs, but the senior partner argued cases before the court. Juan turned over his file to the senior partner that afternoon. When he arrived at Altura Prado, his mother and her husband were having coffee in the nook. The children were in bed and Naomi was consoling Naiwa in the rear yard.

"I have a fresh pot of coffee on if you'd like some," Sarah said to her son as he entered the kitchen and kissed her on the cheek.

Tommy filled Juan in on what he knew about the four murders and what Raul's involvement was. "I'd like you to handle his defense."

"I'm not a trial lawyer. I can give you a list of attorneys in Santa Barbara that would be more qualified than me," Juan said.

"Everything seems to be pointing at Raul. I think someone has set him up, and I want a lawyer who believes in his innocence and a man I can trust. Raul is nearly a family member. He's planning to marry your sister next month. I've watched you over the past year. You're ready. You can handle this," Tommy responded.

"Listen, I'd like to help Raul. The problem is that I've been under close scrutiny at my firm since these hangings, because I'm Sioux. I overheard two women talking to Mr. Grant about me. One distinctly said that she understood that I had been a renegade. I don't know how much credibility I'd have in front of a white jury. Besides, I don't know if my firm will allow me to take the case. I still have to contribute financially to the firm. The amount of time I'd have to spend on trial preparations and before a jury would be expensive."

"I'll talk to your supervisor and make him aware that I'll pay all the legal fees. Raul didn't do this. I don't know who's responsible, but you, Jefferson and I will have to figure it out."

"Christina and I have broken up. Her parents were not too pleased that she was in love with a half-breed. With the Ghost Shirt murders becoming the major topic of conversation in Santa Barbara, they insisted she stop seeing me. There's lot of animosity out there, and right now it's aimed at people like us. I respect your wishes, but I don't think I can help."

Sarah had been listening to the exchange between her husband and son. "If we can't help each other out of this situation, who can we turn to? We're all we have. I'd handle the defense myself if I had the training you have. You can handle this. Do it for us. Do it for me and your sister."

Tommy watched as the smile crept onto Juan's face. He kissed his mother on the forehead. "I'll do my best."

Over the next few days, Juan received permission from his boss to represent Raul. It probably helped that Tommy put up five thousand dollars in cash as a retainer. Tommy also posted a bond, and Raul was released to the ranch. He was back, but was very depressed, and his work suffered for it. Tommy had to take over managing the vaqueros, and most of his orders were directed to Cesar, who worked for Raul. James Jefferson took leave from the Pinkerton Agency so he could concentrate full-time on the investigation. The four men met at the Ranch on a Saturday morning to determine how to proceed.

"This whole thing seems to be moving too fast. We need to slow the process down so we can figure out what this is all about. Raul doesn't have any Sioux blood, and I don't think anyone can prove that he made the Ghost Shirts; it would surprise me if he even knew about them. My guess is that someone in this valley knows about them and is the one we're looking for." Tommy kicked off the meeting.

"Are there any Sioux in the area other than you and Juan?" Jefferson asked

"There's old Charlie and his sixty-year-old invalid son. Maybe the one we're looking for is fair-skinned and is passing as a Mexican or a white man. Then there's the question whether we're looking for one or more people. If it's one person, he has to be young and strong. A couple of those victims were over one hundred eighty pounds," Tommy responded.

"Perhaps we should make a list of all the young men in the area who would be fit enough to pull this off. There're only twenty-five hundred people in the valley, and half of them are women. We could start ruling out the elderly and those who wouldn't be physically capable of the hangings. I'll bet we could narrow it down to less than fifty. I don't think anyone who's lived here all his life would know anything about the Ghost Shirt, so they could be eliminated. It's time-consuming, but it's a task that I've done before. There's always the possibility that the one we're looking for may have completed his mission and is planning to move on. We should be aware of that possibility," Jefferson said.

"Raul, I know you found two of the bodies and that you had a discussion with the fourth victim, but there has to be a logical explanation why you were singled out. Did you have a confrontation with somebody over the past year or two? Can you remember anyone you crossed paths with?" Juan asked.

Tommy did the translating for Raul. "He can't remember having any arguments with anyone since he's been my foreman."

"Perhaps we need to determine if Raul has a reasonable alibi for each of the hangings. That's something, along with trial procedure, that he and I need to think long and hard about. I can't emphasize enough that emotion is high in the valley. Tommy and I are Sioux, my mother was married to a Sioux, and you're going to marry a Sioux. I won't say that a jury will be prejudiced, but in this case, you may not be considered innocent until proven guilty; you may be guilty until proven innocent." Tommy translated and Raul nodded to Juan his understanding.

"Raul, I want you to make yourself available to Juan. Take as much time off as necessary; you'll be on the payroll during the entire time. You're an expert when it comes to ropes. Juan can ask the sheriff to let you see the four ropes used in the hangings. Why don't you see if you can run down the place where that brand is sold or made? It may be Santa Barbara, Ventura, or some place north of here. Don't forget to check catalogs. If you have difficulty with the words, ask Sarah to help," Tommy said.

"I'm going to spend some time thinking about the reason for the hangings. I know of no incidents involving a Ghost Shirt in this area. Oh, I've seen them, and I wore one once when I performed the Ghost Dance. The placing of the shirts on the bodies seems to be symbolic, but of what? They remind me of similar shirts I saw at the Standing Rock Reservation when I visited my father. When Sarah and I visited the Pine Ridge Reservation this summer, Chief Red Cloud showed us some old Ghost Shirts from that reservation, but none were like the ones found on the four bodies. I think the animosity behind these hangings started somewhere else and was brought here. That somewhere else may be the key to unraveling this situation," Tommy said.

"Each of us has discrete tasks to perform. Why don't we meet again in two weeks to compare notes? There's another thing that's puzzling me. How did the shirt get into Raul's room? Someone had to come onto this ranch and plant it. Now, that would be difficult at night because we have two vaqueros patrolling the perimeter of our buildings. So, someone had to come in the daytime. That would be hard to do, unless it was a scheduled delivery or it was someone who was buying some of our stock and went into the barn. Sarah checks on any delivery here at the ranch. She'll have a list of those vendors and who delivered the goods. Raul, when was the last time you wore those chaps that held the Ghost Shirt?" Tommy asked.

"About the middle of last month," Raul replied in Spanish.

"That'll help Sarah narrow down who was here. Juan, you need to get us some time. If you can't, I'll talk to Judge Winters, who's the senior judge in Santa Barbara. My wife and I contributed to his latest campaign," Tommy said.

CHAPTER 21

1890

WHITE BIRD was eighteen years old and had progressed from pounding spikes into rails to assistant bookkeeper. During the two years he worked for the railroad, his language skills had improved, and he had only a trace of an accent. In the late eighteen hundreds, most of the railroad workers, looking for a better way of life, were either Asians or Europeans. As Jacob Light, he befriended an older man from Switzerland, who taught him mathematics. White Bird, or Jacob, as he was known to his fellow workers, didn't drink nor smoke. Of course, he was ridiculed by many of the roustabouts in the camp, but he was undaunted. There was an inner feeling that his lot in life was going to improve. Spending money on liquor, tobacco or women wasn't in his plans.

Getting the job as assistant bookkeeper was a boon for a former Sioux brave. He heard the position was becoming available because the incumbent was moving to Chicago to work for his brother. He put on a clean shirt and asked to talk to the head bookkeeper to see if he could be considered for the position. "What makes you think you can do the work?"

"I'm young, eager and especially good in math. What I don't know you could teach me."

Frank Stewart, who had been running the bookkeeping section for ten years, was taken back by the boldness of the young man in front of him; he liked that in young people. "Okay, I'm going to give you a reading, writing and mathematical test. If you do quite well, I'll consider you for the position."

Jacob was never told what his scores were. Two days after taking the tests, he was told by the yard boss to report on Monday to the bookkeeping office. Once he was up to speed, the duties of the bookkeeping section in the railroad office were divided equally among his supervisor and himself. The railroad had a contract with Fort Robinson, in Nebraska, calling for all vouchers for transported goods to be paid quarterly. Jacob informed his supervisor that the invoices for the fort the past quarter were two months overdue. His supervisor suggested that he travel to the Army Post and present the invoices in person to the Commanding Officer. "We need to get at least a promise to pay. We don't want to stop hauling their supplies and manpower; we just want to be paid," the head bookkeeper told him.

He left the next morning on the train to Alliance and then by stagecoach to the fort. He had a two-hour stop-over in Alliance, and Jacob went to one of the livery stables where he had applied for work after leaving the

Wounded Knee site. He saw the man who had told him that if he didn't leave he'd call the sheriff. The proprietor didn't recognize him, but he sure was polite to the well-dressed young man.

He didn't know what to expect when he arrived at the fort; he'd never been on a military installation. While at the fort, the home of the ninth cavalry, he would learn that Fort Robinson was originally located at the site of the Red Cloud Agency. It was a means of keeping an eye on the inhabitants of the agency. Several years later, the fort was moved to a site about one mile away, where it remained. There were as many as four hundred fifty soldiers stationed here, many of whom were black and designated as the "Buffalo Soldiers." It was here that Crazy Horse was killed in 1877. More important to Jacob was the probability that some of the soldiers who took part in the massacre at Wounded Knee came from Fort Robinson, or had been reassigned there.

It was late in the day when he arrived by coach at the fort. He immediately presented himself at the Adjutant's office, gave his name, stated his reason for coming, and asked to speak to the Fort Commander. "Major Shurlock has retired for the day. You can speak to him tomorrow morning at eight."

"Can you provide a bed and something to eat while I'm here?" Jacob asked.

"They'll have a bed for you in the enlisted barracks. See Corporal Knight, and here's a pass for the evening and morning mess. After you check in with Knight, you can head over to the mess hall; it'll be open until seven."

He found the enlisted barrack and was given a bed for the night; then he went over to the mess hall and got in the chow line. He sat with a couple of white enlisted men and noticed that the black soldiers were seated together at the other end of the hall. "Why are the black soldiers sitting at that end? There's less light and it's further from the food," he asked the soldiers he was sitting with.

"They're black and that's where they belong." By the tone of the response, he assumed that there wouldn't be any further discussion on the subject.

It was still light when he finished dinner, so he strolled around getting acquainted with the layout of the fort. The enlisted barracks were on one side of the fort while the officers' quarters were on the opposite end. The parade grounds and cemetery were to the rear of the enlisted barracks. In the center of the fort was a long single-story building which included shops and stores such as the settler's store, the veterinary office, post headquarters and the adjutant's office; all were connected in a straight line. He counted at least thirteen different entities housed in that row of buildings.

Jacob made his way back to the barracks. A few kerosene lamps were lit in the north end of the housing unit. Some of the men were playing cards; others were cleaning weapons, and the rest were lying on their cots. He sat on his bed opposite a soldier who was field stripping his weapon and engaged him in a conversation. He was curious about the black soldiers. He couldn't remember seeing them before. "Where do the black soldiers live?"

"They have separate barracks, closer to the company cemetery."

"I saw about twelve of them in the mess hall."

"That's about half of their contingent. We don't have much to do with them. They have their own officers."

"Do they fight alongside you?"

"Not generally, though they were at Wounded Knee with us, sort of in a back-up position. I don't think they saw any action."

"Was the entire Ninth Cavalry at Wounded Knee?"

"You ask a lot of questions for a young fellow."

"No offense. I was just curious, that's all."

"We were there. We put it to those redskins once and for all. They'd been causing too much trouble, and we were sent to put a stop to their killing and thieving. I think they'll think twice before they take on the Army again."

He was angry, but he didn't want to show any emotion and then be asked a lot of questions. He decided to lie down. The bed was hard and the blanket thin, but he got through the night, had breakfast, and waited for Major Shurlock outside his office at eight. He waited thirty minutes before the commander was available. "What's this all about, young man?" the major asked as Jacob presented him the vouchers.

"These are the unpaid vouchers for the past quarter. As you can see, they're signed by your first sergeant. The railroad would like to be paid."

"I don't have that much money here at the fort. I'll

wire higher headquarters and tell them to pay the bill. Is that okay with the railroad?"

"Yes, sir."

As he was leaving the commander's office, he walked by the desk of the First Sergeant. Standing before the Sergeant's desk was a soldier White Bird recognized from Wounded Knee. "Private Simon Higgins reporting as ordered," the soldier said.

Higgins was one of the four men who had fired point-blank at his parents. He now had two of the men identified. He caught the morning stage to Alliance and the noon train back to Sidney. He felt a sense of euphoria, having accomplished a great deal by identifying another of the men who had killed Maiden Dream and his parents. With luck he'd find the other two. Maybe they were stationed at Fort Robinson or possibly at the Pine Ridge Reservation. Today, he learned there was a detachment of soldiers stationed at that reservation. Perhaps it was time to visit his brothers and let them know he was alive.

CHAPTER 22

1900

THERE WERE at least seven customers in the general store, trying to take advantage of the month-end sales. John was filling an order from King Ranch when a tall, thin man entered the store and asked one of the other clerks if the owner was available. The worker immediately went to fetch the owner. When his employer appeared, the two men shook hands and went into the business office, but left the door open. John busied himself with straightening out some of the shelves while inching closer to the office, trying to hear what the two were talking about. The stranger was sitting in a chair taking notes with his back to the open door, while his boss was standing behind his desk. A little paranoia started to set in. John wondered if the tall lanky man was a law enforcement officer, and more than likely a Pinkerton man.

Behind the business office was a small storage room. John made his way to the back of the store, and after being sure no one else was in the area, he placed his ear against the wall separating the two areas. He could hear snippets of their conversation, but not enough to piece together the dialog. He was able to distinctly hear one phrase the stranger spoke: "We know he's in this area."

John returned to the front of the store just in time to see the man exit the store. He waited and intercepted the owner as he was walking to the hardware section of the store and inquired of his boss, "What was that all about?"

His supervisor smiled and said, "Oh, he's just doing a survey in the area."

He didn't think it wise to press the issue, so he just smiled and went back to his duties. With the arrest of Raul Mendoza for the four hangings and with a subsequent trial scheduled in two months, John felt a sense of relief. He'd accomplished his mission and hadn't drawn any suspicion to himself. Or at least he thought so until now. He just couldn't accept his owner's explanation of what had transpired.

He learned from another employee that Raul's attorney was Sarah Sanchez' son. In addition, the word around town was that Juan had no trial experience. He didn't know who else was working the case with Raul, but in any event, John knew that the main threat posed to him was not Juan, but Tommy Sanchez. If anyone could create a problem at this stage, it would be him; that man was nobody's fool.

He thought of moving to another town. But this was a nice place to live and everyone treated him fairly. Quitting his job and moving to another locale really wasn't an option; it could create unnecessary suspicion. His employer had returned to his office, so John knocked on his door. "Yes, John?"

"I wonder if you'd mind if I took an extended lunch hour?"

"How much time do you need?"

"Two hours should be enough. I'll make note of it on my time card."

After he grabbed his coat from the closet, John walked outside and sat down on the bench in front of the general store. He waited to see if the man who'd spoken to his boss was still in town. Fifteen minutes later Jefferson came out of the blacksmith shop and went into the livery stables. He was carrying his note pad in his left hand and John could make out a shoulder holster as the man's coat flapped open while he walked. Rather than sit in the open, John walked across the street to the diner and sat at a window seat. This gave him a commanding view of Sagunto Street and any movement the man might make while he was visiting other businesses in Santa Ynez.

The threat of any immediate danger was negligible, but he was still concerned about the tall man, though it could be just as his owner said, a survey. The waitress came over and took his order of a ham and Swiss cheese sandwich with potato salad. She'd come into the general store several times, probably shopping for her parents; he waited on her once. Her name was Doris Trudel; she was friendly and appeared to be about his age.

John watched Jefferson come out of the livery stable, look around and then walk toward the hotel, where his horse was tethered. Apparently his business in town was complete, because he mounted his horse and rode west out of town.

As he was sitting there, his thoughts turned to Claire Wilson. He'd been to Sunday dinner four times and had progressed to the picnic stage of his courtship. He liked her very much, but didn't know if she was the one to settle down with. She let him kiss her and feel her breasts several times, but when he tried to put his hand between her legs, she got angry. "Is that all you think about?"

"No. I think about you, and I thought you liked me enough to go further in our relationship."

"I do like you, but we've gone far enough. If you're serious about a long-time relationship, you can talk to my father."

"Maybe I will."

Jefferson had at one time been a Pinkerton detective in New York City. The Molly McGuires had been running free in the city, and the Pinkertons had been hired to keep tabs on them. Jefferson became friendly with one of the McGuires, and the two men shared a few drinks occasionally. But Jefferson became suspicious of his new friend and wondered out loud who was infiltrating who. As a result of his suspicions, he became adept at spotting people who were trailing him. He could also size up an area and be conscious of who was in his immediate area and who didn't seem to belong there.

He saw the young man come out of the general store and sit on the bench out front. When he went into the livery stable, he watched the same person go across the street and sit at a table, near a window, facing the street. He was sure it was the same person that the general store owner told him was John Smart. He wondered out loud why the young man was interested in him—perhaps he knew.

CHAPTER 23

1893

WORKING for the railroad over the past two and one-half years, with the last twelve months as the assistant bookkeeper, had been rewarding. He was a quick learn, and as his competence grew, so did his supervisor's reliance on him increase. Initially, he was given simple assignments, and as his knowledge expanded, he was given more complex issues to handle. One morning he was summoned by his supervisor and told that there was a special task he wanted him to handle. An awards ceremony was taking place at the Pine Ridge Reservation in two days. Medals had been shipped late by the Army, and they were anxious that they reach the reservation in time. Army Headquarters in the Nebraska area contacted the railroad and asked if one of their employees could deliver the prizes to the senior officer in attendance prior to one p.m. the day after tomorrow.

"I suggested to our station manager that you could handle this. You'll travel by railroad for most of the trip and finish it off via stagecoach. Do you think you can handle this?"

"Is there anything else you want me to do while I'm there?" Jacob Light asked.

"No, just deliver the box of medals to General Miles. These are special medals and come all the way from Washington, D.C. General Miles is already at the reservation; he's staying at the Indian agent's quarters. All you need to do is deliver them to him personally and come back home. First thing tomorrow, take the train north to the end of the line and then the stagecoach the rest of the way. You should be there by tomorrow evening; we're counting on you. Here are the medals; take special care of them." He handed over a medium-sized box to Jacob.

It was a long, monotonous trip. The train was late at the last stop and he nearly missed the stage; he arrived late the next evening. After getting multiple directions, he found the Indian agent's quarters, but General Miles was asleep. He spoke to the sergeant on duty and told him what he was bringing. "I'll take the medals from you and give them to the general when he awakes tomorrow morning. The ceremony is at one o'clock at the Wounded Knee Memorial. Perhaps you might want to attend. I hope you brought your own food and something to sleep on. We have just enough room and food for the medal recipients."

Jacob stepped out into the warm May evening and walked to the center of the reservation. There were two braves sitting against several boulders in the open space near the parade grounds. He asked them in Sioux if they knew Joseph Horn Cloud and Dewey Beard. They pointed him in the direction of their tent. He stumbled in the dark and one of dogs nipped him in the leg. Eventually, he made his way to his brothers' lodge. There were three men inside. They didn't recognize him at first, but then Dewey Beard's face lit up. "White Bird, you're alive!"

The four embraced, and the other three couldn't stop hugging him long enough to ask him what happened and why they hadn't heard from him for three long years. He told them of his ordeal and why he left. He'd been living in Sidney during that period.

"The three of you survived. How could that be? The soldiers were shooting at anyone that moved, even those who were wounded. Tell me what happened."

Dewey Beard related his experience to White Beard. "Somehow, we were separated from you and our parents and at the fringe of the group, when the soldiers disarmed everyone. As the tensions grew, we started to move further away, and when they opened up with the Hotchkiss guns, we ran as fast as we could, but there were soldiers everywhere. One fired his musket over my shoulder and I couldn't hear out of that ear. I wrenched the gun away from him and shot him and made my way to the ravine. Soldiers stood on both sides of the ravine and shot at me and anyone that moved. I was wounded and very weak. Women and children were crying and were shot and fell at my feet. I heard that Daniel White Lance was dead, but as I climbed out of the ravine I saw him on a horse."

"I was separated from the other two immediately after the shooting started; I had only a knife, no gun. People started falling down. Soldiers shot at me and then turned around and shot at those who were running to the ravine. I was shot in the shoulder and fell down. Three others fell on me or next to me, and the soldiers thought we were all dead and moved away. I lay there about ten minutes and that's when an officer came riding up. I jumped up and pulled him off the horse and stabbed him in the chest and took his horse. That's when I saw Dewey, who was bleeding from his shoulder and leg. I helped him on the horse and we rode away," Daniel White Lance said.

"Like my brothers, I started to run as soon as the shooting started. But I ran in the opposite direction. I wasn't alone. Others were running and trying to find an avenue of escape. We made our way to Drexel Mission, about eight miles from Wounded Knee. I wasn't with those who burned the Catholic mission, but I was with Chief Two Strike when we beat back Forsythe and the soldiers he brought with him," Joseph Horn Cloud told his brother.

"We all stayed away for a few days and then made our way here. We've been here ever since. What about our mother and father?" Dewey Beard asked.

White Bird told them about the four soldiers who fired point blank and killed their parents and Maiden Dream and even tried to kill him. When he was finished, he looked around their tent and saw several Ghost Shirts hanging inside. "What's this all about?"

"Joseph and I started a memorial at the Wounded Knee massacre site. We remembered the Ghost Shirts hanging inside our teepee when we were young; we made several shirts. The shirts have to be a part of the memorial, since the Ghost Dance was the reason the Indian policemen came to arrest Sitting Bull. That death caused many of us to leave and be at Wounded Knee. You'll see the memorial tomorrow. That's where they're holding the ceremony," White Lance said.

"You can't be serious. You're not going to attend a ceremony honoring the people who killed our parents and friends," White Bird said.

"The ceremony is twofold. Soldiers will be getting medals for the atrocities they committed against our people, but we will also be honoring our people who died and the monument that we've established."

"I'll go with you, but I'll hate all the soldiers honored."

The next morning the four brothers shared the little food they had and started the trek to the Wounded Knee site. They arrived an hour before the ceremony, and Daniel White Lance and Joseph Horn Cloud showed White Bird the primitive monument they had fashioned out of rock. Then the four brothers walked up the hill overlooking the battlefield where the Hotchkiss guns had rained down death on the Indians. Since they still had time before the ceremony, White Bird took them to the makeshift graves of their parents and his beloved Maiden Dream; the crosses he staked in the ground over the bodies were gone. "We'll come back this week with better crosses. We thank you for taking the time to honor our parents," Dewey Beard said.

At noon General Miles, his staff, thirty soldiers who

functioned as honor guards, and the twenty-three recipients of the Medals of Honor arrived in wagons. Fifty inhabitants of the reservation walked behind the wagons. "We were promised extra rations if we showed up for this event. You can't hate us for trying to stay alive," Dewey Beard told White Bird.

The faces of the Sioux were drawn as they stood in a line facing the reviewing stand. During the presentations, they didn't look at any of the soldiers. Jacob sensed a feeling of dejection and betrayal. At that moment, his resolve took on more meaning; he would exact revenge. He didn't have a plan in mind, but whatever he decided to do would involve the four who had fired point-blank at him and his parents. He assumed that the twenty-three soldiers who were receiving medals came from Fort Robinson. He scanned their faces to see if either of the two he previously identified were in that group. They weren't, but the two he hadn't seen before were there, but weren't receiving medals. They were there as members of an honor guard for the recipients.

Jacob was surprised that General Miles conducted two ceremonies. One ceremony was for the twenty receiving Medals of Honor for Wounded Knee and another was for three soldiers for their action at Drexel Mission.

After the ceremony, Jacob asked his brothers about Drexel Mission. "That took place the next day after Wounded Knee. Some of our braves escaped and were furnished with weapons by the Brule Lakota group led by Chief Two Strike from the Rosebud Indian Reservation.

Forsyth had taken a few men and tried to capture our people who burned a Catholic mission. We kicked his butt, and he had to be rescued by the black Buffalo Soldiers. The black soldiers are considered to be inferior because of their color, and yet they came to his rescue. He not only lost the battle, but General Miles used that loss at his court martial," White Lance said.

"What happened to Forsythe?" White Bird asked.

"He was acquitted by the court martial. I understand he made General," White Lance responded.

Most of the soldiers were taking pictures, including the two he was watching. White Bird left his brothers and strolled over to the two soldiers and asked if he could take a picture with them. They readily agreed; in fact, they took two pictures, one for them and the other for White Bird; he told them his name was Jacob Light and that he worked for the railroad in Sidney. He gave them his name and address and asked if they would write their names on the back of a piece of paper. They could send his copy of the picture to the station in Sidney. They wrote the names of Jarod Butler and Samuel Spenser.

"Are you career soldiers?"

"No, we're going to leave the Army in two years and move to California."

"Are there just the two of you?"

"There are two others at the fort who're going with us."

"Are they your brothers?"

"No, their names are Simon Higgins and Hiram Whitman."

As he strolled back to his brothers, he was offended at the cheering and backslapping of the soldiers who received medals for killing his loved ones. How could this happen? It was so unfair. Each cheer brought further resolve as he went in search of his three surviving relatives. He found them down by the creek where he had buried the three. Dewey Beard was always clever with wood, and with what little there was available, he had fashioned crosses for their parents and Maiden Dream. White Bird knelt down and cried. "We didn't have to wait till later. We found adequate wood nearby," White Lance said.

The next morning he prepared to leave, but the two Ghost Shirts hanging inside on the teepee wall intrigued him. Joseph Horn Cloud had risen and was standing behind his brother. "Would you like to have one of them?"

"Oh, I can't ask you to part with one, but if you could make one for me and send it to Sidney, I'd be grateful."

His brother reached up, took one of the shirts off the wall, and handed it to the brother he hadn't seen in years.

Parting for the four brothers was very emotional. The three brothers from the reservations made White Bird promise to come back for a visit. He agreed, but deep down he knew that this may be the last time they would be together. He had a mission in life now, and nothing was going to dissuade him from that goal.

CHAPTER 24
1900

IT'D BEEN two weeks since the four men had last met to assess Raul's chances and follow up on certain issues. Today, Sarah joined the four in her kitchen and served them a lunch of cold turkey, potato salad and apple pie. Afterward, she joined the group seated in the nook. "I don't know if I can keep awake after that big lunch." Juan hugged his mother.

John Jefferson had a file in front of him, and he was the first to speak. "I'm about half finished with my task. I've talked to all the business owners in Santa Ynez and Los Olivos, and I have a few candidates that might fit a profile that we established. The majority of young men ages twenty-two to twenty-six meet that criteria, but most have lived here all their lives and never left the valley. I've put them in a separate file. I'm eliminating them initially, because I don't think any of them could be our man. If my analysis doesn't work, we can revisit them later.

"When I finish with the ranches in the valley, I intend to go to Buellton and Los Alamos. My guess is that the number of possibles will not exceed twenty. I did find a potential at the livery stable. There's a young man there by the name of

Jed Smith, who's only been in the valley for two years and had a recent run-in with the law. A rental customer left his jacket in the rig he returned. When he went back to the livery, he found the jacket, but nearly one hundred dollars was missing from an inside pocket in his coat. The owner and constable questioned Smith about the missing money. He finally admitted taking the money, but said he was just holding it until the customer returned; there was still twenty dollars missing. He surrendered the money only after he was threatened with jail if he didn't hand over the money.

"There's another interesting thing about Mr. Smith. When I finished asking the owner some more questions, Smith followed me to my other stops. Oh, he didn't come in, but he was out there just the same. I've got him high on my list. I was followed one other time. It was after I talked to the proprietor of the general store in Santa Ynez. Now I didn't see that individual at any time, but I know someone was shadowing me. It could be anyone."

"Could it have been Smith?" Tommy asked.

"As I said, it could be anyone."

"Who works at the general store that might fit your profile?" Sarah asked.

Jefferson looked at his list. "There was only one employee working there that could fit our characterization. His name is John Smart, but he's white with light brown hair."

"I know him. He delivers supplies from the general store. He's very polite, and as you said, very white. I've got him on my list of people who either delivered things or had access to the ranch in the past ninety days," Sarah responded.

"Small and Smith are white. It's possible that the person we're looking for is white or light-skinned Mexican and is just leaving the Ghost Shirt and painting the victims' faces red to throw us off the scent," Tommy said.

"Whether he's Sioux or white, I'm pursuing everyone that meets our criteria," Jefferson added.

Raul didn't have any luck running down the rope. He went to the local general store and then to three locations in Santa Barbara before taking the train to Ventura and striking out. Raul was speaking in Spanish and Tommy was translating. "I'll go to Los Alamos, Santa Maria and San Luis Obispo early next week, if that's okay with you, Patron?" Tommy nodded.

Raul continued. "One of the vendors suggested that the rope could be a special order and wouldn't show up in a retail store. But someone has to manufacture the rope, and if I can find that company, perhaps they can tell us if it was a special order, who purchased it, and if it was sent to Santa Ynez."

"The trial judge has a full calendar for the next two months, so we have a short reprieve. Tommy, you've been very generous, but I need some help. I'd like to hire another attorney who's more familiar with trial procedures than I. His name is Whitford B. Tate. He's well respected by his peers and has twenty years' experience in capital crimes, including five murder trials." Juan said.

"We need a contract with Mr. Tate, a set fee for his services and I want to interview him," Tommy responded.

"I'll set it up for the end of the week."

"Raul, I'd like to go over any alibis that you may have for the days of the hangings. Why don't we go to your room in the barn after this meeting? I'd like to see where the shirt was found and whether anything else is missing. I may also have to hire an interpreter, because your English isn't that good," Juan said.

"I could be Raul's interpreter," Sarah chimed in.

"I'd rather not use you. I want to be the only Sioux at the trial. Emotions are still running high, and I want to avoid attention to anyone who's Sioux, even if by marriage. You were going to determine which vendors had access to the ranch from February 15th to March 20th," Juan told his mother.

"I did, and have narrowed my list down to twelve, of which eight are young and strong enough to lift a grown man, and that includes John Smart. Here's my list. After each name, I have the dates they were at the ranch. Some had access more than once during that time frame."

"Tommy, you haven't told us what action you intend to take," Juan asked.

"I've been thinking about this since the last time we met. I believe there a vendetta in play here. Where it started is the question. I don't believe it was here in the valley. If not here, then where? The shirt, the rope, the method of hanging and the boots in three of the murders are the same. The method of hanging doesn't lead us anywhere, and the style of rope, even if found, may not reveal anything. We have the boots, but they're too big for Raul. That's a plus, but I don't know what a prosecutor will make of that fact. That leaves the shirt. I've seen that style of shirt in two places. One is the Standing Rock Reservation, where my father was killed, and the other is the Pine Ridge Reservation, which is close to the Wounded Knee site. My father's death and the Wounded Knee massacre occurred within fifteen days of each other. I think it's worth the effort if I go to these reservations and see what I can find out. There's also the fact that one of the hangings took place on the anniversary of my father's death and another on the anniversary of Wounded Knee."

"If our killer is someone on Jefferson's or Sarah's list, then I believe our killer is watching one or all of us. Let's not tell anyone where I'm going. I'll leave in three days and be gone for at least two weeks. The rest of you have enough on your plate to last two weeks."

CHAPTER 25
1895

OVERALL, the Army paid its obligations to the railroad, but the time between the agreed-to pay date and the actual date varied. It was Jacob Light's job to monitor this account, and, when necessary, go to Fort Robinson and ask the Commandant to assist the railroad in its collections. Jacob had dealt with three different commanding officers during the past three years; each was amiable to assist. It helped even more when Jacob brought a bottle of malt whiskey with him on these trips; in fact, it was expected. His supervisor suggested the incentive, and the railroad paid for the gift; it worked. For Jacob, there was an added incentive for the trips. He was able to keep track of his four new acquaintances while handling company business.

At twenty-one years of age, he felt mature beyond his years. As a teenager, he had survived a bloody massacre, was able to survive that winter and then find employment. He now had a responsible position with the railroad, his own office, and was sharing the secretary with his supervisor. Though his office was small, measuring six by eight feet, it gave him the feeling of importance. He had repainted the walls and hung some posters that depicted life in the west. Neatness didn't only apply to his office; he took great pride in his appearance, even though he had to be thrifty on the compensation he received. He shaved daily and had his pants and shirt cleaned and washed weekly by one of the wives of the linemen. Many of his former fellow workers addressed him as Mr. Light.

On his excursions to Fort Robinson, he didn't overtly try to create friendships with the four men he targeted; he just seemed to find himself in their vicinity at various time with some or all of the four. He restricted his communication with the men to saying hello or good morning. Over the next two years, Jacob made friends with one of the Adjutant's assistants. When he realized the assistant wanted to visit his wife in Omaha, he arranged for a round-trip pass for the man. From that point on, that soldier was more than willing to help. It was he who told Jacob when the four were scheduled to separate from the Army and where they intended to go.

Jacob knew there was plenty of time remaining; they had three years before separation. Yet he felt a sense of urgency, because he hadn't formulated his plan of revenge. In fact, he didn't have a clue how he could move against the four.

Over the next two years, Jacob increased his reading and writing skills. A retired teacher took an interest in the young man and provided him with initial training and then some of her books. Jacob became an avid reader. It was evident that this increase in his language skills contributed to the promotion to his current position with the railroad. Over the past two years he'd saved nearly two hundred dollars out of his salary. Jacob, at the age of twenty-three, with a good job, also became what one could describe as a good catch, and Rosita Riley became his new friend.

They met at a barn raising inside the city limits of Sidney. He didn't want to go; he was uncomfortable at parties, but he didn't have anything to do on that Saturday. So, he showed up. He planned to leave as soon as lunch was over. That's when they started the hoedown. He'd seen her looking at him, and that in itself made him nervous. But when she came over to him, he was tongue-tied. "Would you like to dance?" she asked him.

"I don't dance."

"Oh, it's easy. I'll show you." He didn't want to dance, but found himself being led to where two guys were strumming on a banjo. He was awkward at first, but soon he enjoyed it, and when it was time to leave, he was reluctant to go.

Her father was Irish and her mother, Mexican. She was nineteen years old and spirited. It had been a year since they started keeping company; they had been intimate on two occasions. Rosita took that as a betrothal. This was his first female special friendship, other than his platonic relationship with Maiden Dream. With Rosita, he may have been in over his head. He liked her very much, but that paled in comparison to the pledge he made to get retributions for the slaughter of his parents. And then there was Maiden Dream—what about her? He still felt a sense of loyalty to his dead sweetheart. But Rosita was fun, and he liked being with her. They enjoyed picnicking and walking around the small town on Saturdays and Sundays. He'd been to her home on at least six occasions for Sunday dinner and always felt welcome. He liked her parents and even her younger sister. It was assumed by the family that he and Rosita would be wed. But the payback for what had happened at Wounded Knee must be his first priority

When asked by her parents what Jacob's intentions were, Rosita said they were unofficially engaged, and that Jacob was saving up for a ring. Her mother wanted to know when they could make the announcement. She said by the end of the year. Every time she and Jacob were together, she pressed the issue, and Jacob started to resist. He knew that he couldn't trust her with his mission, and she was becoming a nag about the marriage.

The scenario was always the same. "We've been seeing each other for a year. That's sufficient time to tell whether we like each other enough to get married. You tell me you love me and I say I love you, so I need to tell my mother when we can set the date."

"I do want to marry you, but I must save a little more. The older men tell me the first year of marriage is difficult if we don't have enough money. You don't want to live in a shack, do you?"

"My father said he would help, and we could live with my parents until we saved enough."

And so it went. He liked the sex, but she seemed more

reluctant lately, as though she was holding back to force him to commit. When he found out the exact date the four were being mustered out of the Army, and that they were going to settle in a little valley in California north of Santa Barbara, he told Rosita that her family could announce their plans to wed as soon as he came back from a trip. She knew that he went to Fort Robinson each quarter and once to Pine Ridge, so she wasn't suspicious; she assumed he'd keep his promise.

Over the next two months she showered him with all kinds of affection and promised that she'd be the best wife a man could want. Although she insisted that they not be intimate until marriage, she was more than willing to share the fruits of life. In fact, she initiated most of the foreplay between the two. Jacob was starting to feel pangs of conscience, but not enough to dissuade him from his goal. *Those men must pay,* is all he could think about for the last month.

He was at the depot when the four happy ex-soldiers changed trains at Sidney. They saw Light and told him they were on their way to Santa Ynez, California. Hiram Whitman had a cousin who had a small spread in that valley and was going to employ the four as cowhands.

It was three days to payday. He planned to leave on the train to California at noon on Saturday. On Friday, he collected his pay and withdrew his savings from the bank and threw out most of his belongings; he only wanted to carry one bag. Not only was it easier to travel with one bag, but it wouldn't raise any suspicions with Rosita and divulge what his real intentions were. He made sure the Ghost Shirt given to him by his brother, Joseph Horn Cloud, was neatly folded, covered with a newspaper, and placed in the bottom of his bag.

The night before he left, Rosita snuck out of her house after her parents were asleep and joined Jacob in his small room in back of the railroad station. "I have to get home before sunup so that my parents won't know that I was with you." She smiled at him as she slowly took off her clothes and climbed onto his bed.

She was especially lusty that night; it was as though she sensed this would be the last time they would be together. Initially she didn't want to go all the way, but after more petting, she relaxed, and gasped as he spread her legs and entered her. Both lost track of time, and as the sun started to rise, Rosita sprang out of bed, threw on her clothes, and said she'd see him off at the station.

"I'll be back on Tuesday. You can plan a party at your parents' home the weekend after I return."

"I love you," she called out to him as she raced through the door.

She seemed so happy and so trusting. Jacob realized then that he might never find another woman as good as she, but she was in his way and wouldn't understand the oath he had made.

On Saturday morning, she waved to him from the platform as he boarded the train, four days after his prey had departed from Sidney. If he didn't feel guilty before, he sure did now. Jacob Light had been with the railroad for almost eight years, and during that time he'd received a pass for unlimited travel on the train. He also had the advantage of knowing many of the dispatchers at the various stops on the way to California. He used this advantage to check on the progress of the four. When he reached Santa Barbara, he confirmed that the soldiers had taken the stage to Santa Ynez.

• • • • •

The leader of the four was Samuel Spenser—primarily because he was the oldest, by at least three years. The stage stopped at the Central Hotel in Santa Ynez, and the four went inside to get directions to the Singleton Ranch. It was indeed a shock when they were informed that Singleton and two of his friends were awaiting trial for robbing the Santa Barbara Bank. Additionally, they were informed that Tommy and Sarah Sanchez now owned the small ranch. They had their mustering-out pay, but that could only last them for a few months. They'd been counting on the jobs that Singleton offered.

"Let's go talk to the new owner. Maybe he needs some help. All of us are experienced around horses. He may have something for us for a short term, anyway," Butler told the three.

They received directions to Altura Prado Ranch, rented a buckboard, and rode out to introduce themselves to Tommy Sanchez. Sarah saw them coming down the long entryway and signaled Raul and two of the vaqueros to ascertain what the visitors wanted. When Raul reported that they wanted to speak to Tommy about work, she went indoors to see if he was available. Tommy came out to the porch and faced the four. "Gentlemen, what can I do for you?"

Spenser explained that they had mustered out of the Army at Fort Robinson in Nebraska and were counting on the job that Earl Singleton had offered them. They knew it was only temporary work until they could find something permanent. But the problem was that they needed something quick before their savings ran out.

"I'm sympathetic to your situation. Why don't you come into the house and we can talk," Tommy said.

The four took off their hats and sheepishly walked into the kitchen and sat at the nook with Tommy. Sarah asked each if they wanted coffee or something to eat. "Just coffee, if you don't mind," the four said in unison.

"I understand that you men were stationed at Fort Robinson," Sarah said.

"Yes. We were there six years."

"I've been to Fort Robinson. You'll like this part of the country much better."

Tommy asked about their experience, and they shared with him what they had done in the Army the past six years. Each had worked at training horses for the cavalry. "I can hire you on a temporary basis until you find something else. If it's okay with the four of you, we can get you started tomorrow."

Spenser and the other three looked at each other and accepted the offer. "Raul Mendoza is my foreman. I have about a month's worth of work for you on this ranch, and then we can move you over to the other ranch that borders our place. I can only promise you a total of six months' work. If that's okay with you, we have a deal." The four nodded their approval.

"You'll bunk here while you're on this ranch, and then in the bunkhouse on the other spread when you move over there. I know you're hungry. My wife will serve you at the nook, if that's okay, and then I'll introduce you to Raul."

The four men seemed grateful for the hospitality shown by Tommy Sanchez and his wife. Hiram Whitman couldn't keep his eyes off Sarah. She could feel the intensity with which he watched her every move, and it made her uncomfortable. She realized she couldn't be alone with this man for any length of time or he'd take advantage of the situation. The look Whitman was giving Sarah wasn't lost on Tommy Sanchez, and he looked directly at the man when he said, "I don't expect any of you gentlemen to take advantage of any situation here at the ranch."

CHAPTER 26

1900

THE DECISION to travel to Standing Rock reservation and then on to the Pine Ridge Reservation was finalized. After much discussion, Sarah decided to stay behind. Tommy would take one of the vaqueros with him.

"Tommy, I'm sorry. Naiwa is too distraught. She sees her chances of happiness going away. I need to spend some time with her. She's neglected her children who're trying to assimilate into a new life, and she's not there for them. Chatan is still being picked on in school by the older boys. It's not a physical confrontation, but it's bullying just the same. I'd hate myself if something happened to my family while I was gone with you. Please understand I love you above all else, but I need to do this."

Tommy picked up his wife and sat down on an overstuffed chair in their parlor and held her while she cried. "You have nothing to apologize for. You have to handle the situation at home, while I have to find a killer and clear Raul. He and Naiwa deserve the chance to see if they can be a family, and perhaps have the love that you and I share."

Cesar Redullo had been employed on the ranch for

the past five years and was Raul's main vaquero. Tommy decided that he would accompany him to the two Indian reservations. Preparations were quick, and at the beginning of the next week, the two left for Los Angeles and then on to Denver. Each took only one bag for clothing and some small supplies, along with their rifles and handguns. Although the world had become more civilized at the turn of the century, they were traveling to mostly frontier locations. It was always good to be prepared.

Accommodations on the train were limited. They slept in their seats and ate in the stations at each stop. It was when they switched to the stage that things were a little loose. The stage from Pierre to Mobridge didn't show. It was on the other side of a rock slide, and the prognosis wasn't good. They slept in the stage station that night. Luckily, the route manager found a carriage by noon the next day, and off they went to the Standing Rock Reservation by another route. The trip took six days to complete.

But that wasn't the only excitement that they shared during the trip. Just outside of Pierre, one of the convicts being escorted by a deputy sheriff tried to escape. His leg irons had been removed so he could go to the restroom in the last car. Somehow, he overpowered the deputy and tried the door to the rear platform, but it was locked. He then ran back through the car, seeking an avenue of escape. Just as he ran past the seat where Tommy and Cesar were sitting, Tommy stuck out his foot, and the convict fell on his face. Cesar jumped on him and held him down until the deputy returned and was able to restrain the prisoner. Tommy and Cesar were applauded by the passengers, and some came up to the two men and shook their hands. Cesar liked the attention, and he couldn't help smiling the remainder of the trip. He was born in Santa Ynez and had never been out of the valley. He was in awe of the trip north and peppered Tommy with all kinds of questions.

Although they were received warmly by his Sioux brethren, the squalor of the camp made them very depressed. Tents were in tatters, older inhabitants were leaning against tents, and garbage was everywhere. It seemed as though the occupants of the reservation were marking time, waiting for their exit to another world. This was the village of Tommy's youth, and it brought back many memories of a happy childhood. None of his relatives who fled this place after Sitting Bull was murdered remained. He hoped to see some of them when he visited Pine Ridge Reservation. None of his brothers were alive, but he had seen two of his nieces when he and Sarah had visited Pine Ridge the previous year. He and Cesar met with Daring Wolf, one of Spotted Elk's surviving sons, and the elected leader of the village. Tommy was able to practice the language of his youth, and although it was a little strange at first, he soon was happy that he retained most of it.

They'd arrived late in the afternoon, and after a long trip they were hungry and thirsty. Although he had little food to spare, the chief, out of courtesy, invited Tommy and Cesar to his lodge. Tommy had bought some food at their stop in Mobridge and shared it with Daring Wolf and his family. He could see the joy in her eyes as he handed the food to the chief's wife. The three children didn't have to be invited to eat. They took their portion and consumed it immediately. Tommy said he wasn't hungry, and gave his portion to the children. Throughout the entire meal, Daring Wolf stared at Tommy. Finally he spoke. "You're the son of Sitting Bull, Tatanka Iyotake."

"Yes, and I'm very proud of it."

"You are most welcome in my lodge. I apologize for not recognizing you right away."

"We came a long way to seek a truth." Tommy told Daring Wolf the story of the hangings and how the Ghost Shirt fit into the crimes.

"What is that you wish to know?" his host asked.

Tommy showed him one of Ghost Shirts used in the executions of the four men in Santa Ynez. Juan had asked the Santa Barbara County Attorney's office for one of the shirts, so they could investigate its origin. "Can you tell if this shirt originated in this village?" Tommy asked.

The chief examined it carefully. "It seems as though each family had a distinctive shirt for themselves and their relatives. It was like a contest at first. Each lodge tried to outdo the others. There were some remarkable designs. I know this shirt. Let me think." The tribe elder sat passive for a few minutes before he continued. It was though he was looking into his past.

"I'm fairly sure that this is the type of shirt used by Running Bear and his family. I remember seeing it hanging in his lodge. One of his sons came up with the design and his wife made them. I don't know where the material came from."

"Can I talk to Running Bear?"

"He was killed at Wounded Knee along with his wife and one of his sons."

"Are there any surviving sons?"

"I believe they're at the Pine Ridge Reservation."

"Do you have any Ghost Shirts here on the reservation?"

"No. We have no spirit for the dance anymore. If we revive it, the soldiers will come and arrest us. My people are afraid. They don't even want to talk about the way it was. There is no hope here."

"Do you remember the Ghost Dances?"

"Yes, I had my shirt and I danced in many. I think Jack Wilson was a false prophet; he didn't spend any time here after your father died. The dance led to the death of your father and the massacre at Wounded Knee. We were fools to believe his teachings. How could the buffalo return and the white cede what he gained through aggression? The dance brought us nothing but pain."

As they left the next day, Daring Wolf cautioned them on outlaws that were known to attack travelers in the area. Tommy looked at Cesar and told him what the chief said. The vaquero nodded.

CHAPTER 27
1900

IT WAS just eight months ago that Sarah, he and the family were hosted by Chief Red Cloud at the Pine Ridge Reservation. Tommy looked forward to seeing the great warrior one more time. He and the vaquero retraced their steps through Pierre and then went west by train to Rapid City, South Dakota.

Tommy had grown up in this area; he remembered the days of his youth and the turning point that changed the lives of those who lived in the Sioux Nation. The Treaty of Laramie had given ownership of the Black Hills, South Dakota, to the Sioux. But in 1874, George Armstrong Custer led an expedition into the Black Hills and announced the discovery of gold in French Creek. The hordes of gold seekers came and established the towns of Deadwood, Lead and Rapid City. Initially, the Army helped evict those who violated Sioux territory, but soon political pressure grew to a point where the Army was ordered not to intercede or help the Sioux protect their Black Hills. It was President Grant who forced the issue. He sent the Army *en masse* to protect settlers and prospectors. Soon the Sioux were in a fight that they could never win. The killing of General Custer, although a great victory for Sitting Bull and Crazy Horse, would be the final issue that would bury the once promising Sioux Nations.

They spent the night in the old town of Rapid City, had dinner and retired early. The next morning Tommy rented a carriage, and he and the vaquero made their way to the reservation; it was a three-hour ride. He'd wired the old chief that he was coming, and Red Cloud was as warm as before. This time he had a surprise for Tommy. Sitting Bull, or Tatanka Iyotake, had sired five sons and three daughters. One daughter was living at Pine Ridge. Her name was Standing Holy, or, as others called her, Mary Sitting Bull.

That evening they gathered at Red Cloud's tent and Tommy met his niece, her husband and their daughter, Angelique Spotted Horse. This was a real treat for him, because he hadn't seen his kin since he left on his own. The young girl was attending the Indian School on the reservation, and she and some of her female classmates performed a dance in his honor. He was somewhat embarrassed because he'd lost track of his family and didn't recognize any of them. Throughout the evening, they peppered him with questions about his family, and especially Helga and Thomas Jr., who were the same age as his grand-niece. Tommy told them where he lived, what the ranch was like, and where the children went to school. They were astonished at how far California was from the Pine Ridge Reservation and constantly asked him questions about his father.

Tommy learned that many of his father's wives and daughters had fled to the Badlands in the Black Hills after the old warrior was murdered. His relatives hid out for two years before they were found and brought to the Pine Ridge Reservation.

He was candid with Red Cloud and shared with him his reason for coming back. "I'll introduce you to the brothers. They are fine young men who've devoted their lives to the memorial of Wounded Knee. They've been able to raise some funds, but most of what has been accomplished has been through their own sweat. You must visit the memorial before you leave."

Tommy spent the night as the guest of Red Cloud in the old chief's lodge. Cesar stayed with Standing Holly and her family. The next morning Red Cloud escorted Tommy and his vaquero companion to the tent of Joseph Horn Cloud and his two brothers. When he entered the tent, followed by Tommy, the three brothers stood up out of respect for their chief. As he introduced Tommy, the brothers appeared to be somewhat speechless. "This is indeed an honor for us to meet the son of Sitting Bull. Welcome to our humble abode," Dewey Beard said.

It was nearly lunch time and he didn't want to embarrass the three brothers. He asked if they would share the food he brought. The five sat on the floor of the teepee and talked of the old days. Tommy learned that Dewey Beard was a survivor of both Wounded Knee and the Battle of the Little Big Horn. He was very proud that of having met Sitting Bull and Crazy Horse. Dewey Beard was astounded when he found out that Tommy was married to the widow of Crazy Horse and that the great warrior has sired two children.

Tommy took out the Ghost Shirt he had brought with him and showed it to the three brothers. "It's similar to the shirts our family made. I remember when my mother would sew the feathers onto the sleeves," Daniel White Lance said after he examined the shirt and the decorations.

"Did your father or mother design these shirts?"

"No, I designed the shirts," Dewey Beard said.

"Do you still make these shirts?"

"Yes, I've made these shirts when I can find enough material."

"Have any of you travelled to California?"

White Lance answered for the three brothers. "We have never been away from this reservation since the massacre at Wounded Knee. Before that, we never left the Standing Rock Reservation. Why do you ask?"

"A crime has been committed using this shirt, and I was wondering how something like this could travel halfway across the country."

"It must have been a serious crime if you travelled this far to speak to us," Joseph Horn Cloud responded.

"Yes. I have come far, because a friend of mine has been accused of this crime. I'd hoped that I could find the source of the shirt and the person who designed it."

"Perhaps you should talk to our other brother."

"I understood that he and your parents were killed at Wounded Knee."

"Well, it's true that our parents were murdered, but our brother White Bird survived. He's been working for the railroad in Sidney, Nebraska, for several years. He might be able to shed some light on your problem."

"Thank you. When we leave here, we'll stop in Sidney to see White Bird. I'll tell him how warmly you received us."

"One more thing: our brother goes by the name of Jacob Light in the white world. He is a fine man, but he's not Sioux; he's white. He was captured on a raid of a wagon train when he was one year old, and our father and mother adopted him. He was raised as one of us. He is the finest brother we could ask for, and we're the only family that he ever knew. He was devoted to our mother and father and was tortured by their killing."

"Can you give me a description of your brother, so that I might recognize him?"

"His complexion is fair, he has brown hair, and he's slightly bigger than you in height and weight. He has very large hands and a mark on the back of his right hand. It's like a cross; he was burned during the wagon train raid. We've not seen him for over five years, so he may have changed some," Dewey Beard said.

As soon as Tommy heard that the brother had been in Sidney, he realized this was the man Spenser had taken pictures with at Wounded Knee and was the man they were looking for.

Tommy couldn't leave without a visit to Wounded

Knee. He was escorted by the three brothers the next day. The monument was simple but effective. He stood in front of the symbol and thought about those who died there. He wondered if this was the reason for the string of hangings in his town. He didn't know what he would have done if any of his loved ones had been victims here. He knew that life had not been fair to the majority of his people. Theirs was a hard life, with little hope for the future.

CHAPTER 28
1900

IT WAS A SLIM LEAD and something that might point them in the right direction. They took the stage back to Rapid City and went to the train depot to buy their return tickets. They planned to visit Sidney, Nebraska, and talk to White Bird. The train south of South Dakota had derailed the day before; they were told that there would be at least a two-day delay before they could continue on. Tommy wired Sarah and told her about the change in their plans. Cesar had a brother in Deadwood, and he asked Tommy if he'd mind if he went there for a day while they were waiting. He hadn't seen his brother in ten years. Tommy suggested they both go.

Deadwood had grown to a thousand people and was as wild as when Tommy passed through there during his youth. The town was illegally founded in the mid-1870s and served as a base for miners going to the Black Hills. It was lawless in its early years, with numerous saloons featuring gambling and prostitution. Murder was common, and punishment for those crimes was not always forthcoming. Deadwood gained notoriety in 1876 when Jack McCall shot and killed Wild Bill Hickok. The famous gunman and subsequently his friend Calamity Jane were buried in the Mount Moriah Cemetery outside the town.

The stage arrived around noon, and they booked two rooms in the Bella Union Hotel and Saloon for a night. They agreed to meet back at the hotel at six that evening, and then Cesar went in search of his brother, who worked on a cattle ranch near town. Tommy walked around town and picked up a couple of small souvenirs for Sarah and the other members of the family. He saw a barber shop and decided that this would be a good time to get rid of the stagecoach dust in his pores and on his clothing. A shave and a good bath would be good on a warm summer day. He took his time with the bath, giving the barber enough time to brush his suit and quick wash and press his shirt. He felt good and strolled back to the hotel, had a cold beer, and then went upstairs and took a nap. Juan returned that evening and thanked Tommy for the opportunity to visit his brother. His visit, though short, was fulfilling. They decided to have dinner in the saloon on the first floor after Cesar washed up.

They walked down the stairs, through the registration desk, and into a very large room which served as bar, poker room and restaurant. A piano player was banging out a ragtime tune while waitresses were milling around the bar and serving customers in the restaurant and poker areas. A waitress seated them at a table with a view of the rest of the room. He and the vaquero ordered rib eye steaks and a glass of cold beer. The meat was cooked just right, and they were on their second beer when two cowboys started an argument over one of the waitresses; one of the riders was young and the other somewhat older. It was obvious that the younger man was no match for the older and larger cowboy, but he wouldn't give way. Tensions were increasing, and neither would walk away. The older cowboy suckered the younger one into reaching for his gun while he was drawing. The young man was shot dead.

Someone went for the sheriff, and he arrived in a few minutes. As soon as he walked in, the room became silent. The lawman asked what happened. The older cowboy said the deceased drew first, and therefore it was a fair fight. Two other witnesses came forward and corroborated the older man's version. The sheriff asked two men to take the body to the undertakers and was about to leave the saloon when Tommy spoke up. "It wasn't a fair fight, sheriff."

The sheriff looked around. "Who said that?"

"I did," Tommy said. The vaquero next to him was tense and had his hand on the gun in his holster. He didn't know why his Patron would want to get involved.

"What do you mean, it wasn't a fair fight?"

"That man over there faked the kid with his left hand while he was going for the gun with his right. It wasn't self-defense. It was calculated."

"Two others said the kid went for his gun first."

"They were wrong." Tommy wasn't backing down.

The sheriff turned to the shooter. "You're coming with me."

"I'm not going anywhere. You have two witnesses who

said the kid drew first. That ought to be enough for you," the cowboy said.

"It would be if they didn't work with you. You'll have a trial by jury and they can speak at your trial."

The sheriff turned to Tommy. "You'll have to make out a statement and appear for the trial."

Just then, there was a commotion at the other end of the saloon, and all the patrons in the large room moved to one side or the other. A large man dressed in black walked slowly toward the sheriff and his prisoner. Jack Cassidy was the owner of the Bar T Ranch and the *de facto* boss in the area. He didn't like it when any of his men were arrested. Most times, he wouldn't pay their fines; he'd go to the jail and just demand their release. He was known to have a bad temper and a fast gun. "Sheriff, you're not going to arrest my man, especially since there are witnesses that say it was a fair fight. I don't care what the stranger says. He doesn't live here, and therefore his word doesn't count for much. In fact, I'll bet he's going to retract his words right now." Cassidy turned and faced Tommy and the vaquero.

"Well, stranger, are you going to tell the sheriff that you made a mistake?" Cassidy was loud enough so everyone could hear. The size of Cassidy alone would scare most men. He was at least six feet tall and over two hundred pounds. He stood swaggering in front of Tommy, not ten feet away.

"It wasn't self defense; it was murder," Tommy responded.

"That's enough, Cassidy. I've got my job to do." The

sheriff grabbed the older cowboy by the arm and started leading him out of the saloon, but two men with guns drawn stopped him and took the sheriff's gun.

"You can't get away with this, Cassidy. I'll arrest you as well."

"You can do whatever you think you can get away with after this stranger tells everyone here that he was wrong. If not, I'm going to shoot him where he sits and I'll call it self-defense. I'll bet I can get a few witnesses to back me up."

There was a stand-off that Tommy hadn't anticipated. The vaquero was tense, but he was ready for action. Tommy put his hand on the Cesar's arm to calm him just as he rose from the table. He turned toward Cassidy, who was standing ten feet in front of him. "Do you really want to go through with this? You're not going to like the outcome. I know how good you are with a gun, so I can't take any chances and just wound you. I'll have to shoot you between the eyes." Tommy was standing away from the table facing Cassidy. His coat was pulled back, exposing the gun on his right hip.

The silence in the saloon was unbearable; no one dared cough. It seemed like an eternity as both men stood facing each other. "Who the hell are you, Mister?" Cassidy asked.

"I'm Tommy Sanchez, the son of Sitting Bull."

The color drained from Cassidy's face and a joint murmur permeated the entire room. He glanced sideways to see who was looking. For a moment it looked as though he'd back down.

"Don't let him buffalo you, Jack. You can take him," one of his cowhands yelled out.

This must have given Cassidy another ounce of courage, because he started to draw, but only got as far as touching the handle on his gun. He fell over backwards with a bullet between his eyes. It seemed like the entire saloon let out a gasp. Tommy waved his gun at the two men holding the sheriff; they immediately dropped their weapons. "I think you can make the arrest, sheriff. My friend and I will be down as soon as we finish our beers and give you our statements."

"You think it's over, but it's not. You haven't got out of town yet," yelled one of the men who'd been holding the sheriff.

Tommy sat back down at the table and finished his beer while several of the patrons carried Cassidy out the front door. The music started again, and the waitresses began to make their rounds. "I've heard the rumors about the fast gun, but I wouldn't have believed it, if I wasn't here tonight. He seemed to know you."

"He did, but he'd gone too far and didn't know how to back away. He always had that problem."

CHAPTER 29
1900

JOHN was fairly certain that he had covered all his bases and that Raul would be tried for the hangings. If there was a problem with his strategy, it lay with planting the Ghost Shirt in Raul's quarters. He didn't know how many service and supply providers made frequent trips to the Sanchez' Ranch, other than himself. But sooner or later, someone was going to check out those providers and start checking to see who could have embedded the shirt.

He thought about this for several days and decided that he would personally deliver the next load of feed to Altura Prado and see if Sarah Sanchez recognized him. If she did, then he'd have to deal with it. Normally, the ranch placed an order twice a month, and usually one wagon was enough to fulfill the request.

On Tuesday, a vaquero delivered an order for Altura Prado, and John loaded the supplies in the store's wagon. He notified his supervisor that he was driving out to the Sanchez' Ranch. As was normal, he drove to the barn and unloaded the supplies in the usual places. As he backed up the wagon, he was startled to see Sarah Sanchez standing on her porch looking directly at him. But what surprised him the most was that she was holding a rifle in her hand, and he wondered if there was going to be a confrontation. "Did you see a bobcat in the barn?" she asked.

He didn't know what to say. It was when she repeated the question that he responded. "No, I didn't see anything."

"What's your name?"

"John Smart."

He was staring at her as she raised the rifle. When she fired, he dove for cover under the wagon. Initially, John thought she was shooting at him. When he heard the animal cry out, he crawled out from beneath the buckboard and walked over to the bobcat lying at the entrance to the barn. Sarah walked around the wagon and over to the cat and pushed it with the end of her rifle to make sure it was dead. "That sucker has been after the chickens and cats for two weeks. In fact, it killed four of our chickens."

"That was some shooting. Where did you learn to shoot like that?"

"My first husband taught me to shoot. My present husband refined my skills."

If John had any idea that he could eliminate Sarah Sanchez easily, he was mistaken. She didn't seem to be a frail female. In fact, she was quite lethal.

Sarah asked the young man to wait on the porch for her as she entered the house. She returned with a pitcher of lemonade and offered him a glass. "I'm sorry I startled you. That bobcat has been a thorn in my side and I wanted to get it. I've seen you here before. How long have you lived in the area?"

"I came here two years ago. I answered an advertisement from the general store."

"Where did you previously live?"

"I lived in San Diego."

"That's interesting. My husband was in business in that town. In fact, he and his partner formed an electric trolley line. Do you still have family there?"

"No, Mrs. Sanchez, my parents are dead. I think it's time for me to return. My boss is understanding, but I don't want to take advantage of his good nature. Thanks for the drink."

Sarah watched him as he hopped up on the wagon, turned the horses around, and headed down the entryway. There was something about the pleasant young man that she couldn't put her finger on. She knew he'd been here before and wondered if he could be the one that placed the Ghost Shirt in Raul's chaps. He definitely was white.

CHAPTER 30
1900

THEY PLANNED to go by way of Sidney, Nebraska, on their way home and talk to the surviving brother of Joseph Horn Cloud. But something told Tommy that he had to visit Fort Robinson and see what he could find out about the four victims. Before they left Deadwood, Tommy and Cesar checked in with the sheriff. "Are you coming back for the trial?" the sheriff asked.

"I'm not planning on it. You have statements from us. Perhaps with Cassidy out of the way, others won't be too timid to tell the truth."

"You're a mind reader, mister. Three more witnesses came forward last night and corroborated what you said; not only that, but the two who said it was a fair fight withdrew their statements. I don't like to see anyone killed, but Cassidy ran roughshod over this town for twenty years. People weren't free from his intimidation and that of his hands. This town and the Badlands have been considered illegal up until now. Perhaps this incident will give impetus to an assimilation of the entire Badlands into the state of South Dakota. You did us a favor last night.

My impression is that you knew Jack Cassidy, though he didn't recognize you at first."

"I hadn't seen Cassidy in thirty years. We rode some together when we were in our twenties, but we weren't friends. What I remember most was that he had to have his own way, or there would be a confrontation."

"His son is arriving by stage tomorrow. Do you think there'll be any trouble between you two?"

"Cassidy was married early in life and didn't have much to do with the son. I met the younger Cassidy when he was a teenager, and he wasn't anything like his father. When you see him, tell him I'm sorry, but I had no choice. I don't think the son will have a vendetta that he has to settle, but just in case, I'll leave my address with you." Tommy wrote his address on a piece of paper and handed it to the sheriff as he and Cesar left the building.

"He may not, but those two cowhands who had a gun on me are hard cases. They may make an attempt on you before you're out of the area. I can have a deputy with you until you leave."

"We don't think that's necessary, but we'll stay alert until we board the stage."

But Tommy and Cesar remained alert until the stage left town. Then they relaxed once the coach got underway; in fact, Tommy dozed off for a bit. They were two hours into the ride to Fort Robinson when they felt the stage start to slow down. Tommy woke up, stuck his head out of the side window, yelled up to the driver and asked what was wrong. "There's a big log blocking the road. It's wedged between two trees. We'll have to move it before we can continue," the driver responded.

Tommy sensed something was wrong; he looked at Cesar, who grabbed his rifle. As soon as the stage stopped, he and Tommy went out the right-hand door just as two shots were fired into the cabin. They threw themselves to the ground and rolled behind a boulder. Tommy called for the driver, but he didn't answer. They sensed the shots had come from a grove of trees on the other side of the stage, but weren't completely sure. However, their guess was confirmed when several more shots were fired at them as they looked out from behind the rocks. After five minutes, Tommy turned to the vaquero. "We can't sit here and do nothing. Our best bet is to circle back around and see if we can come up behind whoever is shooting at us. You go around to the left and I'll do the same to the right. Confirm before you shoot. I don't know what happened to the driver, and I don't want you and me firing at each other."

As soon as Cesar made his move, Tommy crawled around to the right, keeping the stage about forty feet away from him. He was moving on all fours for a minute, then stopping to listen for movement before he crawled forward. After he went another twenty feet, he heard some movement up ahead and assumed it wasn't Cesar. As he continued to move on his belly another fifty feet, he heard them whispering. When he was within ten feet of two men lying on their stomachs, each with a rifle aimed in the direction of the stage, he stood up. "If you two want to live, leave your rifles on the ground, stand up and raise your hands."

No sooner had he given the command when both turned in his direction. As they were aiming their rifles, he shot both in the head. Just then Cesar came forward and kicked their rifles away. It didn't matter; both were dead. "These are the two who had their guns on the sheriff last night, Patron."

"I can see that," he responded.

They found the driver leaning against some rocks. He'd been shot in the shoulder and was experiencing some pain. Cesar examined the wound, cleaned it out, and bandaged the injured area. "The wound doesn't look too bad."

"Do you have any heavy rope with you?" Tommy asked the driver.

"Look in the boot. I think you'll find what you need."

With Cesar's help, the injured driver was able to climb up into the boot and turn the horses around. Tommy wrapped the rope around the log that was lying across the trail and tied it to the rear axle. He directed the driver to move forward, and the log was pulled to the side of the road. Cesar and he buried the two Tommy had shot. They'd wire the sheriff of Deadwood when they reached the fort and give him the location of the bodies. The driver indicated he'd rather go to Alliance than to the fort. He felt that the medical services were more professional in the town versus the fort. After they found a doctor to look at the driver's wounds, they wired the sheriff in Deadwood where to find the two that were shot, and continued on to the fort by rented carriage, once they were sure that the driver wasn't in any danger.

The commandant was off post when they arrived, but as it turned out, it was the adjutant who helped them. He'd been at the post when the four victims were discharged. Although he was initially reluctant to divulge any information to Tommy, once he heard what had happened to his former soldiers, he was helpful. "I can't let you see their personnel folders, but I can answer any questions you might have."

"I think the main question is whether they were involved in any action or skirmish where Sioux were killed or injured."

"There wasn't any action while they were stationed here from 1893 to 1896. Prior to that, they were assigned to the Seventh Cavalry under Major Forsythe. As you know, the 7th intercepted the Lakota at Wounded Knee, and when the tribe failed to disarm immediately, they were fired on and most were killed."

"Were any of the four singled out for medals or any awards at Wounded Knee?"

"No. Many did receive medals; in fact, there were twenty Medals of Honor awarded for the action, but none for any of those four."

"Was there any other action that they were involved in other than Wounded Knee?"

"No."

"Were any of the four involved in any incident here at

the fort that may have gotten out of hand and someone retaliated?"

"No. They were here, did their jobs and left."

"Off the record, Major, what do you think?"

"Off the record, I think Wounded Knee was a tragedy. Forsythe overstepped his orders and massacred most of the Sioux. General Miles had him before a court martial board, but he beat it. You can't give out all those medals and court martial the commander. It's possible that someone survived Wounded Knee and is taking his revenge."

CHAPTER 31
1900

THEY ARRIVED in Sidney, Nebraska, late in the evening and found two rooms at the Sutter Hotel. Tommy and Sarah had come through here the previous summer, so Tommy was familiar with the layout of the town and where the depot was located. The next morning they went to the depot and asked for the station manager. A young man greeted them; he told them he'd only been there for two years and didn't know anything about a Jacob Light. Unfortunately, they had had a complete turnover of personnel and no one at the depot had been there longer than he. He did have Jacob's personnel folder and a grainy picture of the young man. There was a notation in the file that he departed on payday, June 26, 1898, and was never seen again. "Mr. Sanchez, for all we know, Jacob could have met with foul play."

"Did he have any other jobs with the railroad while he was here in Sidney, besides bookkeeping?"

"Yes. He worked laying track for over two years. Maybe some of the older men remember him. You can take his picture and check with them, but I want the photo returned before you leave. There are a few of the old timers repairing track about a mile east of town. We have a three-wheeled hand car that you can borrow and go out there. If you've never operated one, they're easy to move. You push from behind to get it started and then you move the beam up and down to keep it moving. You'll get your exercise in today!"

"Did Jacob travel to Fort Robinson while he was working at the depot?"

The station manager looked in the file and saw that Jacob went to Fort Robinson on seven occasions to collect delinquent accounts. "The file doesn't indicate who he interfaced with at the fort. My assumption is that he probably talked to the commander or the adjutant."

Tommy thanked the young man, and, with the picture, he and the vaquero got on the hand car the station manager offered and made their way east. It took about ten minutes before they reached a gang of twelve workmen. Tommy looked for the oldest of the group and asked him if he knew the man in the picture.

"What's he done?"

"Nothing. His name was given to us by his brothers. We're hoping that he can help us out."

"I remember him, but he's been gone some time. He worked alongside me for two years. What I remember most about Jacob was that he was a nice young man and a hard worker. I think he had a girl friend in town. I don't know her name, but I think she works in one of the saloons on Main Street."

No one else seemed to remember Jacob, so Tommy

and Cesar pumped the hand cart back to Sidney. They indeed had a good workout. "What do you want to do, Patron?" Cesar asked.

"I think we need to make an effort to find the girl."

Tommy thought they'd have a better chance of finding her at night if she worked in one of the ten saloons in town. Around six that evening they entered the first one they came across and then continued down one side of the street and then crossed over and repeated the process on the other side. It was at the seventh watering hole that they met Rosita Riley, who wasn't shy about telling them all she knew about Jacob Light.

"He said he was going out of town on business and would be back Monday so we could announce our engagement. The son-of-a-bitch walked out on me and the child I was carrying. My father beat the hell out of me and threw me out of the house. I started working here and when my time came, my mother found a place for me and cared for me and the baby until I was able to work again. I haven't seen my father since Jacob left. This is where I've been for two years and this is what I have to look forward to for the rest of my life."

"Do you have any pictures of Jacob?" Tommy asked.

"I did, but I threw them out several years ago. I waited and I waited and then I just gave up on him."

"Did he by any chance say where he was going?"

"No. I only know that he got on the westbound line. I was on the platform waving goodbye to him. What a loser I was!"

"Did he have any friends or acquaintances that are still in town?"

"If they are, I wouldn't know about it. He was closed-mouthed about everything."

"Did you know that he was raised by a Sioux family? They were killed at Wounded Knee; he was nearly killed there as well."

"He's not Indian; he's white. I've seen Jacob without any clothes. He really is white."

"Did he mention Wounded Knee to you?"

"No."

"Did he mention his brothers?"

"No. I guess I really didn't know Jacob at all."

CHAPTER 32

1900

COMING HOME to the ranch in the Santa Ynez Valley was always a pleasure for Tommy Sanchez. The greeting he received from his wife and children made the trip worth the effort. Sarah was anxious to know what he found out, but she waited until he had spent some time with the children before she asked. When he was ready, they sat down at the nook and he summarized his trip to the fort, the two reservations, and the run-in with Jack Cassidy in Deadwood.

She put her hand to her mouth when he described the encounter with Cassidy. He waited until she composed herself before continuing. When he finished, she asked, "Did you come to any conclusion about who could be hanging these men?"

"No, but I have a theory that's plausible. I believe that the impetus for these murders lies at Wounded Knee. It's possible that a brave by the name of White Bird witnessed the killing of his parents, survived the massacre, and is exacting his form of justice. I spoke to his three brothers, whom he visited five or six years ago, the girlfriend that he left behind, and the people at the depot in Sidney. He was employed by the railroad there for almost six years and went by the name of Jacob Light. He's an Indian brave who in reality is white. I think that's the reason we're having such a problem finding our killer. We need to be looking for a young white man."

"White Bird, or Jacob Light, survived a Sioux raid on a wagon train. He was taken and raised by a Sioux family. I have a picture of Jacob Light, alias White Bird, but it's too grainy. I promised to return it to a young man who loaned it to me in Sidney. I figured that solving the four murders was more important than giving the picture back. I can always send it to him." Tommy handed the picture to Sarah.

"I agree that it's grainy, but the face is very familiar. I could swear that I've seen this young man in the valley recently."

"It's entirely possible."

"That makes Jefferson's summary of all young men who're capable of lifting the victims right on the mark."

"I have a description of Jacob and a report that he has a birth mark on his right hand. Now, mind you, this is only a theory, because Jacob may not be the person we're looking for; he may, in fact, not be alive. No one has reported seeing him in the last four years. Jacob disappeared four days after the soldiers resigned from the army. We know that the four traveled through Sidney. Jacob may have been waiting for the time when he could follow them to California."

"What's your next step?"

"I think we need to discuss my theory with both Jefferson and Juan and get their opinion. I'll make up a message and wire it to Santa Barbara and have a vaquero deliver a copy to Juan."

"Do you remember me telling you about the bobcat that's been killing our chickens?"

"Did you catch it?"

"Shot it dead at the entrance to the barn. I also scared the hell out of the young man from the general store. He thought I was shooting at him. He dived under the wagon he used to bring supplies we ordered."

"Was it John Smart?"

"I believe that's his name. Why?"

"I think he's our man."

Two days later Juan and Jefferson arrived at the ranch around noon. They decided to meet in the kitchen, without Raul. Sarah provided lemonade and sandwiches. Tommy took his time and outlined his trip and what he had found out. "Here's a copy of the picture that the Sidney depot manager loaned me and a written description of Jacob Light provided to me by the same person."

"I've seen this man, though I don't know where, but I've seen him," Jefferson said.

"No offense, Tommy, but even if we found Jacob Light here, nothing points to him as the killer. He may be the killer, but unless someone can come forward to say they saw Light hang one or more of the victims, he's free as a lark. I think we have to find an alibi for Raul. Right now he's pissing me off. I can't get any cooperation from him. He says he's innocent, but I can't convince him to help us," Juan said.

"I'll talk to him, but let's not lose sight that Light may be in the valley. That analysis Jefferson did, identifying men that could be strong and young enough to be the killer, is still our most valuable asset. Have you been able to narrow down the list?" Tommy asked Jefferson.

"I think that there are about twenty men in this valley that could possibly be strong enough to commit the murders. I suggest that I keep this list and we do some checking on them. To me, our main priority is to concentrate on those around twenty-six years of age; one might be Jacob Light. You think it's him, don't you, Tommy?"

"I do. Finish your analysis, but I think I know who it is."

CHAPTER 33

1900

GETTING Raul to focus on the upcoming trial was frustrating Juan. He asked Tommy to intercede and act as an interpreter during his pretrial preparation with Raul. They met at Juan's office. His intent was to establish an alibi for Raul at the time of each of the four hangings. "I want you to take your time and think about where you were when each of these men was hanged, starting with Simon Higgins."

The lessons in English that Sarah was giving Naiwa and Raul had some impact. But Raul was reverting to his native language, and Tommy had to translate. This helped, but it was still cumbersome for Juan, who wanted to hear his client speak directly to him. "Higgins was hanged on a Monday night, December 15. He left the Grange Hall at ten that night, talked to a few acquaintances, and then walked to his room. What was your schedule that night?"

After conversing with Raul and making sure he knew what was being asked, Tommy responded,"He doesn't remember."

"Doesn't remember or doesn't want to remember."

Juan fired back. This wasn't the first time he'd been down this road with an uncooperative client.

Tommy spoke sternly to Raul. He told him to cooperate or he'd be convicted and hanged. That last scolding seemed to make an impression on him. Juan's Spanish was weak, so he couldn't quite understand all the nuances of the language. "He thinks he was on the south range checking the herd that whole day. He didn't get back to his room until early the next morning."

"Was he by himself, or did he have some of his men with him who could confirm his whereabouts?" Juan asked.

"He said he was alone."

"That doesn't help. What about December 29th, when Butler was hanged?"

"I can vouch for Raul on that evening. He was cooking the half steers during our annual Christmas party. He didn't leave the backyard until ten that evening. Then he and I went over some cattle figures until midnight. From what the doctor tells us, Butler died between eight and midnight. I would think that would be one alibi that could stand up in court."

"The next hanging was February 13th. What does the doctor say?" Juan asked.

"He said it was sometime between dawn and noon that morning. Raul got there round ten and found Whitman in the barn, so he was there during that time frame."

"Did he go by himself?"

"Yes, he was delivering two horses for me," Tommy responded.

"The hanging of Spenser, on March 31, gives me the most concern. There was a witness to the argument between Raul and Spenser, and then the reverend is murdered. Can Raul account for his time on that date?"

After a brief discussion with Raul, Tommy said that Raul was angry when he got home and went for a ride to the south pasture so he could clear his head.

"He's either one unlucky son-of-a-bitch or someone is setting him up. We can argue a good case for the Butler hanging, but the other three are problems. I think we need to find the real killer, or a jury just might convict Raul for at least three of the hangings. That newspaper editor is still stirring everyone up. He's practically convicted Raul in public opinion. I don't know if we can get a fair trial in Santa Barbara. However, any judge who wants to be reelected or reappointed won't allow this to be tried elsewhere."

"Our client is distraught. He needs to concentrate and see if he can remember anything about the Butler hanging that could help us. He was there. He must have seen something that could help," Juan said.

"I'll talk to him, but the best thing I can do for him is find the killer," Tommy said.

CHAPTER 34
1900

THAT EVENING, Tommy telegraphed Jefferson and asked him to come up the next day to discuss the pending trial. He and Sarah talked about what to expect and who should attend the trial in support of Raul. "I don't think Naiwa is up for it. She is distraught and cries constantly. I'm worried about her mental state. If he's convicted, she may withdraw into herself, and you and I will have to raise her two children."

"Who do you think put the Ghost Shirt in Raul's room inside the barn?" Tommy asked Sarah.

"I don't think it was anyone that worked for us. It had to be a vendor or their worker. We have supplies, hay, groceries, and sometimes clothing delivered. I sign for everything as it's delivered and then inventory it later. So if twenty bags of oats were delivered, I'd count them the next day. Generally, a vendor or his employee has access to the barn for the items we store there. It's interesting that you raise this issue. Last week, John Smart, who works at the general store, delivered a load of oat hay, and stacked it in the rear of the barn. He seems like a nice young man, but he did have access to the barn, and consequently,

Raul's room. I'll check the invoices to see if he'd been here before."

"Why don't you check those invoices now and see who was here prior to April first? It may prove to be meaningless, but I want to check everything possible. Jefferson replied to my wire and he'll be here tomorrow afternoon."

The ride up from Santa Barbara was tedious, but Jefferson wanted to contribute as much as he could to Tommy's quest to find out what happened. He left at nine in the morning and was sitting at the nook in Sarah's kitchen at three.

"Want something cold or a hot cup of coffee?" Sarah asked the old lawman and current Pinkerton agent.

"Could I have a cold glass of water first and then a hot cup of coffee?" Sarah laughed but complied with his request.

As soon as Tommy joined the two, Jefferson placed two pieces of paper on the table in front of the three of them. The first sheet had a list of characteristics that he felt someone who hanged these men would have. Down the side of the first sheet he listed the names of thirty men. In a column to the right of the names he listed those characteristics each individual met. On the second page in one column he listed ten men who met most of the qualifications, while a second column identified five men he considered the top five candidates.

"This is my initial attempt to identify young men who could fit the profile of the killer that we identified. Of the thirty I initially identified, I further reduced that list to ten and then to five. You can review all the lists and change them based on some information you have that I wasn't privy to. I know this is the first time you've seen this matrix and you may have other traits that you want to consider, but at least this is a good start."

"I think you've done a fabulous job. I don't want to add any other features. Let's look at the five you identified. If they don't work out, we can keep going back as far as the original list," Tommy responded.

Sarah and the two men looked at the names of five individuals. They were William Watson, Frederick Holden, Jonathan Gooddale, John Smart and Joseph Hollis. "Watson rides for Big Bend Ranch. He was born here and has family in the area. He's also a friend of Cesar, one of your vaqueros. Holden came here two years ago and is an apprentice to the blacksmith. Gooddale was born in Santa Barbara, where his father is a minister. He came to the valley a year ago and works in the post office. John Smart works for Josh Ingram at the general store; he's been in the valley for two years. He worked on the wharf in Santa Barbara for two years before he got the job working for Ingram. I don't know where he was prior to Santa Barbara. Joseph Hollis is a bartender at the Lucky Lady Saloon. He's been here ten years. He's constantly in trouble and has been in jail twice for fighting," Jefferson summarized.

Sarah looked at the names and compared those with her invoices. "Smart has delivered supplies in February and March. Hollis delivered beer in February for our vaquero party at the ranch. Holden has been here three times this year to shoe some of our horses. His last visit was the middle of February. Gooddale made a special delivery in mid-March. As far as Watson's concerned, I've seen him here several times this year visiting Cesar. I think all have had access to the barn and could've planted the shirt. But if I compare your analysis to Tommy's theory that it was a young white man who was raised by a Sioux family, then it looks like it could only be John Smart or Frederick Holden, and as a long shot, Jonathan Gooddale. I'd rule out Watson, because he was born here and Hollis has been here for ten years."

"By the way, Smart was here while you were gone. He delivered a load of hay from the general store and yes, he was in the barn."

"What about the other five in the first column of ten?" Jefferson asked

"A Jacob Whatney delivered flowers for Naiwa one time. I remember him. He didn't leave my sight, so I think we could eliminate him. The others, to the best of my knowledge, have never been here. I think we need to concentrate on the three you suggested. My question is, how do we do that?" Sarah responded.

"I think that's something I should do. I've done this type of work before. You realize that our suspect could be someone other than the thirty I identified. What do you think, Tommy?" Jefferson asked.

"I agree with everything you said, and like Sarah, I think we should concentrate on Smart, Holden and

Gooddale, though I think it's Smart. I plan to visit their places of employment so I can get a feel for them. I won't get in your way."

Jefferson was staying in the guest house for the remainder of the week while observing where the three worked and where they lived. He kept to himself except that he shared dinner with the entire family each night. After dinner on the last night of his stay, Naiwa and Naomi gave the children baths and Tommy helped Sarah with the dishes. Jefferson had retired for the evening and planned to leave early the next morning.

When they finished cleaning up, Sarah turned to Tommy. "What do you have on your mind, Indian man?'

"I was thinking of that nice white butt of yours. The thought of my patting it has filled me with huge anticipation."

"Has it now?" With that comment, Sarah threw the dish towel in Tommy's face and took off running into the bedroom with Tommy in close pursuit. As she reached the bed, she turned and threw her head scarf at him. He didn't slow down. He grabbed her around the waist and both tumbled into the bed. Then the real race began in earnest, as to who would be able to remove their clothes first; it was a dead heat. Tommy was smiling; Sarah was laughing.

"We haven't done this in a week. Are you losing your passion because I'm older?"

"We'll see who's lost any passion."

CHAPTER 35
1900

RAUL and his two attorneys arrived at the Santa Barbara County Courthouse two hours prior to jury selection. This was the first time Juan had tried a case in this building or any building; he was nervous. In fact, he was somewhat in awe of his surroundings as he stood for a few minutes outside the entrance on Figueroa Street, taking in the view. Five years ago he'd been a renegade with no future. Today he was here in the people's court trying a murder case. Every day he thanked God and Tommy Sanchez for his good fortune. In front of the building was a triangular-shaped gable supported by huge granite columns. Adding to the Mediterranean flavor was a dome over the central space of the structure.

Sarah and Tommy arrived in the midst of a demonstration. Anacapa and Figueroa Streets were roped off and police were redirecting traffic. They had to walk two blocks back to the court house. The crowd was unruly, and it definitely had a prejudice against the defendant, Raul Mendoza. Several in the crowd held nooses aloft; others shouted out, "Hanging is too good for him! Let us have him."

Sarah was slightly unnerved, and Tommy quickly ushered her into the courthouse. No one tried to stop them, but several pointed out Tommy and yelled, "We're going to give you Indian lovers what Sitting Bull got."

"So much for innocent until proven guilty," Sarah said to one of the demonstrators as she walked by him.

Jury selection took nearly the entire day. Those who made up the selected twelve jurors were ranchers, ranch hands, and Santa Barbara city residents. Juan had hired an experienced trial attorney and it was his task to screen and interrogate prospective members of the jury pool. Most potential jurors had very little knowledge of the crimes committed. Only a few had read the newspaper articles, but even those few didn't know the magnitude of the offenses. Only three potential jurors were excused. Juan entered a plea of not guilty for Raul Mendoza. He also requested a court-appointed interpreter.

Opening arguments were fairly sterile. The prosecutor, Jason Turner, realized he had nothing but circumstantial evidence to base his case on. So he embellished on that set of circumstances and vowed to prove beyond a shadow of a doubt that Raul committed the crimes as charged. Turner knew he needed another two months before he was ready for trial. But the newspaper editor was pressuring the sheriff, who in turn was pressuring the prosecutor's office, and therefore he was forced to move early.

Juan still hadn't made up his mind whether to have Raul testify on his own behalf. The vaquero had been a difficult client, and if it had not been for Tommy Sanchez, he would have asked Raul to secure other representation. The main problem was Raul's unwillingness to cooperate in the defense. The view that Raul maintained was that he was innocent and that it was an imposition for him to be tried for something that he didn't do.

After he laid out his case in his opening statement the next morning, the prosecutor started calling witnesses. The first witness was the county sheriff, Tyrone Bates, who was on the stand the entire afternoon. He testified what the approximate time was for each hanging and what evidence they recovered at each of the scenes. Under questioning, he discussed the type of rope used, the boot marks found under the bodies at three of the murder scenes, and each of the Ghost Shirts found on the victims. When the Ghost Shirts were placed into evidence by Turner, there was a loud murmur that permeated the court room. The judge pounded his gavel and called for silence.

Under questioning, the sheriff stated that Raul was not at his residence, High Meadow Ranch, the night that Higgins was killed.

"Did you ask him where he was?"

"He said he was out all night looking for strays."

"What about Jarod Butler?"

"Butler was at a party at Thomas and Sarah Sanchez' home on December 29th, the night he was killed. We interviewed several people who were at the party, and they testified that Butler was seen talking to Raul Mendoza around seven o'clock and that the two men appeared to be having an argument."

"Could Mendoza have left the party, made his way to the livery stable, hanged Butler and made his way back?"

"It's possible. At the end of the party, most of the people who worked for the Sanchezes were busy cleaning up. We couldn't find anyone to confirm that Mendoza was there the entire cleanup time."

"Is it true that Mr. Mendoza was the person who discovered Jarod Butler hanging in his barn?"

"According to the statement given by Mr. Mendoza, he delivered two horses that morning to the Butler Ranch. It appeared to him that no one was on the ranch at the time. So he decided to put the horses in a holding pen and then look in the barn. That's when he found Butler. He went into town and reported the hanging to the town constable, Charles Little."

"Who did the investigation?"

The Santa Ynez Town Constable initiated the investigation, and subsequently my office took over the responsibility."

"Did you hire any consultants to help with the investigation?"

"No."

"Did you have help from an unpaid individual?"

"You must be referring to Mr. Sanchez."

"Did he help in any capacity?"

"Yes."

"Why don't you tell us the circumstances?"

"As was the case with Mr. Higgins, the Town Constable asked Mr. Sanchez to look at the murder scenes and give his opinion."

"Was he helpful?"

"Very. He's a very astute individual. He pointed out the clues and gave us an avenue to investigate the hangings."

"Pretty convenient, don't you think? Here's a man who knows all about Ghost Shirts and Ghost dances, who may be leading you down a path. Have you arrested anyone yet?"

"Raul Mendoza."

"Have you any other suspects?"

"No."

"Well, your so-called expert may have led you down a path that didn't produce any results. Is it possible that was his intent?"

Juan jumped to his feet and objected. "Mr. Sanchez is not on trial here. If the sheriff and his office want to ask someone for their opinion, what are they supposed to say, sorry, you have to handle that yourself. Wouldn't that be good citizenship?"

The judge ordered the prosecutor to move on. "Tell me who found Mr. Whitman?"

"Raul Mendoza."

"Tell the jury the circumstances whereby he was the one who found the victim."

"Mr. Mendoza's horse had a shoe problem, and he walked the horse from the post office to Whitman's livery.

The barn was locked, so he went around back and peered in the window. That's when he saw Whitman hanging in the middle of the barn."

"What did he do next?"

"He went to the town constable, who sent for Mr. Sanchez."

"Oh, Mr. Sanchez is involved in another hanging?"

"He wasn't involved. He was asked to look at the murder scene."

"Tell me in your own words what you found when you investigated the death of Rev. Samuel Spenser."

"The reverend was found by the cleaning lady, who ran to the town constable. Subsequently we learned that the deceased had had a heated argument with Mr. Mendoza the day before."

"Was there anything peculiar to these four hangings that convinced you that it was the work of the same person or persons?"

"Yes. The rope used in all four deaths was the same brand. The noose was the same and the method of hanging seemed to be the same."

"Were you able to determine the origin of the rope?"

"No, sir."

"What else was similar?"

"The Ghost Shirts placed on the victims were, in essence, the same."

"Anything else?"

"There were peculiar boot marks in the dirt under three of the victims."

"Were you able to determine the origin of the boots that made those marks?"

"No, but we found the boots in a garbage heap behind the church, within a few hours of finding Rev. Spenser."

"You said *we* found the boots. Who specifically found the boots?"

"Mr. Thomas Sanchez."

"Is it true that he also found some clothing at the same time?"

"He found a shirt, pants, gloves and a hat that may have belonged to the killer."

"Boy, wasn't that convenient?"

"I object." Juan stood up immediately and told the judge that Mr. Sanchez was not on trial. He was asked by the constable to look at the scene.

"Objection sustained." The judge directed the prosecutor to move on.

"What did you do next?"

"I met with the County District Attorney and we agreed that Raul Mendoza was a person of interest, primarily because of the argument with Rev. Spenser. Based upon this evidence, Judge Holden issued a warrant to search Raul Mendoza's residence."

"And did you inspect the defendant's quarters?"

"My deputy and I went to High Meadows Ranch and showed the warrant to Mr. Sanchez, and then we inspected Mendoza's quarters."

"And what was the result of this inspection?"

"We discovered a Ghost Shirt hidden in one of the

legs of Mr. Mendoza's chaps. The Ghost Shirt matched the ones found on the four victims. At that point, I arrested Mr. Mendoza and had my deputy take him to the jail in Santa Barbara."

"Do you think these murders were the work of one or perhaps more than one individual?"

"I believe that Mr. Mendoza was the only one involved."

"It's still possible that more than one individual was responsible for the hangings, isn't it?"

"It's possible."

"As I understand it, there were no boot marks found under Spenser's body."

"Yes and no. There were hardwood floors where Spenser was hanging, and we didn't get a definitive boot mark. We did find some scuff marks, and followed those first to Mr. Spenser's quarters and then to the gravel road outside. The boots were found in some trash behind the church."

"Was Mr. Mendoza familiar with the four victims?"

"The four men were employed by Mr. Sanchez for six months. Mr. Mendoza was their supervisor."

"Was there animosity between any of the four and Mr. Mendoza?"

"Not that I am aware of."

"Was there any animosity between any of the four victims and Mr. Sanchez?"

Raul jumped to his feet immediately. "I object. Mr. Sanchez is not on trial here, and I find it inappropriate for the district attorney to make unfounded allegations and innuendos."

"Objection sustained. Move on, Mr. Turner."

"He's trying to imply that you had a part in the hangings," Sarah whispered in Tommy's ear.

"I know. Let Juan handle it."

Turner apparently wasn't finished with Tommy. "During your investigation into the four hangings, did you hire or request any assistance from individuals outside the sheriff's department to look at the murder scenes or help in your analysis of the cases?"

"Mr. Thomas Sanchez."

"During your testimony, we talked about the help that Mr. Thomas Sanchez gave to your investigation. Would you say that Mr. Sanchez is a violent individual?'

"No."

"Well then, is Mr. Sanchez the same person who shot the hats off three men on Sagunto Street and then beat one of the three unmercifully?"

"That was before my time. I'm not aware of the circumstances."

"Was this the same Mr. Sanchez who tracked down and killed Jason Brown who kidnapped Mrs. Sanchez?"

"Mr. Sanchez didn't kill Mr. Brown."

"Who did?"

"No one knows."

"Then how do you know that he didn't kill Jason Brown?"

"He told me he didn't."

"Wow."

"Is Mr. Sanchez the employer of the defendant, Raul Mendoza?"

"Yes."

"Don't you find it odd that we have Ghost Shirts placed on four victims and the one most knowledgeable person in this area is a former Sioux brave who's also the employer of the man charged in the murders?"

"I don't think that has anything to do with these murders."

"What about finding the Ghost Shirt on the Sanchez Ranch?"

"I believe we found the shirt in Mendoza's room."

Sarah turned to Tommy and again whispered, "He's really trying to implicate you."

Tommy nodded. "He doesn't have a case. He's hoping to throw everything he can at the jury, hoping that something might stick and they'll take the bait."

"Doesn't it bother you that you and the town constable have based your strategy to find the killer or killers of the four men hanged on the suggestions of Mr. Sanchez, who's also the employer of Mr. Mendoza, who's charged with the killings?"

"I don't see it that way."

The prosecutor said he had no more questions for the sheriff, and Juan said he'd defer any question to when they presented the defense's case.

The only other witness called by the county was the woman who said she overheard an argument between

Samuel Spenser and Raul. She stated that she was passing outside the church when she heard the two men shouting at each other. Though she was outside the church, they were loud enough for her to hear them. She couldn't make out exactly what was said, but she told the court about an Indian woman who came running out of the church while the two men were arguing. Turner stretched out the testimony of this witness until late in the afternoon and then rested his case. The judge adjourned for the day and directed the court to reconvene at nine the next morning. Juan was ready.

That evening, Sarah, Tommy and Raul stayed at the Arlington Hotel. They arranged for transportation to Stearns Wharf, where Juan and his colleague, Frederick Hamilton, joined them for dinner; Juan couldn't reach agreement with his first choice, Whitford B. Tate. Raul was very depressed and wanted to stay in his room. "We're meeting with your two attorneys to go over tomorrow's testimony. You need to be there," Sarah said.

"What difference does it make? They're going to find me guilty because I'm a Mexican. I'm going to bed."

She looked at Tommy, who shook his head in disbelief. "Raul, I'm your supervisor, and I want you there at the meeting. You don't have to say anything if you don't want to, but you must be there."

"I'm not going." Raul left their suite and went to his room.

"This isn't going to be easy. We may have to win this case in spite of him," Sarah told Tommy.

The first thing Tommy asked the two attorneys when they joined them at the table was, would Raul testify on his own behalf?

"Not if I can help it. I don't know whether he can maintain his composure, and that may prejudice the jury. We think we can win this case without him ever getting near that witness stand. By the way, where is he?" Juan asked.

"He refused to come," Tommy responded.

"Is he going to be at his own trial?"

"He'll be there, even if I have to tie him to a horse."

With Tommy and Sarah sitting in the middle of the spectators in the court house the next morning, Raul was in attendance. It was Juan's turn to cross-examine Sheriff Tyrone Bates. "Tell me, Sheriff Bates—why did you single out Raul Mendoza as a suspect in these hangings?"

The sheriff appeared flustered at first with the question, but he quickly recovered. "Well, he was the only one at Whitman's place when he said he found the body. In addition, he was overheard arguing with Butler at the Sanchez' Ranch the night Butler was murdered and with Samuel Spenser prior to his death."

"Was there anything else that made you suspect Raul Mendoza?"

"No, it was mainly the arguments with the two victims."

"What were the arguments about?"

"I don't know."

"Excuse me, you suspect a man of hanging two men because he had an argument with them, but you don't know what the arguments were about?"

"Yes."

"Sheriff, you don't even know if there were any arguments, do you?"

"No."

"So, if you don't know if there were any arguments and you didn't have a clue that pointed to my client, then tell me why you made him a suspect. Remember, you're under oath, sheriff."

"The newspaper was pressuring my office; the mayor said we had to do something, and a lot of local politicians were saying that the county ought to appoint another sheriff. When the newspaper pointed out that Mendoza found two of the bodies, we decided to get a warrant and see if we could find any Ghost Shirts in his possession. That's what we were looking for when we went to High Meadows Ranch."

"So let me get this straight: the newspaper, the mayor and the politicians put the pressure on you to get a warrant, not good police work. You were actually on a fishing expedition. Isn't that true?"

When there was no answer from the sheriff, Juan said, "You don't have to answer that, Sheriff Bates."

"Sheriff Bates, you said Mr. Mendoza found two of the bodies, namely, Jarod Butler and Hiram Whitman. Did you ask my client why he was at Whitman's place?"

"Mendoza said his horse threw a shoe while he was in Santa Ynez and he walked the animal over to the stable."

"Did you verify whether the horse threw a shoe?"

"Yes. The town constable verified that the horse had to be reshod."

"So he was telling the truth."

"I don't know that. I only know that the horse was reshod."

"Okay. What about Butler, what was Mendoza's reason for going there?"

"He said he was delivering two horses to Butler."

"Was he?"

"Mr. Sanchez said he had an order to deliver two horses that morning."

"Was there any paperwork that would support that statement?"

"Yes, there was a contract."

"So in each case, Mr. Mendoza had a valid reason for going to the victim's place of residence or workplace. Is that true?"

"Yes."

"Now, is it your testimony that Mr. Mendoza had an argument with Mr. Butler, the night he was hanged?"

"Yes."

"What was the argument about?"

"I don't know. We had a witness who indicated the men were shouting at each other, but they couldn't ascertain what was said."

"Where did this take place?"

"At the Sanchez' party the night Butler died."

"Is it possible that there was so much noise that the two men shouted at each other so they could be heard?"

"I don't know."

"It's hard for me to understand how you could possibly get a warrant with such flimsy evidence, which is mostly innuendo or hearsay. You don't have to answer that."

"So according to the doctor's report placed in evidence by the prosecutor, Butler was killed sometime between midnight and eight in the morning. Did you check on Mendoza's alibi for that time frame?"

"He said he was in his room in the main barn."

"Was he?"

"We found one vaquero who said he didn't leave the barn that evening, but we weren't sure we could trust what he said."

"Why was that?"

"He works for Mendoza."

"In your earlier testimony, you stated that the boots that left distinctive marks at three of the murder scenes were found in some garbage behind Spenser's church. Is that true?"

"Yes."

"Do you believe they were the boots used in the murders?"

"Yes."

"Weren't they two sizes too large for Raul Mendoza?"

"Yes."

"It's my understanding that certain apparel was also found behind the church the same night. Is that true?"

"Yes."

"Do you think they were used by the killer?"

"It's possible."

"Wasn't all the clothing too large for Raul Mendoza?"

"Yes."

The sheriff was excused, and since there was no redirect by the prosecutor, Juan recalled Catherine Hollywood, who said she overheard the argument between Samuel Spenser and Raul. She repeated what she had previously said under oath.

"Tell me what the argument was about."

"I told the other lawyer that I couldn't hear what was said."

"So what are you testifying to?"

"Just what I told the court."

"Didn't you come into the church and ask Reverend Spenser if anything was wrong?"

"Yes."

"What did he say?"

"He said he must've been talking too loud."

"Did he seem threatened?"

"No."

"Have you ever yelled at another person in your life?"

"Well, yes."

"Did you hang them?"

"Of course not."

CHAPTER 36
1900

IT WAS TIME to break for lunch, and the judge gave both sides a two-hour recess and asked if they could finish closing arguments that afternoon. Juan and the prosecutor agreed. Tommy bought sandwiches and something to drink for five and they met in a vacant room in the courthouse to go over the case and comment on Juan's closing argument.

Juan's assistant, Frederick Hamilton, who handled the jury pool and advised Juan when to object, said that the case was an easy victory for acquittal in any jurisdiction. "However, I believe that the amount of pressure exerted by the local politicians and the newspaper will make that outcome uncertain. I'm not sure we'll gain an acquittal. I think I should give the closing argument. Juan, you're part Sioux. I believe there's so much prejudice here that it may affect your client. I'm white and he's Spanish. I know it's your call, but that's my advice."

"Juan is a respected member of the bar. I know you mean well, but I can't believe what you're saying. The county doesn't have a case and they know it. Raul is being railroaded. This is ridiculous," Sarah told the others.

Tommy, Sarah and the two attorneys discussed the merits of the defense, while Raul was mute and seemed to be disinterested. They still had an hour left. Juan was using that time making notes for his closing summary, when Jason Turner knocked on the door, stepped in, excused himself and asked Juan to step out into the hall.

Turner led Juan down the corridor of the great building to his office and asked him to have a seat. "I have a proposal for you. Now don't get mad, just read it and then we can talk."

Juan took a few moments to read the short paragraph. Turner was offering a deal. Raul would plead guilty to one count of manslaughter in the death of Samuel Spenser and serve ten years. He would then be eligible for parole after eight years. The district attorney would recommend to the parole board that Raul could be released at the end of the eight years.

"Are you crazy? You have no case, just innuendos. My client is going to be acquitted."

"That's entirely possible, but the way I read the jury —and I've been doing this a lot longer than you—there are four outstanding murders in this county, and someone must pay. I think they'll find your client guilty of all four murders and ask for the death penalty. I'm not trying to take advantage of you because of your youth. I'm telling you the way it is. Why don't you present this to Mendoza and see what he says? This offer is good until we go back into court. Once I give my closing argument, I'll take what the jury offers."

"How do we know that the D.A. at the time of the parole hearing will recommend that Raul should be released?"

"I'll put a memo in the file that I made that agreement."

"That's not much of a commitment."

When Juan reentered the room where the other four were waiting, he remained quiet for a moment before he spoke. "Tommy, I want you to translate what I'm about to say." Tommy nodded.

"Turner has made an offer. If Juan pleads guilty to the charge of manslaughter for the Samuel Spenser murder, the County will recommend a sentence of ten years. They'll also recommend to the parole board that Raul be released after he serves eight years."

When Tommy explained the plea to Raul, he stood up and screamed in Spanish that he didn't do anything. He didn't kill anyone, and why were these people trying to do this to him? He broke down and slumped at the table. He sobbed uncontrollably.

Sarah turned to Tommy. "I can't believe this is happening. What can you do?"

Before he answered Sarah, he questioned Juan. "If he pleads to one count of manslaughter and goes to jail, what are the chances that while he's in prison, they'll try him on the other three murders?"

Hamilton answered, "Nothing in this plea deal will preclude that from happening."

"I think we take our chances in court, and if they find him guilty, we appeal it as far as we can go. I have enough money to pay for the attorneys and any appeals. If he's found guilty, perhaps we can get some sort of bail pending an appeal. What do you think, Juan?"

"This is my first capital case, and I feel I've let Raul down. I'd like to hear what Frederick has to say."

"This is tricky. There is no case. They only have the shirt, and anyone could've planted that. As Mrs. Sanchez said, there were at least five young men who visited the ranch and had access to the barn where Raul's room is. The newspaper has stirred up a frenzy, and the politicians want someone to pay. I think the jurors are honest people, but they have to live in this area. With sentiment high against Raul, it's possible that they could convict. Everyone saw the demonstration yesterday outside the courthouse."

"I can't make the decision for you, Juan, I can only advise. We've been subjected to some form of prejudice our entire lives. I've never rolled over and played dead. I fight back. It only takes one on the panel to get a hung jury. I think you have to make the case for Raul," Tommy said.

After Turner gave his closing argument, Juan rose and walked toward the jury box. "Smoke, that's all the prosecutor has produced. He feels that if he generates enough smoke, you won't be able to see through his case.

It has so many holes in it that nothing sticks. We have my client involved with two arguments, and nobody knows what the arguments were about. We have some witness state that he was shouting at one of the victims at a party that generated so much noise that everyone was yelling to be heard.

"Mr. Turner's case is so shaky that he uses the pretext that anyone who finds a body must be the killer. Mr. Mendoza did find two of the bodies, but had a legitimate reason in both cases for being there. So what did he do when he found the bodies? He notified the authorities. If it's a crime to find a body or help someone in distress, think how people will feel in the future if they find someone alongside the road, either dead or dying. They won't get involved for fear of being accused of the harm done to that person. That would be a tragedy.

"The county's entire case is that the Ghost Shirt was found in a leg of one of Mr. Mendoza's chaps. Is it possible that someone put it there? We have a list of five people, who live off the High Meadows ranch, who had access to Mr. Mendoza's room. In some cases, that individual had access more than once. Could any of them have put the Ghost Shirt in his room to take suspicion away from them? Of course they could. It wasn't a secret that Mr. Mendoza found two of the victims. He was fair game. The county sheriff isn't looking anyplace else.

"Mr. Mendoza has been working for the Sanchez family for ten years. He's a model employee, rising from a young cowhand to be foreman of a fifteen-thousand-acre ranch. His men respect him and he's never been in trouble. Let's stop this charade started by an overly ambitious newspaper editor to increase circulation. Set this man free."

CHAPTER 37
1900

THE JURY retired to deliberate, while Tommy, Sarah, Raul and the defense team went to the Sanchezes' rooms at the Arlington Hotel. It was nearly five o'clock, so they ordered dinner for everyone. Raul had been quiet on the way back from the courthouse, and now he sat in one of the overstuffed chairs, just staring at the ceiling; he refused to participate in any of the discussions. He remained sullen and withdrawn.

"I was very impressed with your questioning of the two witnesses. By all accounts, you won this case. I hope the jury sees it that way. For a first trial, you more than vindicated yourself. You've come a long way from that saloon where Jefferson and I found you. When Turner started questioning the sheriff about me, I thought he was going after you next. He probably didn't know that you were half Sioux and the son of Crazy Horse. Must be something in the lawyers' association that says, 'One will not go after a fellow lawyer.'" Tommy laughed and tapped Juan on the shoulder.

"With the jury deliberating and Raul having to stay here, I need to get back to the ranch. Sarah, it's up to you whether you want to stay here or come back with me," Tommy said.

Juan looked at Sarah. "There's nothing else you can do here. We're just waiting for the verdict. If he's acquitted, I'll bring him home. If he's guilty, I'll file an appeal. Don't worry about me, mother. Your younger children need you."

They took the stage the next morning, had lunch at the Kinevan Kitchen, and were home by four in the afternoon. Their two children ran out of the house to greet them as their carriage stopped in front. They were excited to hug Helga and Thomas, and it took them a few seconds to understand what the children were saying. "Chatan has run away."

Naomi rushed out of the house and filled them in on the situation with Chatan. "He wasn't in his bed when I went to wake him this morning. I looked everywhere, and then I had two of the vaqueros check the barn and the holding pens. He sometimes plays there. When they reported that he wasn't there and one of the horses was missing, I sent them to the fishing pond to see if he was there. I didn't know what else to do. I'm sorry."

"Did anything happen at school yesterday?" Sara asked Naomi.

"He had a few scratches on his face when he came home. Thomas said Chatan got into a fight with the two older boys again. The teacher broke it up before it went too far and sent the two Heller boys home."

Before they went into the house, Tommy called to one

of the vaqueros who'd come out of the barn. "Saddle my horse. I'll be with you in ten minutes."

"What are you going to do?" Sarah asked.

"I'll find him and bring him home. Right now, I'm going to change. Can you fix two days' rations? I think that should be enough time."

When he was outside, Tommy asked the vaquero, "Which horse did he take?"

"Crossfire. That's the one with a cleft in the right front foot. The boy likes to ride him. Cesar tracked him south but lost his tracks around the fish pond."

Most of horses on the ranch were unshod. Tommy believed that horses were more comfortable without shoes. As a precaution, though, Tommy had his horses' hoofs trimmed every six weeks.

Tommy brought the shirt Chatan had worn yesterday, had the two hounds get on the scent, and off they went south. Tommy was a skilled tracker and was used frequently by the sheriff's office to catch escaped prisoners. He'd learned his skill while an Indian brave, and maintained that skill even though he was a well-to-do rancher. It was still light when he reached the fish pond that he had built for recreation for the family, his employees and friends. The tracks from Chatan's horse were visible. Tommy determined from the marks made by the hoofs that Chatan stopped on this side of the pond for a few minutes, probably trying to determine which way to go next. If the vaqueros lost the tracks here, then Chatan had used a ploy to disguise which way he went. Tommy decided to camp there overnight and get a fresh start at dawn. He had an idea of what Chatan did while he was trying to decide which way to go. Tommy allowed the children and grandchildren to ride as far as the pond, but that was their limit. Chatan would be confused beyond this point.

Tommy camped on the north side of the pond and was up as the sun came over the horizon. He found where Chatan had entered the pond and where he came out. The boy entered and exited the pond four times and finally exited the area where the ground was very hard, hoping to disguise his true intent; the boy's father had taught him this skill. Chatan was headed south toward the Santa Ynez Mountains. The boy wasn't aware that Tommy had hunted and tracked throughout the mountains and knew the trails better than those who were born here.

Later that morning, Tommy found where the boy had crossed the river and where he exited. This was an area with abundant wildlife, including an occasional mountain lion. Tommy had killed one here last year that had been feeding on some of his calves. About a hundred yards over the river, the trail broke in two directions. Tommy dismounted and went up one and then the other before he found the tracks he was looking for. The boy had travelled this way about two hours ago.

Sensing that he was getting close to Chatan, he began walking while trailing his horse behind him. He was looking ahead about five to ten feet as he made his way up the mountain. When he heard a rider up ahead, he starting running, pulling the horse behind him as he moved. He came upon Chatan sitting on the ground in a small clearing with his head down; the boy was crying. Tommy walked up slowly and looked down at the cold and tired young man.

"It's time to go home, Chatan. Your family is worried about you." Tommy handed the young man some fried chicken that Naomi had prepared. There was no hesitation; Chatan was glad to be found. Although reluctant at first, Chatan freely told Tommy what happened. The boy's English was getting better, but he used English and Sioux to tell Tommy about the beating he got from the two Heller boys. "When I get bigger, I'm going to scalp them both." Tommy smiled.

"They said you've killed many white men and you're the one who hanged the four men. They said since I was your relation, I was probably guilty as well, and if the court didn't hang Raul, they were going to hang me. They showed me a rope. That's when the teacher came and pulled them off me. I didn't want to be hanged, so I ran away. Are you mad at me?"

"No, I'm proud of you. Good blood flows in your veins. Your ancestors were great men and women."

When they arrived home, the women wouldn't stop hugging Chatan. He looked to Tommy to get them to stop, but his savior smiled and raised his hands as though to say he couldn't do anything.

Sarah took Tommy aside. "What happened?"

Tommy told her the story that Chatan related and

from her expression she was shocked. "Why are those boys so vicious?"

"I'm going to find out."

"Tommy, with the verdict in doubt, we can't afford any situation that could sway a jury."

"I'll keep that in mind, but I can't allow anything like this to happen to any of our family. I'll wait until later and have a visit with the bartender."

Phil Heller knew that Sanchez was in Santa Barbara at the trial and that he'd react when he found out that his nephew had been beaten by his two sons. Phil was carrying a gun these nights. He didn't know if he'd be able to stop Sanchez, but he at least felt more comfortable with the revolver tucked in front of his pants. His normal routine was to close up at midnight on week days and be out of the saloon by twelve-thirty. He locked the back door and slowly looked around to see if anyone was in the alley behind the watering hole.

As he started walking toward his home on Roblar Street, he sensed that someone was watching him. "Is anyone there?" he called out.

"I have a gun." There was a crack in his voice. No one answered.

He gathered some courage, and, with a hand on the gun tucked in his pants, he made his way home. Just then a blood-curdling sound pierced the night air and sent shivers down Heller's spine. He paused for a few moments and started walking backwards, while keeping his eyes riveted on the alley. As he neared Roblar Street, another sound echoed through the night. He couldn't be sure, but it was like an Indian war cry. He turned and ran north on Roblar and didn't stop until he reached his front gate and stopped. Nailed to the front gate was a dead rat. Heller backed up a few steps, and before he could move, an arrow flew over his left shoulder and imbedded in the rat. Heller jumped the fence, ran as fast he could, tripped on the front stoop and slammed into his front door. The impact knocked him over, but he quickly regained his footing and went into the house and bolted the door.

Marie Heller was awakened out of a sound sleep when she heard the crash at her front door. She was a short, heavy-set woman with pock marks on her face. To say she was unattractive would be an understatement. By the time she put on her robe and reached the living room, her husband was bolting the door. "What the hell happened?" she yelled.

"I think Tommy Sanchez is after me. Those damned kids beat up his nephew again, and he swore he'd cut off my ear lobe if they did that."

"Is he outside?"

"I don't know. Someone made a blood-curdling sound as I closed up the saloon and followed me here. Then someone shot an arrow over my head, and it stuck in a dead rat fastened to the front gate."

"Show me."

"I'm not going out there."

"What a coward!" Marie Heller walked out the front door and stopped at the gate. There wasn't anything fastened to the gate, nor was there an arrow any place near it.

"There's nothing here. I think you scared yourself."

When he returned home, Sarah was up and waiting. "What did you do?"

"I just had some fun. Let's see what he does next."

The Heller boys didn't attend school the next two days, nor did their father go to work. One of the vaqueros reported to Tommy that Phil Heller called in sick, but was expected back the day after tomorrow. As was his routine, Heller closed up the saloon at midnight, cleaned up and exited through the back door. Just as he stepped down from the landing, an arrow struck the door behind him and Heller took off running toward home; he didn't look back. As he turned onto Roblar Street, another arrow went sailing by his head, and he sprinted the remaining two blocks. The front gate was open, but he saw a noose hanging from the top of his front door. He rushed to the door, went inside and bolted the door. His wife was waiting for him and asked what happened.

"Sanchez tried to kill me."

"How?" she asked.

"He fired two arrows at me as I was coming home and he put a noose over our front door."

Marie opened the front door and looked outside. "There's no noose here. Where did you say it was?"

Heller carefully looked out the front door. "It was here when I came into the house."

CHAPTER 38

1900

CHATAN attended school on Friday, four days after he was assaulted by the Heller boys. The Heller boys had been taken out of the school and were transferring. Phil Heller quit his job at the saloon and moved the family to Lompoc. But the word was out. The two children and the two Indian grandchildren were given a wide berth at school. No one called them names, and no one suggested that their family was responsible for the Ghost Shirt Murders.

The jury still hadn't reached a verdict, and Juan and Raul came home for the weekend. The judge allowed the jury to go home to tend to their families and return Monday morning at nine. Juan didn't have a clue which way the verdict would go. His consultant told him that the longer it took, the better the chance for acquittal. Sarah told her son what had happened with the Heller family, and Juan couldn't control himself from laughing. "If I could only have been there to see the look on his face when they couldn't find the arrows, rat and noose."

Chatan seemed to have renewed energy and was back

to his old playful ways. Tommy took the four children to the fish pond, and the five of them spent the day fishing.

No one was talking about the Hellers, but it seemed that everyone knew what had happened. Some people were offended, but not enough to confront either Sarah or Tommy. Sarah noticed that shopkeepers were especially polite to her. Men tipped their hats to Tommy when he was in Santa Ynez.

Jefferson and Tommy had been looking at the five candidates who could be the Ghost Shirt murderer. They decided on a strategy whereby Jefferson and Tommy would each look at and evaluate the five individuals. Then they'd exchange their lists. Tommy went out to the Big Bend Ranch on the subterfuge that he was looking for some quarter horse mares. Watson was the foreman and was more than willing to show Tommy the stock. "I like your stock, but I've got a couple of other horses I'm looking at. I'll let you know within a week if I'm interested."

"Just let us know, Mr. Sanchez. I believe we can make you a good deal."

Angus Ricker had been out to the ranch several times to trim a couple of troubled horses. Since Tommy hadn't met his apprentice, Frederick Holden, he asked Ricker to bring his apprentice the next day to trim the shoes on a couple of his mares. He used the subterfuge that he wanted to examine Holden's work in case Ricker couldn't make it one day. Angus introduced the young man to Tommy, and the two struck up a conversation. Tommy learned that Holden was an orphan and adopted by a

Mexican family in Santa Barbara. He'd been on his own since he was sixteen. Ricker told Tommy that Holden was a good worker.

Tommy had seen Joseph Hollis many times when he visited the Lucky Lady saloon to have a beer with some of the vaqueros. Hollis was a troubled young man who was constantly in trouble, and although he'd been a bartender for four years at the Lucky Lady, he'd been fired twice by the owner. The young man had been in the valley for ten years, so he couldn't have worked in Sidney, Nebraska, for the railroad and probably wasn't White Bird, alias Jacob Light. Tommy had no doubt that Joseph could kill someone, especially if he was drunk. He'd wait to see what Jefferson had to say and go from there. He talked to Gooddale's employer and immediately eliminated the young man. He seen Smart many times and was convinced that he was the man they were looking for.

When Jefferson finished his evaluation, he and Tommy met at the ranch. Sarah had some leftover beef and prepared sandwiches and potato salad. The three sat at the table with their notes. They decided to see who they could eliminate. Although Hollis had been to the ranch on two occasions, both Jefferson and Tommy felt that the young man wasn't the one. Watson was born in the valley and both Tommy and Jefferson felt that that fact alone eliminated him. Gooddale was from Santa Barbara. Both Jefferson and Tommy had spoken to the man's father and employer; both were convinced that he couldn't be White Bird.

That left Holden and Smart. Both had come to the

valley one to two years ago. Although each was polite and considered a good employee, neither could be ruled out. Initially, Jefferson didn't have Holden or Smart high on his list of potential killers. What he did was eliminate three from the list they assembled. "I wonder if we should expand our list. I'm not comfortable that either of these could be the killer," Jefferson said.

"What are your thoughts, Sarah?" Tommy turned to her.

"I agree with you both. We have eliminated some from our list, but we didn't establish a clear-cut favorite, nor are we sure that Holden or Smart is our man."

"I looked at all five and gradually eliminated one, then another until I came down to these two. My instincts tell me that John Smart is our man. Holden is a warm individual, while Smart is a cold fish. I have a picture of Jacob Light who worked for the railroad in Sidney, Nebraska. I know it's grainy, but it looks like Smart." Tommy passed the photo around.

"What do you propose we do?" Sarah asked.

"I'm going into town tomorrow, so give me a list of some items you need at the general store."

"You're going to see John Smart, aren't you?" Sarah asked and Tommy smiled.

The next morning, with Sarah's list in his pocket, he took the small carriage into town and tied the horse to the front post. He didn't see Smart as he walked into the store, so he asked one of the clerks if the young man was on duty today. The salesman pointed to the rear of the store. He saw Smart stocking one of the shelves. Tommy took out his list and handed it to him. "My wife indicates you deliver to our ranch. I'm Tommy Sanchez, and if you don't mind, I need this list filled and the order placed in my carriage out front."

Smart looked at the list. "We have these items. I can fill the order in about ten minutes. Will you pay now or charge it to your account?"

"Charge it. I'll be around the store and I can help you load when you have all the items assembled."

When he saw Smart head to the carriage, Tommy followed close behind. After he loaded all the items, he turned and smiled at Tommy and started back into the store.

"Anpetu waste yuha yo White Bird," Tommy said in Lakota Sioux, which meant, "Have a nice day, White Bird."

John stopped, as though frozen, and it looked to Tommy that he was going to respond in Sioux, but caught himself in time. "You think you're pretty smart, don't you?"

"I found out what I wanted," Tommy said.

"You didn't find out anything. So, I know some Lakota words, so what?" He'd regained his composure and walked back into the store.

When he returned to the ranch with the items Sarah wanted, she asked him if he found out anything.

"He speaks Lakota. He didn't deny that he was White Bird, but he didn't confess to anything. It's him, all right, and he knows I know."

CHAPTER 39
1900

TOMMY had installed a telegraph link at the ranch in his office. One of the vaqueros had been trained in sending and receiving messages and was responsible for maintaining the wire and usually received and transmitted any messages to and from the ranch. But Sarah was trained in Morse Code, and just as they were completing their lunch, she received a message from Juan. "The jury has found Raul guilty and he's been taken into custody. Tomorrow, the judge will hear arguments on the death penalty from both attorneys."

It took them both several minutes before they could digest the news. "This is devastating! How could this happen to an innocent man?" A tear ran down Sarah's cheek and she stood by the fire in the kitchen, rereading the message.

"We need to be in Santa Barbara tomorrow to give Raul some support. Naiwa should go, but her state of mind is in a state of flux, that I'm not sure it's a good idea. You should be there, Sarah, so Raul can see we're not abandoning him."

"What about you? Don't you think you should be there?"

"I know, but I think I need to be somewhere else. He's probably going to be sentenced to death, and the only thing that can save him is a confession by the killer. I don't think that's going to happen unless he can be persuaded to do so."

"What do you have in mind?"

"The answer lies at the Pine Ridge Reservation."

Tommy had two vaqueros drive Sarah to Santa Barbara, while he and Cesar took the stage to Santa Barbara and the train to Sidney, Nebraska, where they stayed overnight. Tommy took along one of the Ghost Shirts that the sheriff had placed in his keeping. He telegraphed the Indian agent at Pine Ridge and asked that a message be given to Red Cloud that they would arrive in a day. The next morning, he and Cesar took the train to Alliance and the stage to the Pine Ridge Reservation, arriving around eight that evening. They were warmly greeted by the old chief and given adequate lodging. Tommy and Cesar brought enough food for themselves so they wouldn't impose on their hosts. Joseph Horn Cloud and White Lance had gone to the Wounded Knee Memorial, leaving Dewey Beard alone at their teepee.

Red Cloud sent for the older brave, who was delighted to see the son of Sitting Bull again. He asked if both would like to share his lodge that night. Tommy accepted the hospitality, but informed him that Red Cloud had provided accommodations. "When will your brothers return?" Tommy asked.

"Late tonight. Why don't you come by in the morning? I know they'll be happy to see you again."

They shared their food with Red Cloud and his family that evening, and Tommy confided in the great chief what he had in mind. "It will be hard on them. They are a very close family. I just don't know. I remember White Bird. He was captured by our raiding party and adopted by Running Bear and his family. I don't think he ever regretted being a Sioux brave. He loved his father and mother. Taking another person, even though a baby, and feeding and caring for it, was an imposition on the family."

The old man was smoking his pipe and seemed to be reminiscing. "Do you know anything about Maiden Dream?" the chief asked.

"This is the first time I've heard that name."

"She was White Bird's intended. She was fifteen years old. I was fascinated watching the two try to hide their love from her father. They would sneak away, and when they reappeared you could tell in their faces that they were meant for each other. She and her family made the trek to Wounded Knee along with White Bird and his family. Her father said she could be White Bird's as soon as he proved himself and could take care of her. Apparently, she was by his side when the soldiers fired into our unarmed people."

"So it wasn't just his family that he lost that day."

"No. He buried her alongside his parents. It must have been traumatic for a sixteen-year-old to lose all his loved ones on the same day."

The next morning Dewey Beard came to Red Cloud's lodge and informed Tommy that his brothers had returned. Tommy had brought three winter jackets with him and presented them to the brothers as his gift. They tried them on and wouldn't take them off, even though the temperature was in the seventies. They passed time telling each other what they'd been doing since last they met. Tommy took his time telling them about the trial and the verdict. He knew that what he was going to ask would be difficult, and that the brothers may find his request repulsive.

"I want one of you to come back with me and identify your brother, and then see if he'll give himself up for the crimes he committed."

"You seem pretty sure it's White Bird. What if he didn't do any of the killings?" White Lance asked.

"Then he has nothing to worry about from me."

"What if he doesn't want to give himself up?" Dewey Beard asked.

"Then there's nothing anyone can do. Whoever hanged those four men had to know about the Ghost Shirts. You told me they were similar to those made at Standing Rock. I brought one of shirts used in the hangings. You can see for yourself that it's the same as the ones you have lining your tent. Who else but one of our brethren could have carried out these crimes? And who else but your brother would make shirts identical to the ones your family made while you were at Standing Rock? I knew the four men that were hanged; they worked for me. They seemed like good men, but in war, men do outlandish things that in years later they regret. Those four were at Wounded Knee. I know that your brother made many trips to Fort Robinson where these men were stationed. It's possible that your brother became acquainted with them there. I think your brother saw these men kill your mother and father and he tracked them to my valley and got his revenge. I'm not justifying what he did, nor am I passing judgment. I just want my friend to go free. He's from Mexico and had nothing to do with Wounded Knee. He doesn't deserve to be treated this way."

"My brothers and I must talk this over before we can give you a decision," Joseph Horn Cloud said.

"I must know tonight. I don't know how much time we have before they hang my friend."

At six that evening, Dewey Beard came to Red Cloud's lodging and asked Tommy to accompany him. His brothers had made a decision. Joseph Horn Cloud appeared to be the leader of the three, and it was he who spoke. "I share your pain, but this is a very difficult decision. Had not you been the son of Sitting Bull and a person who's been very generous to our less fortunate brothers, we would not consider your request. My brother, White Lance, and I will accompany you to your home and talk to my brother, if he's there. We will not tell him what to do, but we'll share your concerns with him. We have no money, so I assume you will provide for both of us to and from your home."

CHAPTER 40
1900

THE TRIP HOME was without incident. The brothers were at first very uncomfortable with the stagecoach ride and lonesome for the brother they left at Pine Ridge. Several times they wished he had come along. As the trip continued, their mood changed. They were like little children, pointing out everything they saw from the stagecoach and later the train; everything was a first for them. When they stopped in Sidney, Tommy took them to a restaurant in town; it was their first. They didn't know there was so much food in the world. They didn't care what was on the menu; they would've eaten it, no matter what it was. They seemed to have two helpings of everything. The waitress would smile and giggle at them each time she brought refills on their orders.

Although the trip was long and tedious and they couldn't sleep, the two brothers didn't complain. They were amenable to any suggestion that Cesar and Tommy made. The trip was wearing on Tommy; he'd been gone eight days and wasn't sure he could save Raul. To take some of the pressure off him, Cesar spent most of the time caring for the two brothers. When they arrived at the

Los Olivos Railroad Station, Juan met them with a buckboard. Tommy told the brothers that Juan was the son of Crazy Horse. The three broke out in their native language, and their conversations didn't end until they were in front of the ranch house. The questions about Crazy Horse were never ending. Juan did his best to answer most, but even he couldn't keep up with the inquiries the brothers were making about his past

Everyone on the ranch was glad to see the brothers. They were made to feel like members of an extended family. Tommy, Juan and Naiwa were half Sioux, while Naomi was full-blooded. Chatan and Wachiwi were three-quarters Sioux. Another surprise was to await the two young men when they found out that Sarah had been married to their Great War Chief, Crazy Horse. They followed her and Juan around the ranch like two puppy dogs. Although English was the preferred language of the family, all, except young Thomas and Helga, were fluent in the language of the Sioux. Sometimes the two felt left out. Sarah and Tommy made sure they were included even if they couldn't understand what was said.

Tommy asked Naomi to entertain the two brothers and show them where they were staying while he, Juan and Sarah went into his office. He wanted to know what had happened while he was gone. "The penalty hearing was short. It was as though the judge had made up his mind what the punishment would be. I've appealed the death penalty and expect a hearing within two to three days. The judge wouldn't grant bail pending the appeal.

He didn't give me much time. He apparently is being pressured a lot. I don't have much hope that we'll be successful. There seems to be a rapid sprint to justice. The newspaper is driving everything and the editor is questioning why the judge would even consider an appeal. The only thing that could save Raul is for someone to come forward and confess. Will the brothers be able to help?" Juan asked Tommy.

"I hope so. They seem like honorable young men and I'm sure they'll talk to their brother, but I don't want to take any chances. I want to control their first meeting. Let's hope it's the two we've identified."

"What do you have in mind?"

"I want Holden and Smart to come to the ranch. We can ask the blacksmith to send Holden out to trim some of the horses' hoofs and Sarah can have Smart deliver supplies. That young man could be a problem. He understands Sioux and I believe he thinks I'm on to him. He may not come. I'd like to have the sheriff here as well. He's been a good friend even though his testimony was not beneficial to our side. He was caught in an awkward position and was just doing his job. I'll have Cesar talk with the blacksmith and Sarah can contact the general store. I'll wire the sheriff and ask him to bring Jefferson with him. I don't know how strong the family bond is between the three brothers, but they won't be able to hide their feelings when they see each other at the ranch."

"What if it's someone else?"

"We'll have to take that chance. If Smart or Holden

isn't White Bird, then we'll look at the other three. I won't stop until we're able to free Raul."

Time was not on Raul's side. The soonest Tommy and the others could arrange for the two to come to the ranch was the day after tomorrow at two in the afternoon. At least it was before the appeal hearing in Santa Barbara the next day. To keep the two young Indians in a good frame of mind, he took them and the four young children on an overnight camping trip. They stopped at the fish pond for a couple of hours and let them try their luck at catching a fish before continuing south where the cattle were grazing. The brothers had ridden before; a horse was a premium at Pine Ridge, and they were delighted that they could have one to use for the next two days. They were constantly racing each other, and when the four children got involved, they competed to see who was the best rider. They started back early the next morning and arrived back at the house by noon. Sarah and her daughter had prepared fried chicken, beans and potato salad. The two brothers couldn't get enough. It was as though they had died and gone to the happy hunting ground.

Holden was the first to arrive, and Cesar had him start trimming Chatan's horse, which was tied to the rail on the side of the house. Soon John Smart arrived, and, as was his custom, he parked the wagon out front and came up to the door to ask where they wanted the supplies unloaded. Sarah answered and said she'd like to check the supplies and then sign the invoice. She and Smart went out to the wagon. Both candidates were outside when the two brothers came out the front door with Tommy. The two brothers said nothing, but John Smart turned away immediately, and the expression on his face gave him away. He stood silent for a few moments with his hands on the side of the wagon. It looked as though he was trying to decide whether to run or play out the scene.

Tommy walked up to Smart and touched his shoulder. “Your two brothers are here to see you, White Bird.”

“You set this up. You now think you’re got it all figured out, don’t you?” He turned, smiled at his brothers and walked to them; they embraced.

“You can use the kitchen, if you’d like,” Tommy said.

The three brothers walked into the kitchen and sat at the table. Sarah placed three cups, a pitcher of coffee and some rolls in front of the three and excused herself. By this time the sheriff and Jefferson had arrived. “What’s this all about?” the sheriff asked.

Tommy told him and Jefferson about his trip to Pine Ridge and what he suspected. “So it was an Indian brave who hanged the men?”

“Yes, he was a brave and yes, I think he hanged all four for killing his adopted parents. I don’t know what I would have done, if I were in his shoes.”

“Will he confess?”

“I don’t know, but that’s our only chance.”

Two hours later Joseph Horn Cloud asked Tommy to join the three in the kitchen. He sat down in the nook next to John Smart, with the two brothers opposite him. He couldn’t help but notice how fit the younger man was.

"This is our brother White Bird. I will not tell you what he told White Lance and me; that's between us. My brother will not confess to save your friend."

"Can you tell me why?" Tommy asked.

"I won't admit to anything. Those men deserved to die—they shot our parents. Yes, I know I'm white, but those two people took me in and made me part of their family. I was their son as much as my three brothers. Their lives mean something and they had to be avenged."

"I understand that. I probably would have done the same thing if it had been me instead of you, but putting the shirt in Raul's room was unfair and sneaky." Tommy could feel an instant physical reaction from Smart, but he was prepared for it. The young man restrained himself and didn't rise to the bait.

Tommy wasn't finished. "Did Raul Mendoza ever treat you unfairly?"

"He gave the four men work on your ranch."

"There's only one person who hires people for this ranch, and that's me."

"You're the son of Sitting Bull, my father's hero and the leader of our people."

"If White Bird were to confess, it could only be to our Indian Council at Pine Ridge. This is a Sioux matter, not for a court of white people. I'm a member of that council. If White Bird's willing, I could escort him to the reservation and he would be tried by his own people," Joseph Horn Cloud said.

"That wouldn't solve Raul's problem. He'd probably

be hanged before you had your trial. There has to be another way, but first White Bird has to confess to the sheriff, who's waiting outside to see what happens in here."

"I didn't say I was guilty. You're trying to put words in my mouth. I'm getting out of here."

Smart attempted to push Tommy off the bench, but Tommy had shifted his weight to his right foot and held his position. Smart's face turned red and he used all of his strength to push Tommy again. This time Tommy jumped up from the table and Smart couldn't stop his momentum. He fell on the floor with Tommy staring down at him with a gun pointed at his head. "Stay there for a few minutes until you cool off."

"Without your gun, you wouldn't be able to hold me."

Tommy holstered his weapon, undid his belt and placed both on the table. "I'm not holding it now."

Smart leaped to his feet and charged Tommy, who waited until the young man was almost on him. He went with the momentum of Smart, grabbing his shirt and leaning back while putting his foot on Smart's chest and then kicking out. Smart flew through the air and landed hard on his back. Tommy was up and standing over the young man, who was slow in getting up. When Smart rose, Tommy kicked his legs out from under him and the young man fell again, hitting his head. Tommy reached down to help the man up, but Smart slapped his hand away and just lay there. He began to sob. "I wanted revenge. I didn't want someone else to pay for what I did. I panicked when I saw you going over the scenes with

Jefferson. It was just the spur of the moment. I hadn't planned to put the shirt in Raul's room, it just happened."

The sheriff, Jefferson and Sarah heard the noise coming from inside the house and rushed in just as Smart was confessing to putting the shirt in Raul's room.

The sheriff put cuffs on John Smart and told him he was under arrest. He asked those who witnessed the confession to sign a statement to that effect. Sarah made up the statement and Jefferson, Tommy, Sarah and the sheriff signed. Joseph Horn Cloud and White Lance refused.

"You took advantage of us. We said we'd talk to our brother, but it was up to him to decide if he wanted to confess," Joseph Horn Cloud said

"I didn't do anything. It was his choice; I never put words in his mouth. I think he has remorse. I'll ask Juan to be his attorney once Raul is released. I'll do everything I can to see that he gets a fair trial. Juan is the son of Crazy Horse and a former Sioux brave. He'll work hard on your brother's defense. He's an honorable man."

CHAPTER 41

1900

JUAN presented the confession to the county prosecutor, Jason Turner, with Sheriff Tyrone Bates present. Turner immediately said the trial was over and Raul Mendoza had been convicted. But the sheriff was adamant that Raul was unjustly convicted and that John Smart was the killer. The County Prosecutor said it was up to the trial judge to determine what should be done next.

Juan presented the confession to the trial judge and asked that Raul be released immediately. The prosecutor said he didn't have a position on the matter, though the statement seemed to be valid. The judge was reluctant to make a hasty decision until he talked to John Smart. When he was brought before the judge with a court-appointed attorney, he refused to admit to anything; he remained silent. The judge continued to question him even though Smart refused to say anything. "This statement signed by four people indicates you admitted to putting the shirt in Mr. Mendoza's room. That's for the record. My question is, where did you get the boots that made identical marks under three of the victims?"

John Smart turned to his attorney, who responded, "My client refuses to answer your questions, judge."

"I'll take this matter under advisement and give you an answer in twenty-four hours. Mr. Smart is to be held by the sheriff until I render a decision on the statement that counsel presented."

"Mr. Mendoza is scheduled to be executed the day after tomorrow, judge," Juan said.

"I'm aware of that."

This time Sarah stayed at the ranch and Tommy went to Santa Barbara with the two brothers. Their initial anger at Tommy had given way to almost an appeal for Tommy to intercede with the judge. "The judge is independent; he'll not listen to me. As I told you, once Raul is released, I will help with your brother's defense expenses and provide both of you with accommodations during the trial, should you decide to stay."

That evening, Tommy took the two brothers to a fish restaurant on lower State Street. This was the second time they'd eaten at a restaurant, and the first in an upscale dinner place. They couldn't stop looking around at all the people seated and the pretty waitresses that served them. Tommy admired their courage in coming all this way to try to convince their adopted brother to do what was right. Tommy could tell that they were ashamed at the indifference White Bird had exhibited.

At noon the next day, all parties were called to the judge's chambers. Tommy was allowed to attend, but was cautioned not to speak. "I'm going to set aside the jury's verdict and release Raul Mendoza. Since the sheriff has a valid arrest warrant for John Smart, I expect that he'll be held over for trial for the murder of the four men that Mr. Mendoza was convicted of."

Tommy and Juan went to the jail, and after getting Mr. Turner's approval in writing, Raul was released. The group, including the sheriff, adjourned to one of the many saloons on lower State and had a few beers to celebrate Raul's exoneration. Tommy cautioned the two brothers not to drink too much; he insisted they have only one beer. In front of the two brothers, Tommy explained the promise he'd given them. "I assured the two brothers that you would handle John Smart's defense."

"You know he's guilty as hell."

"Yes. But there are a lot of extenuating circumstances. You and I both know that it could easily be us on trial. We have his same view of justice handed down from our forefathers. If it had been me that witnessed the killing of my parents, I would have killed all four, and I'll bet you would have as well."

What Tommy said gave pause to Juan. He had a great deal of faith and admiration for Tommy Sanchez. Without him, he wouldn't be where he was today. "I don't know if I agree, but if you promised, I will do my best."

"I think the experience you gained defending Raul will be a distinct advantage in this trial. Smart's case could be decided on emotion, especially if you can put the jury in White Bird's place at Wounded Knee and show the callousness of the Army Commander. He has one advantage.

He's white and being defended by a former Indian brave. Think about it."

CHAPTER 42

1900

WHITE LANCE and Joseph Horn Cloud were valuable to Juan in preparing a defense on such short notice. Not only did they provide eyewitness accounts of the massacre at Wounded Knee, but they convinced Smart to cooperate with Juan. He still wouldn't admit to the killings, but he was able to provide a portrait of a young man torn between two worlds, one white and one Sioux. He came to tears whenever he spoke of his Indian parents and the love he had for his brothers, but he wouldn't open up on his feelings for the four he hanged.

The newspaper seemed to be infuriated with the conclusion the trial judge had in releasing Raul. Though the editorials didn't openly state that Thomas Sanchez had a hand in the judge's ruling, it definitely implied as much. The newspaper basically challenged the new jury not to be swayed by the son of Sitting Bull and his adopted protégé, who was the son of Crazy Horse, the murderer of an American hero and his Army at the Battle of the Little Big Horn. Each day there was an editorial that tried to stir up the emotion of the local citizenry, but there were no demonstrations. It was as though the public was tired of the entire situation and wanted to get back to their lives. Whenever Tommy and Sarah attended the trial to see Juan work, they were met with stares and outright scorn. Some who were seated next to them in court got up and moved to another seat, but no overt action was directed at them. "This is bad, Tommy. You'd think we are being accused of killing Custer."

"I'll take care of everything after the trial."

Although there was no overt attempt to confront Tommy or Sarah, he carried his weapon on his hip. Most knew of his reputation and gave the couple a wide berth.

The only evidence, although it was damaging, was the statement signed by the four that they heard John Smart put the Ghost Shirt in Raul's room to cast suspicion on the High Meadows foreman. Joseph Horn Cloud and White Lance gave graphic descriptions of the firing on the unarmed Sioux and the blatant slaughter of women and children nearly two miles from the main massacre.

Jefferson was very helpful. He found a former soldier who had been at Wounded Knee. He testified about the mountain guns on a small hill firing down on the Indians, who stood huddled in one spot and were defenseless.

Mr. Turner didn't seem to have his heart in this trial, but he was still effective in his cross-examination of the three witnesses.

Juan could see the impact the testimonies had on the jury, but he wasn't sure whether that would help get an acquittal. Prior to the trial, Juan's employer had told him that the firm didn't want this case. They said it was bad for business, and if Juan persisted, perhaps he'd be better off at another firm.

"They fired me," Juan told Tommy.

"Perhaps it's for the best. I think you've found your niche. After this trial, you're going to be famous and will be getting a lot of new clients. I can set you up until you've established your own practice. I have a great deal of faith in you, and so has your mother."

The trial took two days, and in the end, the jury found John Smart guilty of all four murders. The jury did, however, recommend that Smart be sentenced to life in prison.

After the verdict, Tommy and Juan went to have a beer at a saloon across from the courthouse. "Well, two trials, two guilty verdicts, though I did get lucky on the first."

"Are you going to appeal?"

"I think it's a waste of time. When I approached Smart about an appeal, he just shrugged and said, 'Let it go.'"

"I've felt for some time that Smart should have been tried by a military court or the Sioux Council at Pine Ridge. The basis of the killings is at Wounded Knee, not here in Santa Barbara. I think a military court is out, because he'd be shot the next day. I don't think White Bird did anything wrong other than trying to place the blame on Raul. I also don't think the four soldiers did anything wrong. They were following orders and doing what everyone else around them was doing. I remember going on raids when the whole village was wasted, even though it wasn't our intent when we went in."

"You're going to do something, aren't you?"

"Don't ask."

CHAPTER 43

1900

THE TWO BROTHERS were distraught. They blamed themselves. If they hadn't come to the valley, no one would've known who their brother was. They knew Tommy Sanchez suspected Smart, but he couldn't prove anything. They were going to return home with a heavy heart and one less brother. Sarah and Tommy were gracious hosts and they loved the valley, but their goal in life was to save their brother.

As they were preparing to leave, Tommy asked if they'd like to go riding with him to the fish pond. They saddled the horses they'd been riding, and the three rode for two hours and rested the horses. Tommy had brought along three poles and some bait. The three sat smoking, fishing and talking small talk until Tommy broached the subject.

"What do you think White Bird's punishment should be for killing those four men?"

"I've thought about that many times. If it had happened on the reservation, he'd be tried by the council. If it was one of our people he killed, then he'd be responsible to provide the family food and shelter until another brave was able to care for the lodge. In grievous cases he would be sent from the reservation and would have to live by himself for a period of time before he could come back. I think this is a grievous case and he would be ostracized for at least ten years and not have any contact with anyone in the tribe for that period of time. I don't think that would be a problem for White Bird. He's lived on his own for at least ten years. You have something in mind, don't you?" Joseph Horn Cloud asked.

That evening, there was a farewell dinner for the two brothers, hosted by Sarah and Tommy Sanchez. Juan, John Jefferson and Tyrone Bates, the sheriff, attended. Raul and Naiwa were there while Naomi watched the four children. Raul was back to his cheery self and Naiwa had come out of her shell and was smiling for the first time in many months. To everyone's surprise, Joseph Horn Cloud asked if they could stay another three days. He knew it was an imposition, but the brothers wanted to hunt for a few days in the hills south of the ranch before they went back to the reservation.

"How long do you think you need?" Sarah asked.

"Three days should be enough, if we could use the horses we've been riding while we've been here."

Tommy nodded that was okay, and Sarah said she and Naomi would give them plenty of food for the trip. The sheriff suggested a couple of trails they might want to explore. He excused himself and went outside, but was back within a few minutes. "Here's a very good map of the trails in the mountains."

He pointed to the two trails he suggested. "The game is good near these two trails, especially if you're looking for mountain lion." The brothers stood up and peered at the map as the sheriff was pointing out different markers along the trails. "Thank you very much, Mr. Bates," White Lance said.

The party broke up, and early the next morning, with Sarah's provisions in hand, the two brothers made their way south. Tommy didn't get up to see them off. He and the sheriff were going fishing soon, and he wanted another few minutes of sleep.

With a bottle of wine produced at the ranch and a half-dozen good cigars, Tommy and the sheriff went to do some serious fishing at the fish pond. "What do you think of the two brothers?" Tommy asked.

"They seem like fine young men. Smart is probably a good kid as well, but I can't condone the hangings. If he had done it the next day after the killing of his parents, I could live with that, but not ten years later."

"What are they going to do with Smart?"

"He's being sent to Sacramento in two days. He's probably going to be at the state penitentiary for the rest of his life. I told my deputy to let the brothers see him if they showed up."

"That was nice of you. Want a cigar?'

"Where do you get them?"

"Oh, I can't tell you that. You'll arrest my source."

"No way."

"Are you heading back tomorrow?"

"No. I've got some business in Los Olivos tomorrow. If you don't mind, I'll stay another night."

CHAPTER 44

1900

THE BROTHERS made it to Santa Barbara by evening and waited in the shadows of the jail house until they were sure that only the night deputy was on duty. It was eleven p.m., and they were still trying to figure out how to distract him long enough to free their brother. Just then the door opened, and the deputy stepped out onto the porch to look at the stars. This was their chance, and they rushed the deputy, knocking him down and putting a gag in his mouth; they dragged him into the jail house. White Lance looked around to be sure no one had seen what had happened, while Joseph Horn Cloud tied up the deputy and put him in one of the cells. They freed their brother, and after a quick embrace, they locked the front door and made their way to their horses. "There's only two. We need another horse," White Bird said.

"We'll take the deputy's. He's not going to need it for a while," White Lance said.

"Where are we going?" White Bird asked.

"We're going to make our way east until we reach Bakersfield, and then we'll go north to Cheyenne and then on to Pine Ridge. We have provisions for about three days and some money to buy more."

"Sanchez will come after us. He won't let us get away."

"The son of Sitting Bull is our friend."

"He'll still come after us. He hates me."

"It was his idea to free you."

The sheriff was notified of the jail break by telegraph at the Sanchez Ranch. "Hell, I helped them escape. I told them about the trails south. Did you know about this, Tommy?"

"I beg your pardon?"

"I didn't mean that—I was just talking out loud. That newspaper is going to fry me alive. I need to get back as soon as possible and form a posse. Will you lead?"

"I'm going to pass on this one."

"I know you're angry, but it came out the wrong way. I'm sorry."

The sheriff walked past Sarah as she came in the kitchen. "What's wrong with Tyrone?"

"The two brothers broke Smart out of jail, and they're on the lam. He wants me to track them, and I said no."

"Where do you think they're going?"

"Home."

CHAPTER 45
1900

HE WAS more than pleased with himself as he sat at a table savoring a glass of sherry. Two murder trials had increased his circulation by forty percent, and the revenue generated by that increase was more than he could have hoped for; he was glad he had bought the rag.

He had proved to all what a power the newspaper could be, and that it wasn't wise to anger Samuel Jacobs, owner and editor. Several politicians and acquaintances walked by his table and tipped their hats. Jacobs liked the notoriety, and vowed to make the paper even more powerful. His next target was that boob of a sheriff; he had let the convicted killer of four men escape. Deep down, Jacobs knew that Sanchez was behind the jail break, and if it was the last thing he'd do, he'd bring down that scoundrel. How dare that half-breed masquerade as a white man?

Staggering a little as he left the saloon, his thoughts were about what or whom he might target next. He unlocked his front door, fastened it behind him, and dropped the key in the dish on the table in the entryway. Immediately he was seized from behind by another man, approximate to his height, but so much stronger. A hand was placed over his mouth while he was dragged into his bedroom. He was somewhat dazed after being struck in the face twice. Tape was placed over his mouth, and his arms and legs were tied to the bedposts. He was lying on his back.

As his head cleared, he saw the masked intruder go into the wash room and come back out with a basin of water and a towel. The stranger put water on his head and then proceeded to shave his head. He couldn't make out who the figure was, because he was completely clothed in black with a black mask.

When his head was completely shaved, the trespasser took out a knife and cut off his right ear lobe. Jacobs tried to scream, but any sound he made was muffled by the tape over his mouth. Tears ran down his face, and his eyes were pleading, but the stranger made no sign of recognition. Then the stranger put something on his missing lobe and it stung, and Jacobs cried again. The interloper put a knife to Jacob's neck, and with a hoarse whisper in his ear, he said, "Leave town tomorrow, sell the paper, and don't ever come back, or I'll cut off the other lobe."

When the intruder left, Jacobs tried to place the voice; he could not. Someone was going to pay for this outrage; he'd get him.

The next morning, his housekeeper found Jacobs lying on the bed with his hands tied and blood dripping down the side of his face. She called the sheriff, who came right over. There was a doctor present when the sheriff arrived, and he was telling Jacobs that the lobe could not be sewed back on. Jacobs turned and saw the sheriff standing in the doorway. "Well, what are you going to do about this? Someone broke into my house and cut off my lobe and told me to leave town today, sell my paper, and not come back or he'd cut off my other lobe. Is anyone safe in this town that you're supposed to protect?"

"Give me a description and I'll get on it right away."

"He was dressed in black, about my height, and very strong."

"What did he look like?"

"His face was covered with a black mask."

"Well, that's not much to go on."

"What do you suggest I do?"

"I'd leave town. I think the man is serious." The sheriff, who'd been chastised in this man's paper, couldn't help but smile.

"You know who did this, don't you?"

"Everyone knows who did it."

"Then arrest him."

"On what evidence? There is none. I told you to be careful, but you're such an arrogant ass; you think you can do whatever you want. Whoever did this means business. My advice to you is, leave town—and the sooner the better."

"I can hire bodyguards, and he'll never get to me."

"When your bodyguards find out who you think is threatening you, they may not want to continue in your employ. You created this problem all by yourself. You wanted to sell papers and went after the wrong people."

EPILOGUE

TRUE TO HIS WORD, Joseph Horn Cloud presented White Bird to the Pine Ridge Indian Council for a trial on behalf of the four soldiers. Their verdict, which Joseph and his brother feared, was a lifetime ban from the Sioux Nation and all its followers. It was to commence in ten days. White Lance and his brother had expected a similar fate for their younger brother, but not one of that length.

Their parting was one of sadness. They loved their white brother and would miss him forever, but they knew in their heart that this was a just verdict and not as great as the court in Santa Barbara had pronounced.

White Bird vowed to his brother that he would devote the remainder of his life to being a good man and one they could be proud of. He spent the next week in meditation at his parents' grave and at the monument at Wounded Knee. He then left the area and headed south toward Sidney. He found Rosita Riley in a dirty saloon on the outskirts of the town and asked her to forgive him. He learned that he had a son who was four years old.

He told her what he'd done and what the verdict laid down by the Pine Ridge Council was. He told her he was still hunted by the authorities, but if she and the child were willing, he would marry her and take them with him.

"Jacob, we've had a miserable existence the last three years, but I don't know if I can trust you. You left me once; why wouldn't you do it again?"

"I understand your reluctance, but I'm a different man today, and I promised my brothers that I would be a good man. My name is not Jacob Light; it's Raymond O'Caliegh. I researched records of the many wagon trains that were lost and found out who my real parents were."

Printed in the United States
By Bookmasters